PROPHET ™

④ JOINING

PROPHET, VOL. 4: JOINING TP
ISBN#: 978-1-63215-254-1
February 2015. First printing.

Published by Image Comics, Inc. Office of
publication: 2001 Center Street, Sixth Floor,
Berkeley, California 94704. Copyright © 2015 Rob
Liefeld. Originally published in single magazine form
as PROPHET #39-45 and PROPHET: STRIKEFILE
#1-2. All rights reserved. PROPHET® (including
all prominent characters featured herein), its
logo and all character likenesses are trademarks
of Rob Liefeld, unless otherwise noted. Image
Comics® is a trademark of Image Comics, Inc. All
rights reserved. No part of this publication may
be reproduced or transmitted in any form or by
any means (except for short excerpts for review
purposes) without the express written permission
of Image Comics, Inc. All names, characters,
events and locales in this publication are entirely
fictional. Any resemblance to actual persons (living
or dead), events or places, without satiric intent,
is coincidental.

PRINTED IN USA.

For information regarding the CPSIA on this
printed material call: 203-595-3636 and
provide reference # RICH – 602102.

For international rights and foreign licensing
contact - foreignlicensing@imagecomics.com

STORY **Brandon Graham**
with **Simon Roy** (chapter 1-4 & 6)
and **Ron Wimberly** (chapter 2)

ART Giannis Milonogiannis   Grim Wilkins
Simon Roy   Sandra Lanz
Dave Taylor   Onta
Ron Wimberly   Brandon Graham
Matt Sheean   Ron Ackins
Malachi Ward   Tom Parkinson-Morgan
Farel Dalrymple   Gael Bertrand
Bayard Baudoin   Rob Liefeld
Joseph Bergin III   Addison Duke
James Stokoe   Ludroe
Aaron Conley   Xurxo G Penalta
Lando   Amy Claire

COLORS **Joseph Bergin III**
with **Ron Wimberly** (chapter 2)
and **Dave Taylor** (chapter 5)
COLOR FLATS Sandra Lanz (chapter 6)

LETTERS **Ed Brisson**

COVER **James Stokoe**

PROPHET created by **Rob Liefeld**

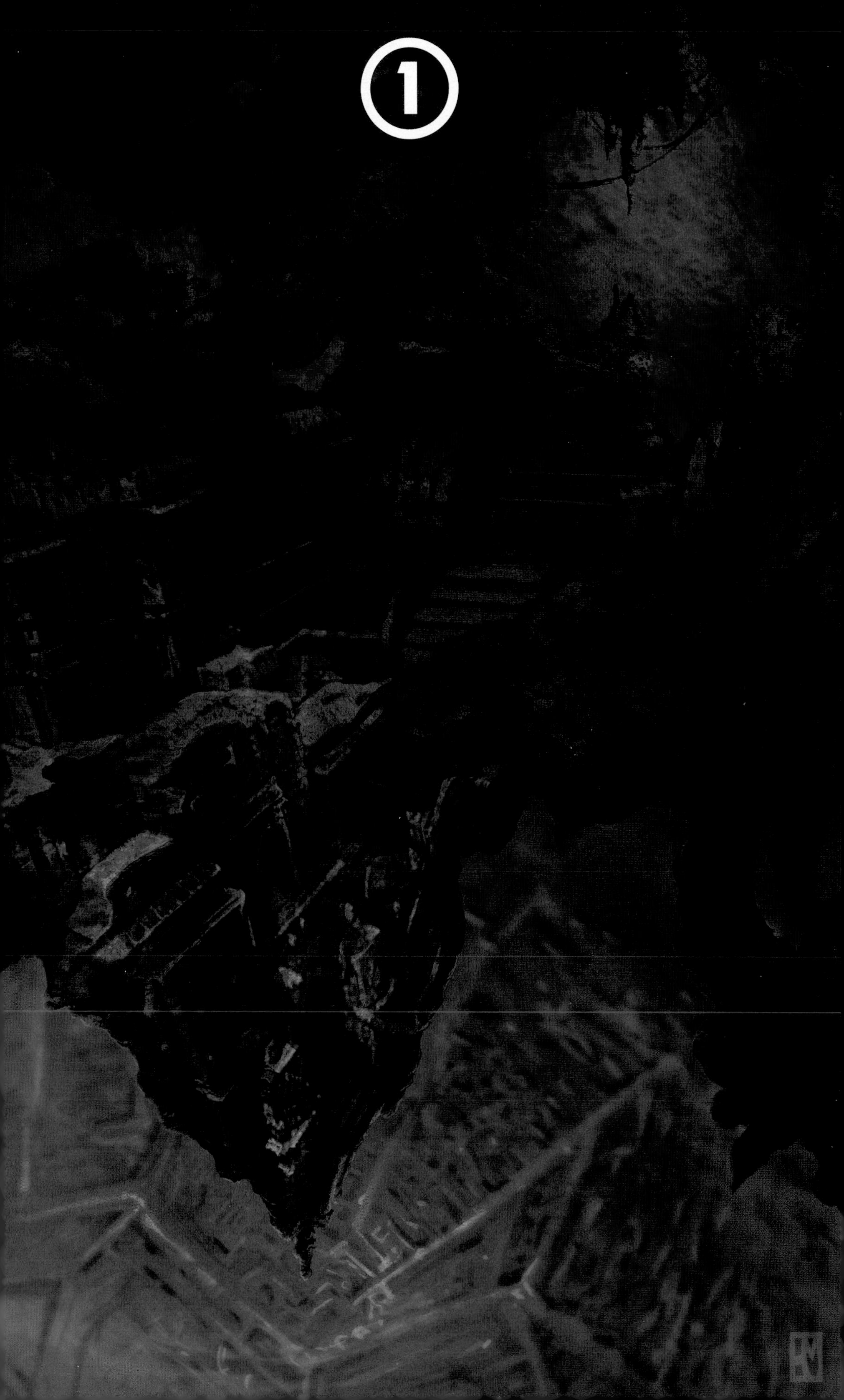

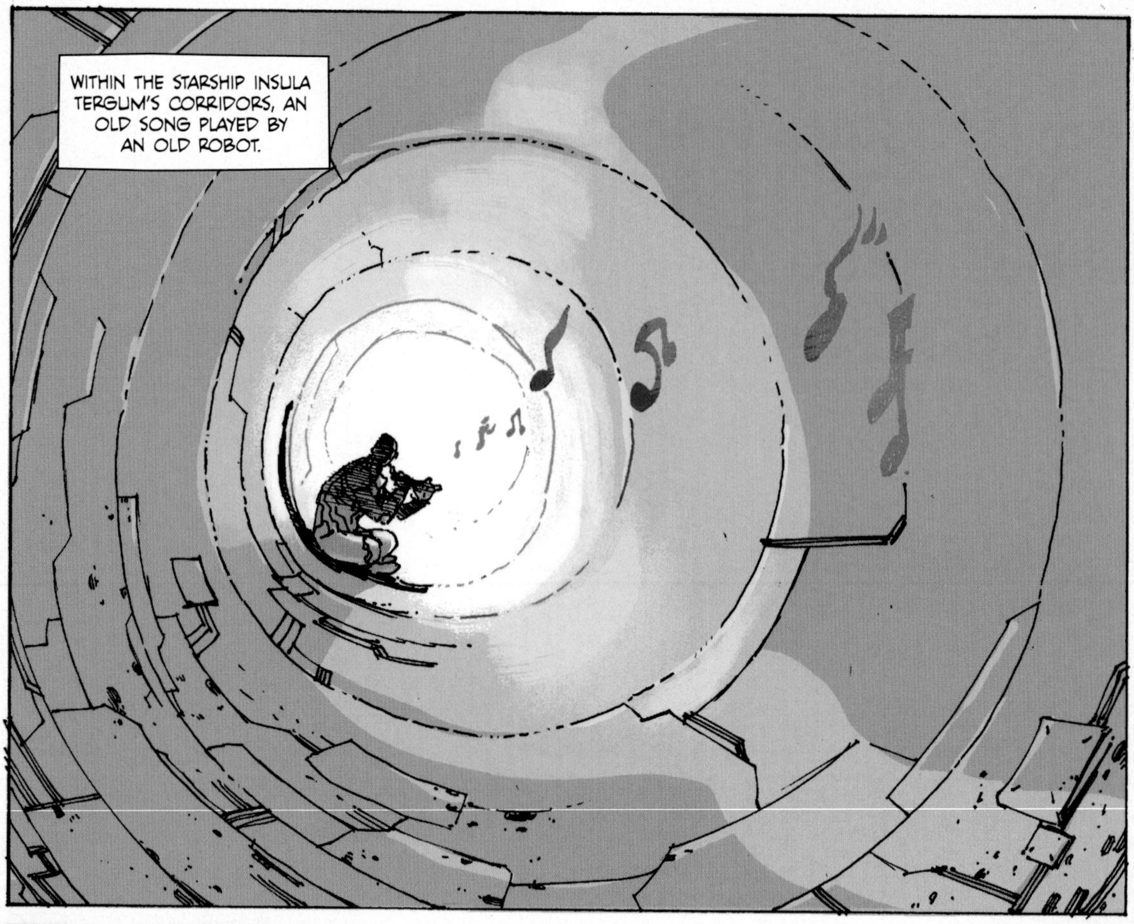
WITHIN THE STARSHIP INSULA TERGUM'S CORRIDORS, AN OLD SONG PLAYED BY AN OLD ROBOT.

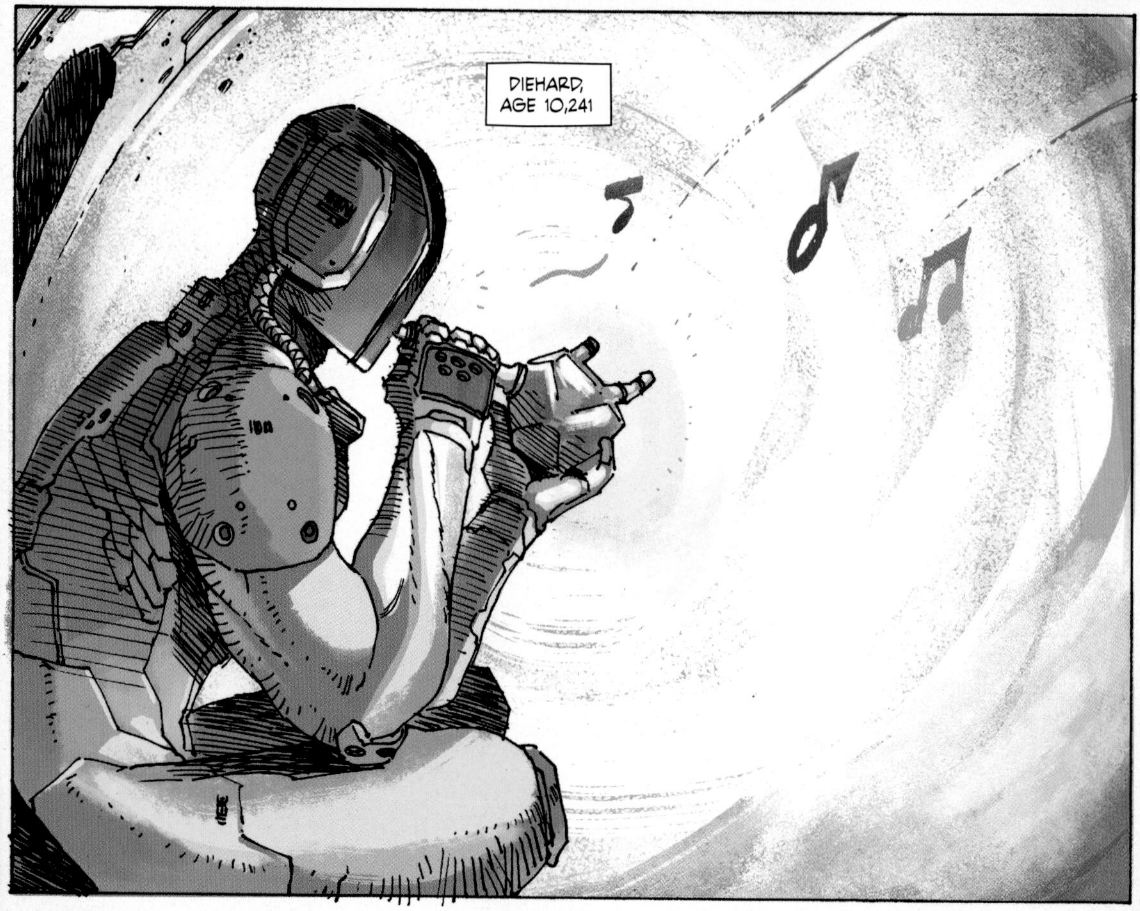
DIEHARD, AGE 10,241

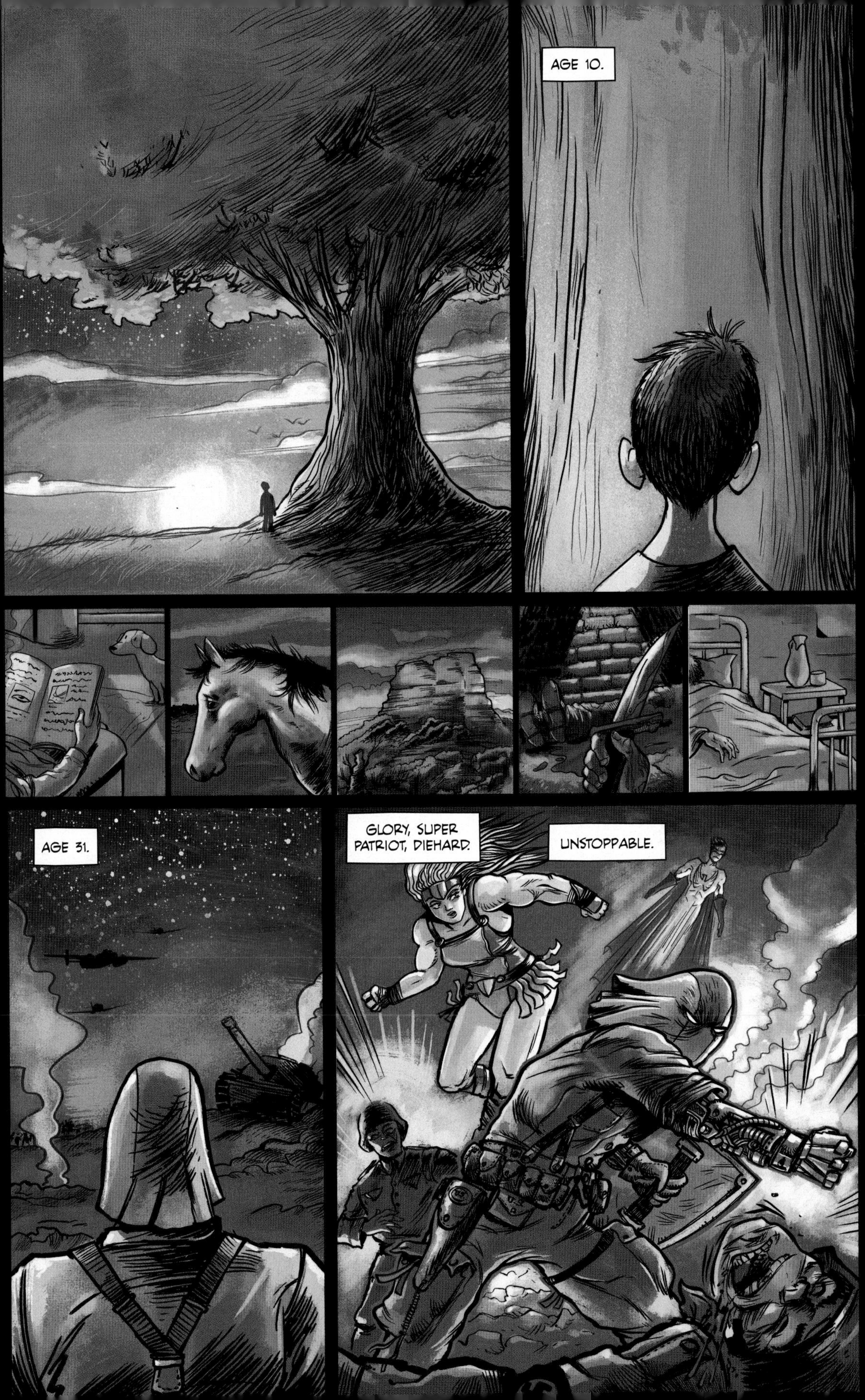
AGE 10.
AGE 31.
GLORY, SUPER PATRIOT, DIEHARD.
UNSTOPPABLE.

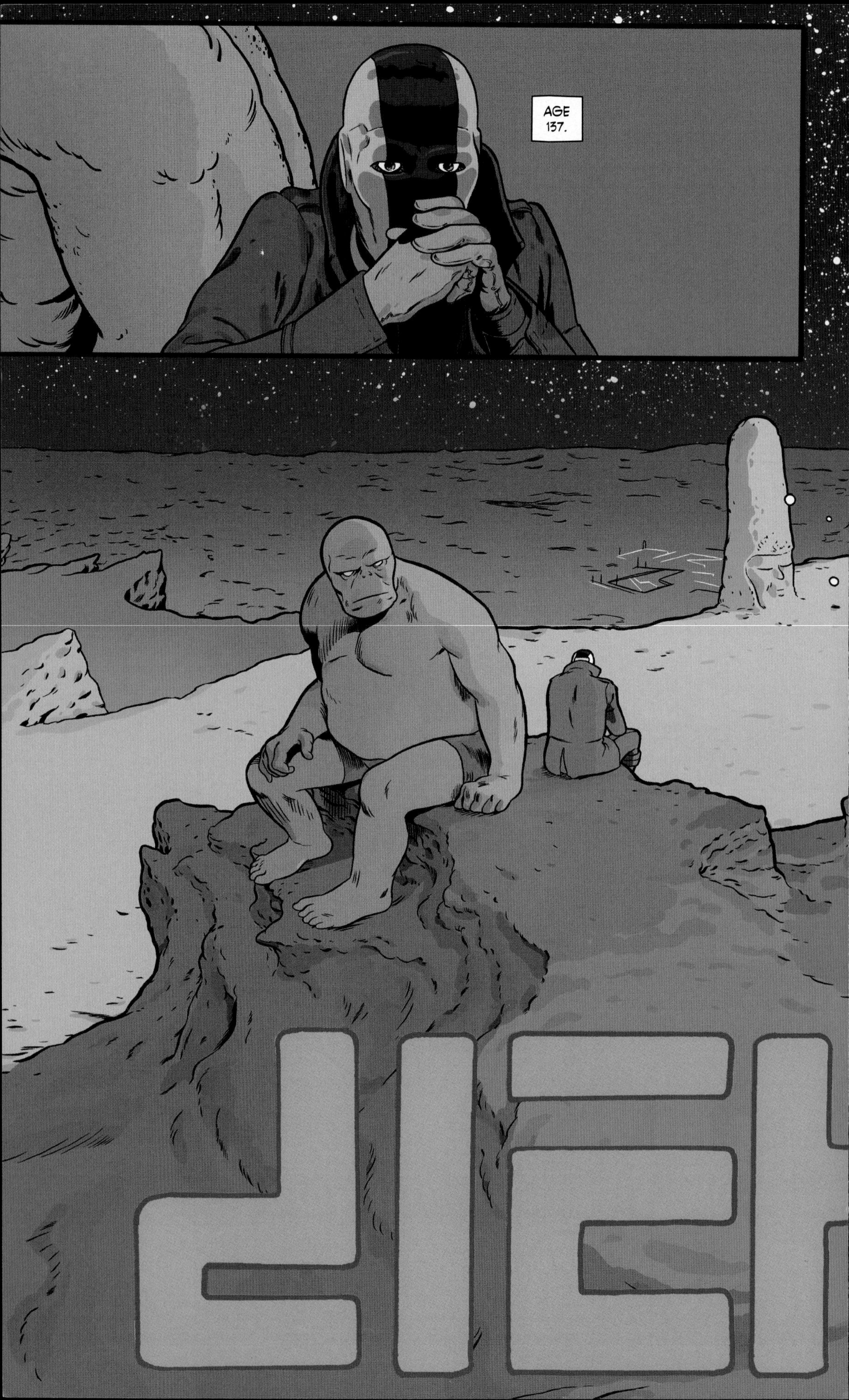
AGE 137.

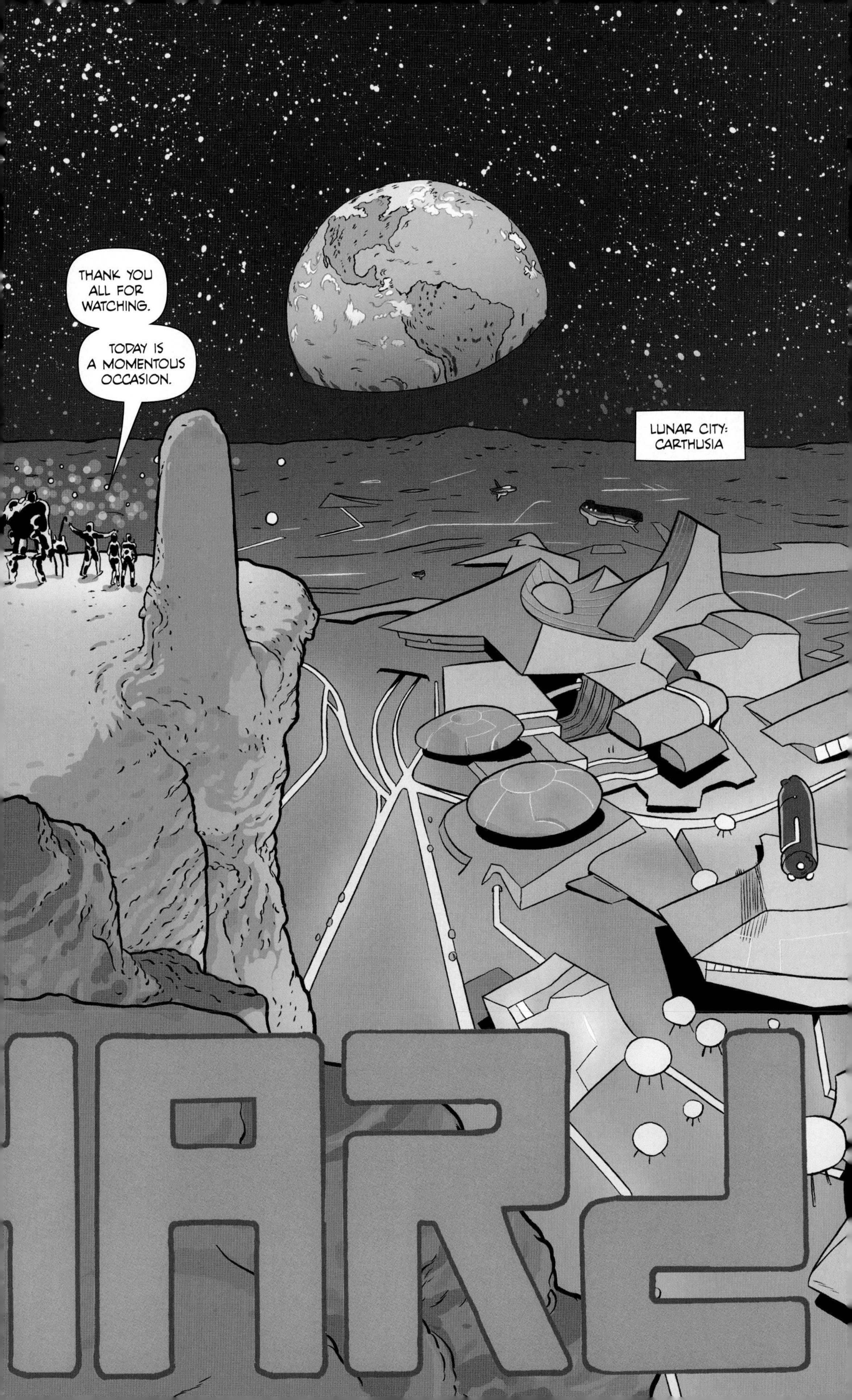
THANK YOU ALL FOR WATCHING.
TODAY IS A MOMENTOUS OCCASION.
LUNAR CITY: CARTHUSIA

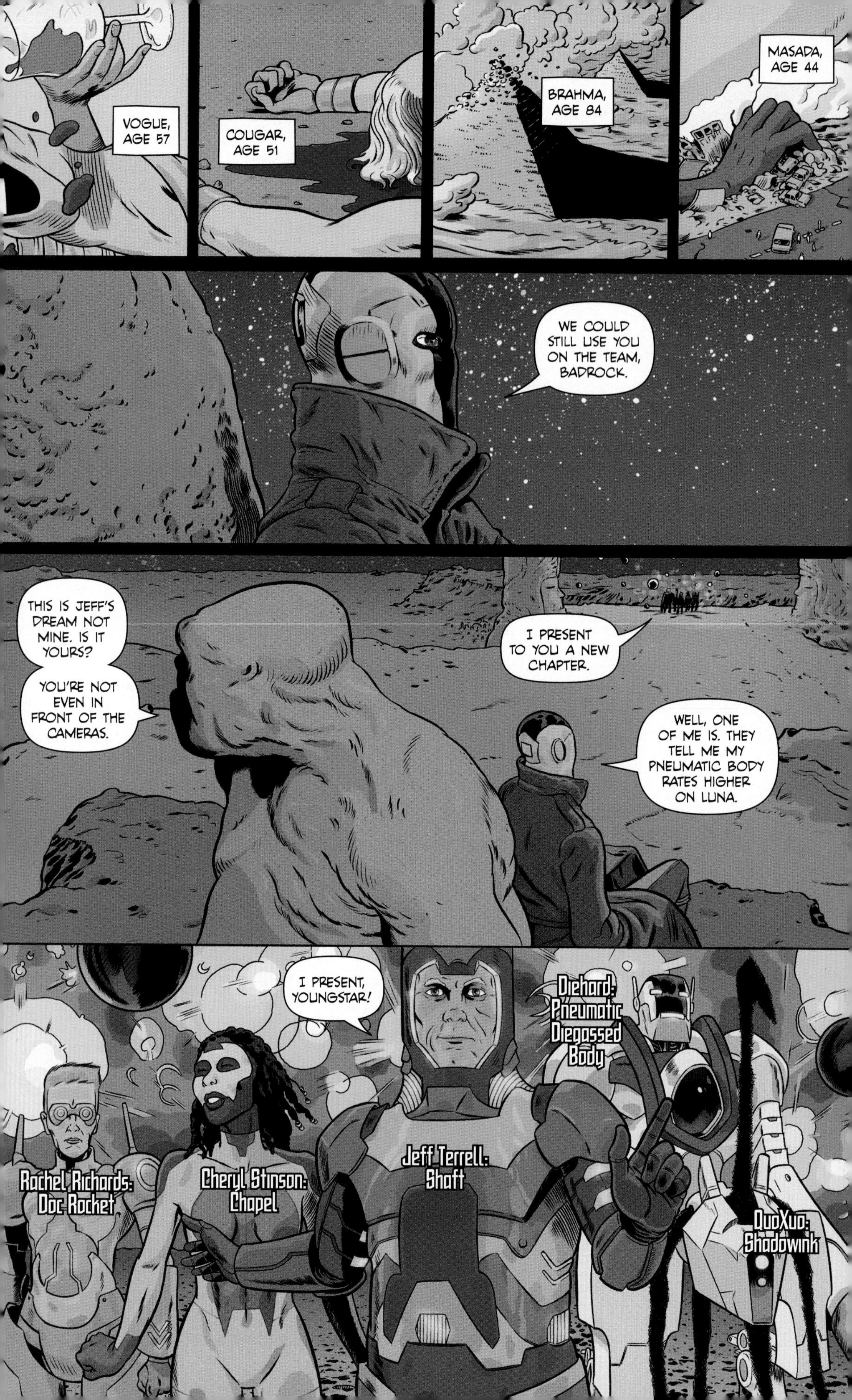
VOGUE, AGE 57
COUGAR, AGE 51
BRAHMA, AGE 84
MASADA, AGE 44
WE COULD STILL USE YOU ON THE TEAM, BADROCK.
THIS IS JEFF'S DREAM NOT MINE. IS IT YOURS?
YOU'RE NOT EVEN IN FRONT OF THE CAMERAS.
I PRESENT TO YOU A NEW CHAPTER.
WELL, ONE OF ME IS. THEY TELL ME MY PNEUMATIC BODY RATES HIGHER ON LUNA.
I PRESENT, YOUNGSTAR!
Diehard: Pneumatic Diegassed Body
Rachel Richards: Doc Rocket
Cheryl Stinson: Chapel
Jeff Terrell: Shaft
QuoXuo: Shadowink

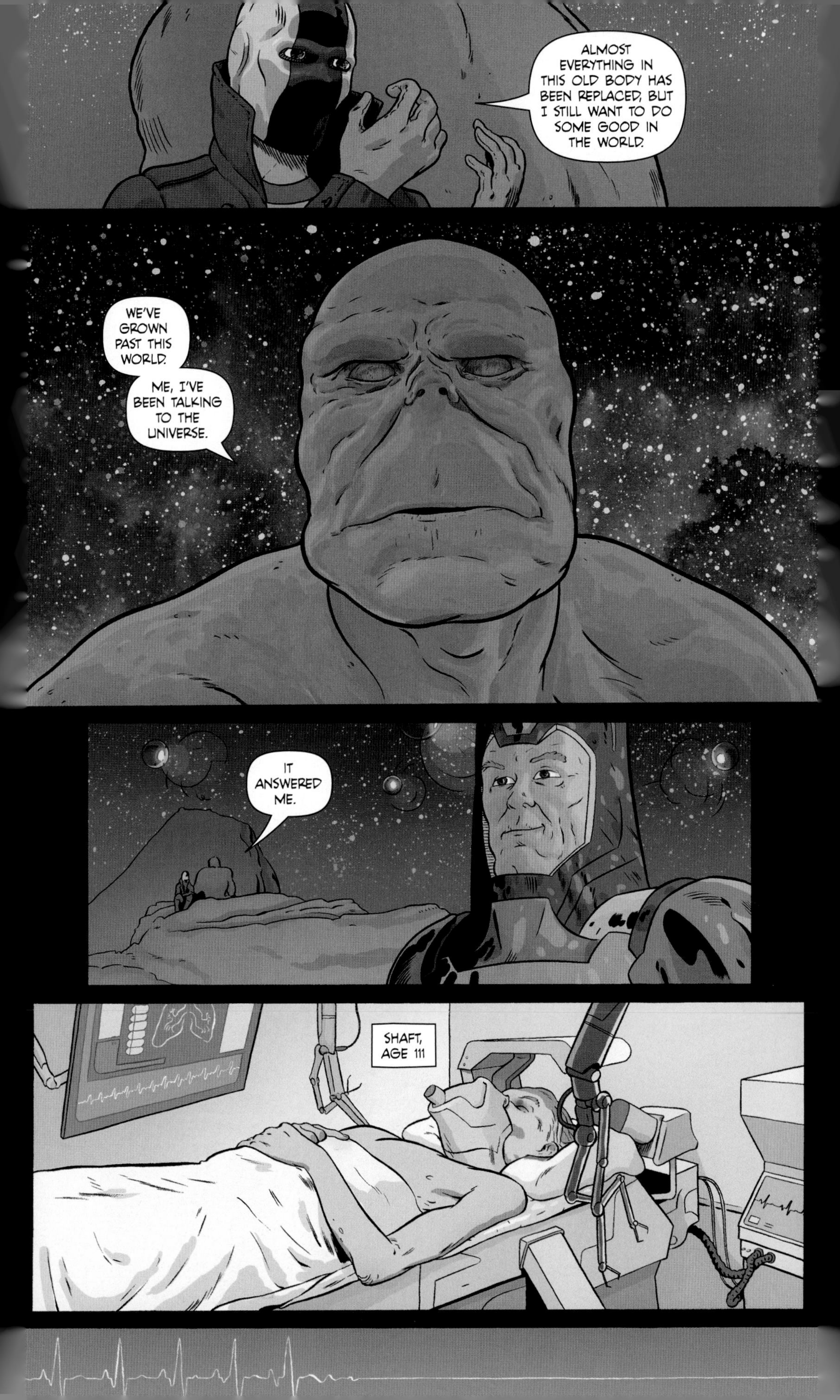

ALMOST EVERYTHING IN THIS OLD BODY HAS BEEN REPLACED, BUT I STILL WANT TO DO SOME GOOD IN THE WORLD.
WE'VE GROWN PAST THIS WORLD.
ME, I'VE BEEN TALKING TO THE UNIVERSE.
IT ANSWERED ME.
SHAFT, AGE 111

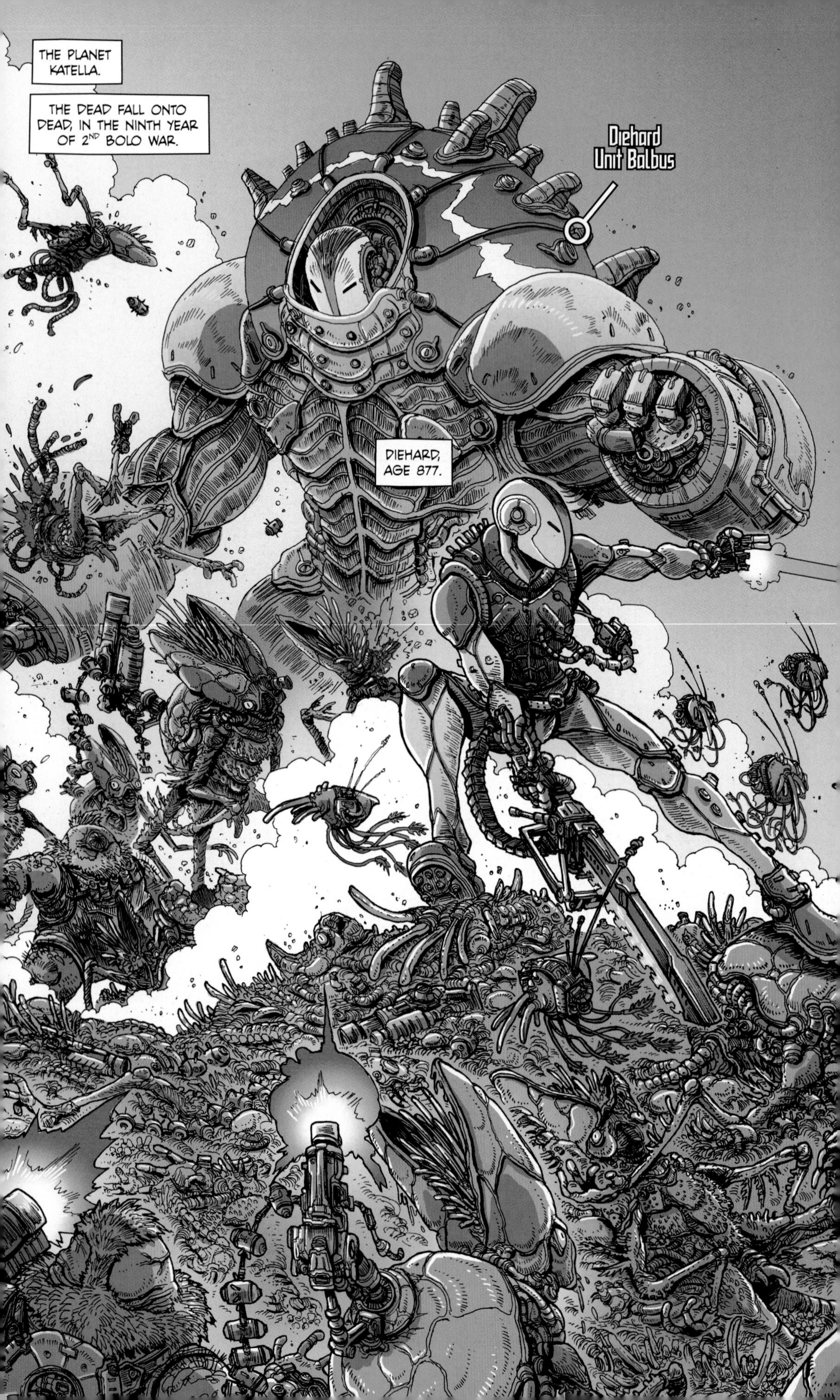
THE PLANET KATELLA.
THE DEAD FALL ONTO DEAD, IN THE NINTH YEAR OF 2ND BOLO WAR.
Diehard Unit Balbus
DIEHARD, AGE 877.

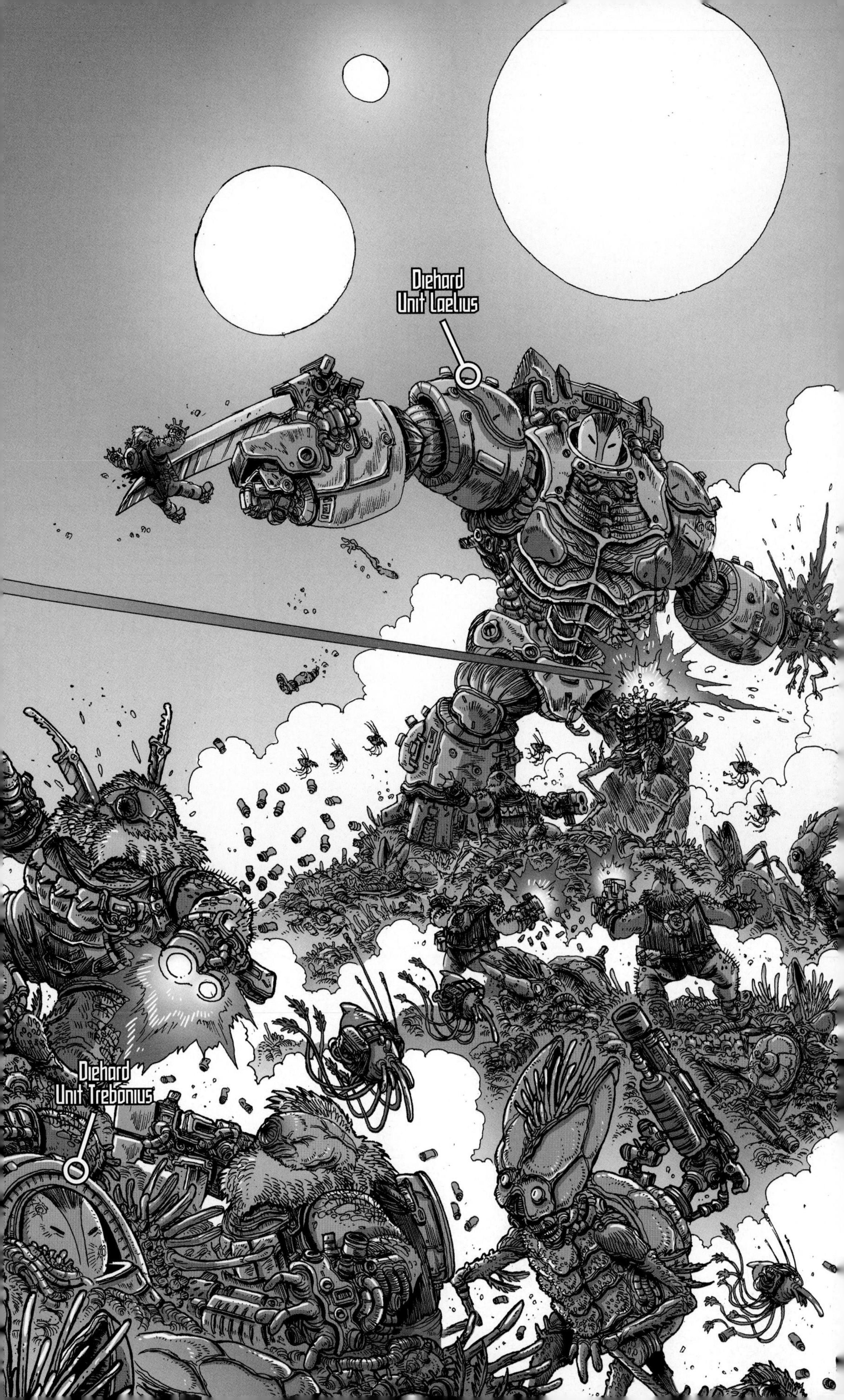
Diehard
Unit Laelius
Diehard
Unit Trebonius

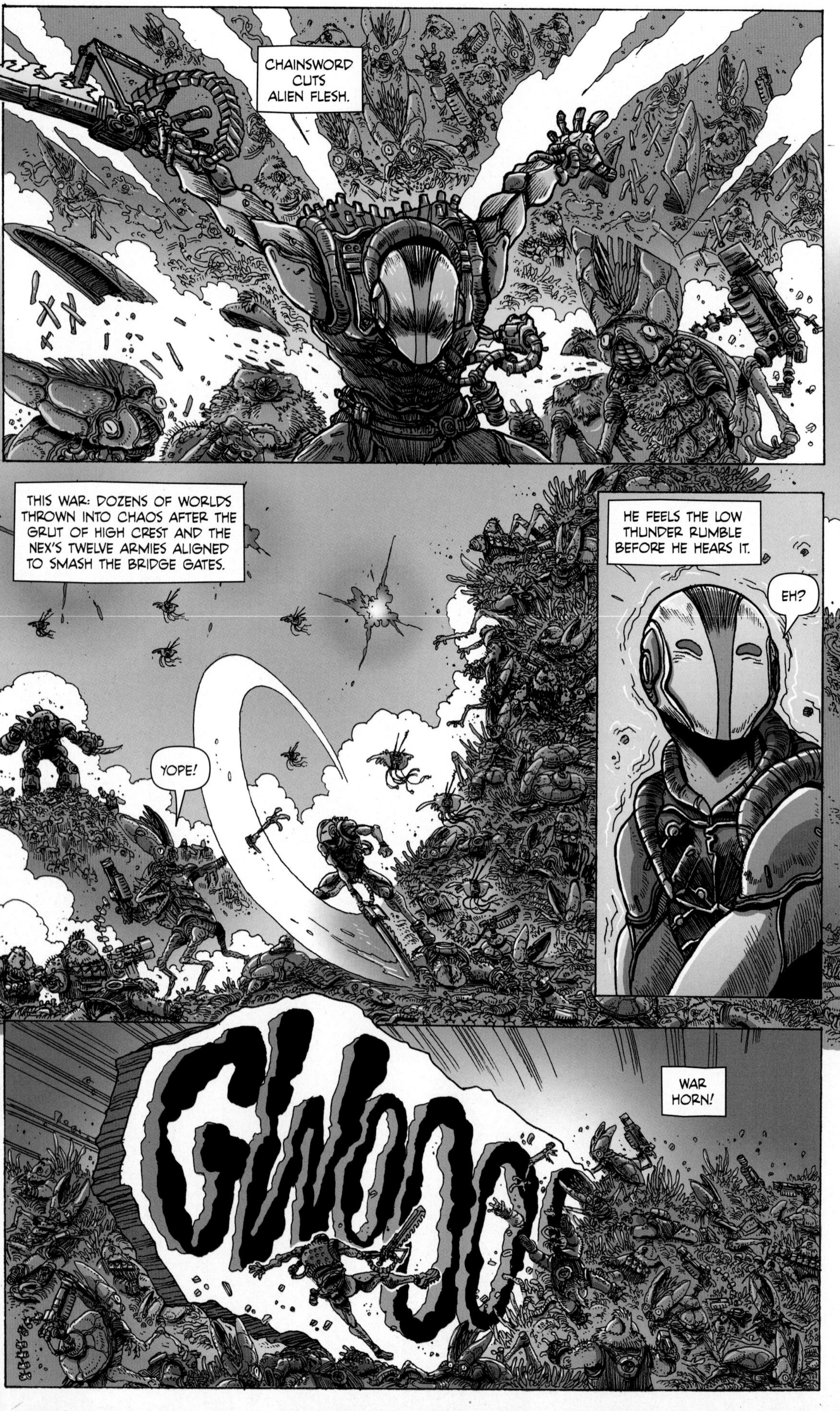
CHAINSWORD CUTS ALIEN FLESH.
THIS WAR: DOZENS OF WORLDS THROWN INTO CHAOS AFTER THE GRUT OF HIGH CREST AND THE NEX'S TWELVE ARMIES ALIGNED TO SMASH THE BRIDGE GATES.
HE FEELS THE LOW THUNDER RUMBLE BEFORE HE HEARS IT.
EH?
YOPE!
GWOOO
WAR HORN!

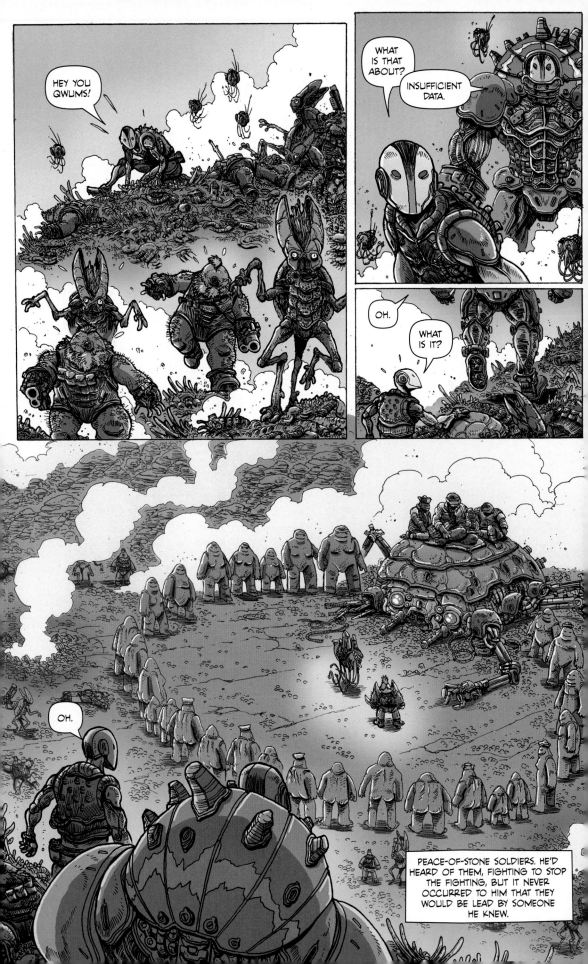

HEY YOU QWUMS!

WHAT IS THAT ABOUT?

INSUFFICIENT DATA.

OH.

WHAT IS IT?

OH.

PEACE-OF-STONE SOLDIERS. HE'D HEARD OF THEM, FIGHTING TO STOP THE FIGHTING, BUT IT NEVER OCCURRED TO HIM THAT THEY WOULD BE LEAD BY SOMEONE HE KNEW.

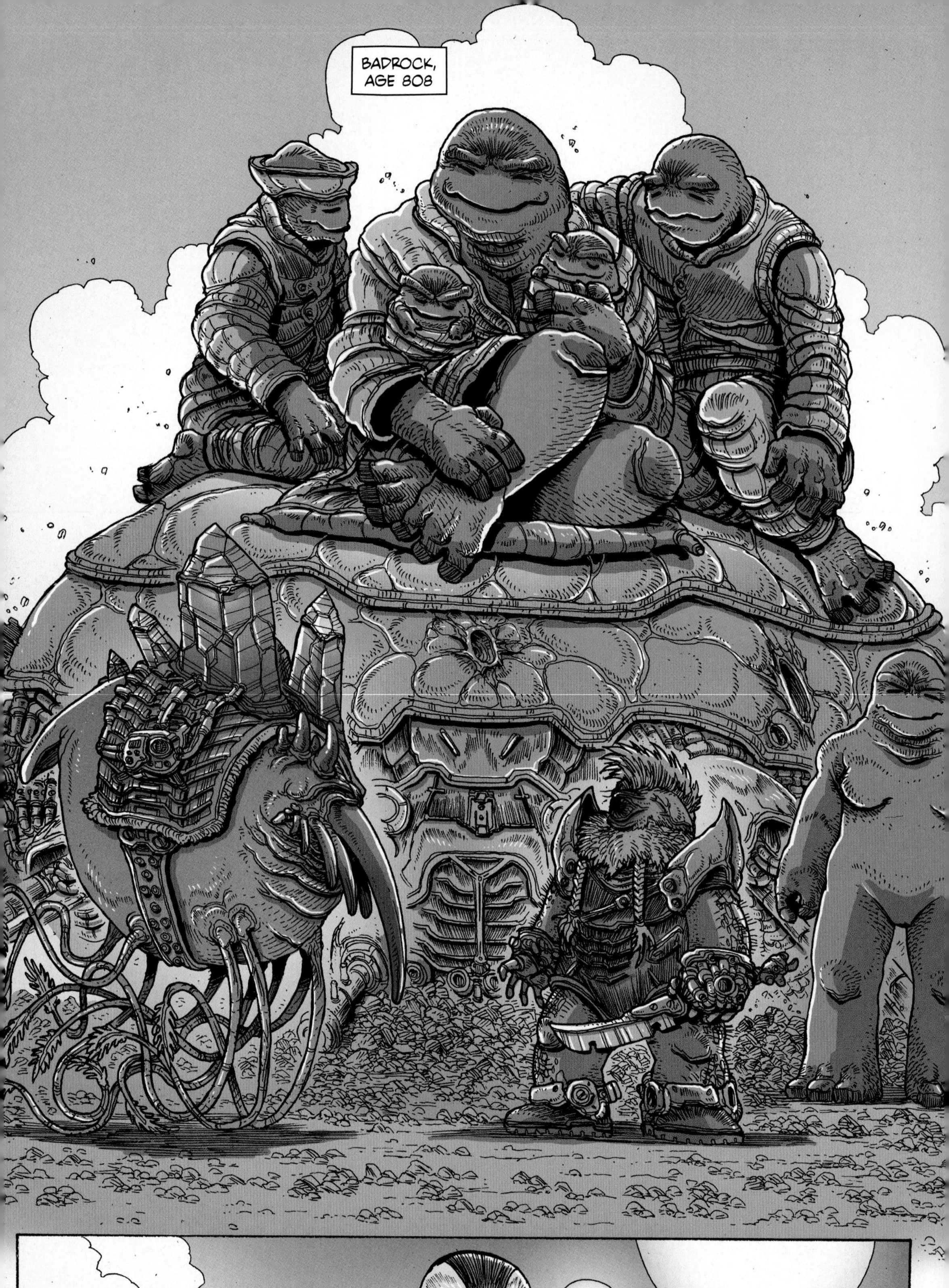
BADROCK,
AGE 808
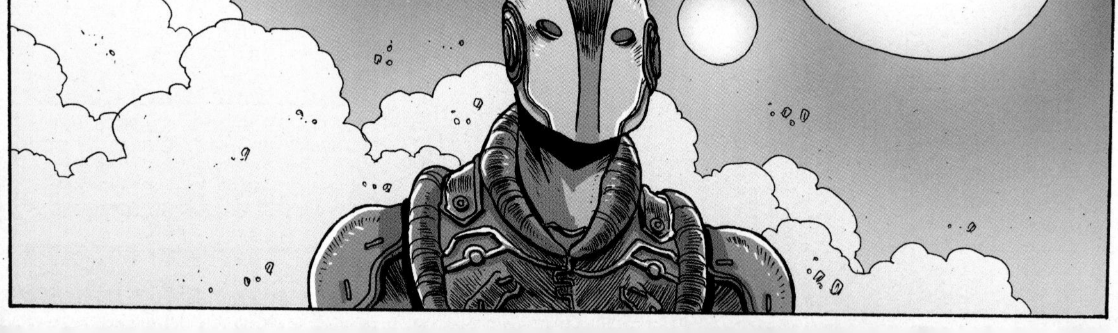

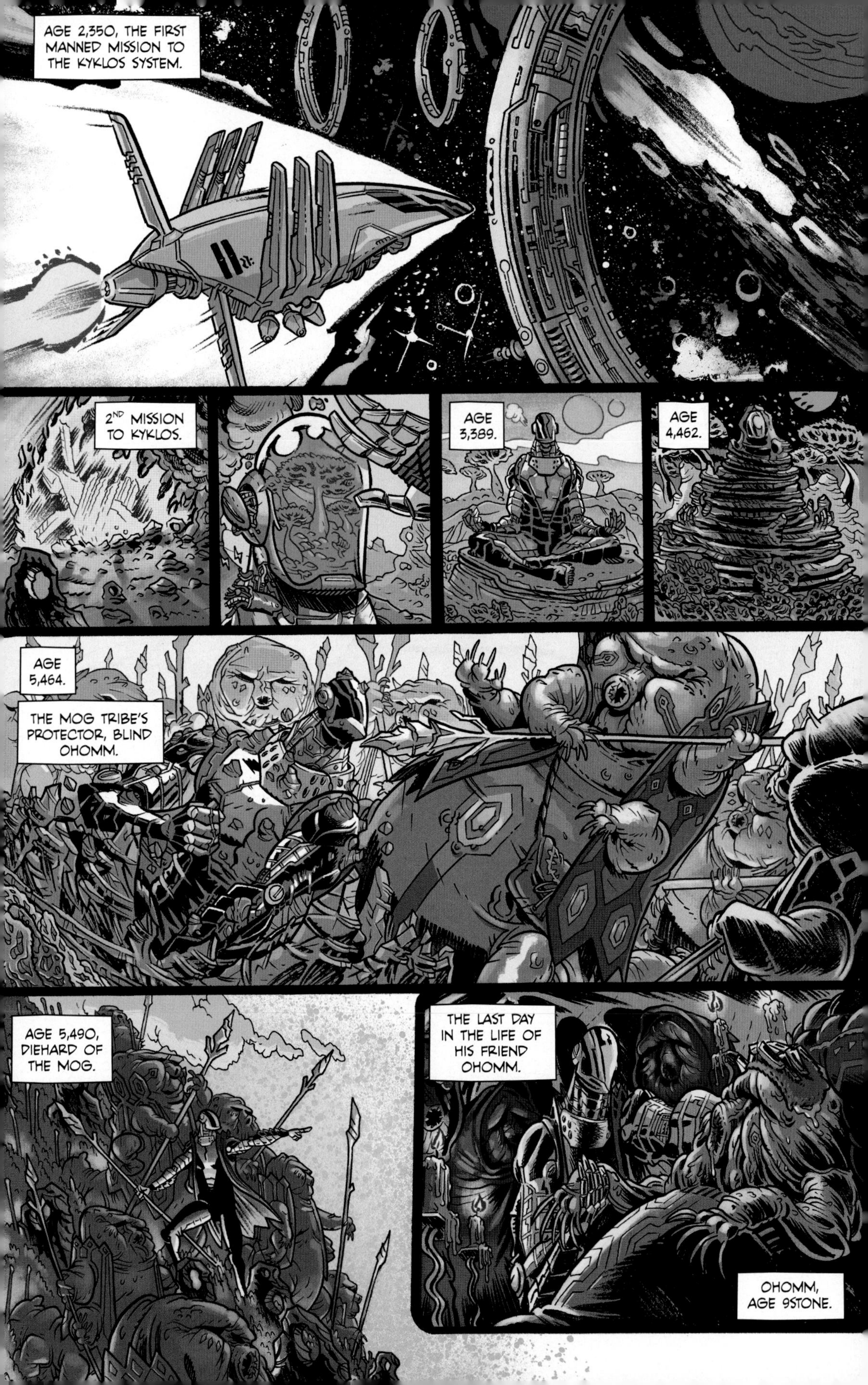
AGE 2,350, THE FIRST MANNED MISSION TO THE KYKLOS SYSTEM.
2ND MISSION TO KYKLOS.
AGE 3,389.
AGE 4,462.
AGE 5,464.
THE MOG TRIBE'S PROTECTOR, BLIND OHOMM.
AGE 5,490, DIEHARD OF THE MOG.
THE LAST DAY IN THE LIFE OF HIS FRIEND OHOMM.
OHOMM, AGE 9STONE.

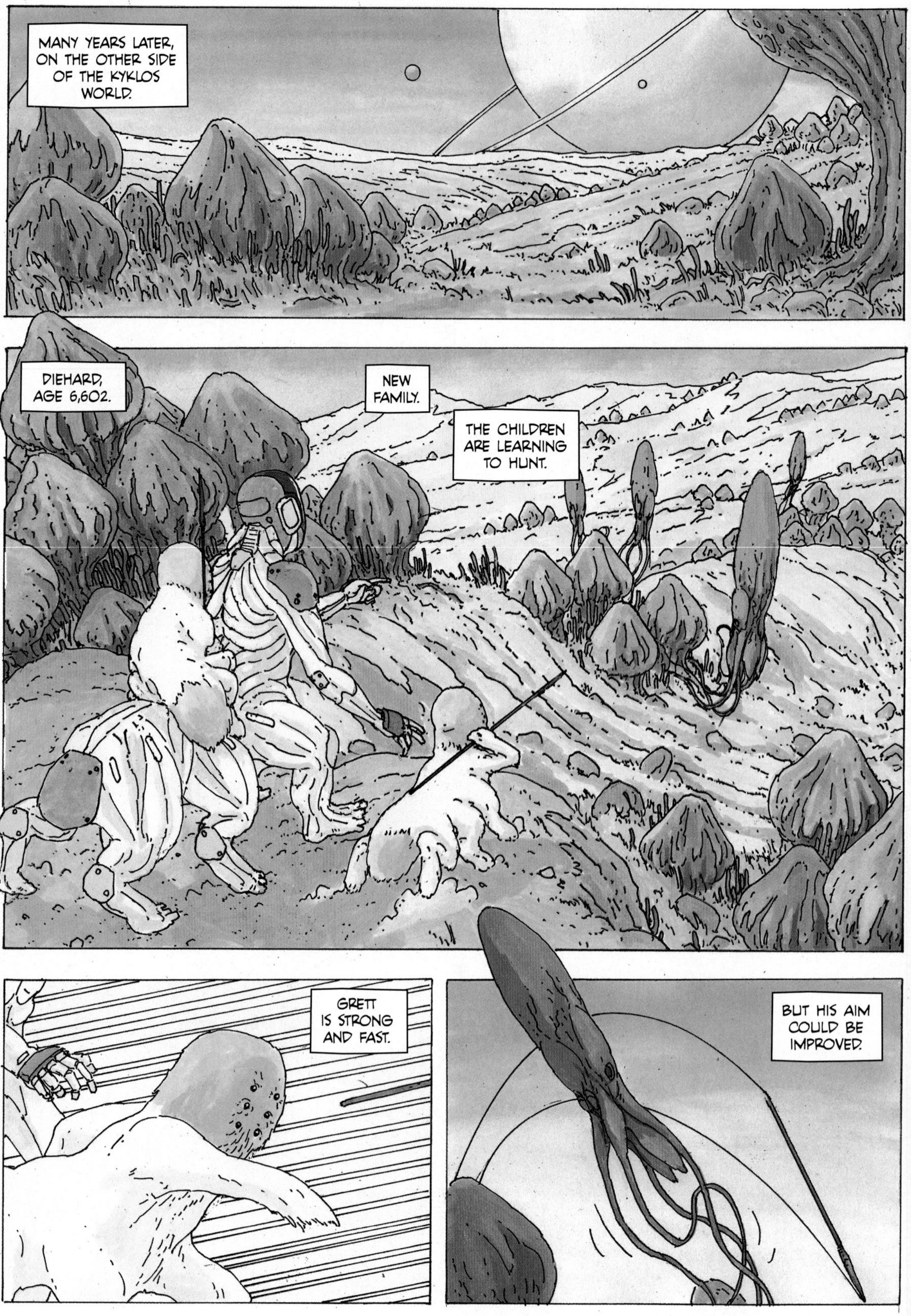
MANY YEARS LATER, ON THE OTHER SIDE OF THE KYKLOS WORLD.
DIEHARD, AGE 6,602.
NEW FAMILY.
THE CHILDREN ARE LEARNING TO HUNT.
GRETT IS STRONG AND FAST.
BUT HIS AIM COULD BE IMPROVED.

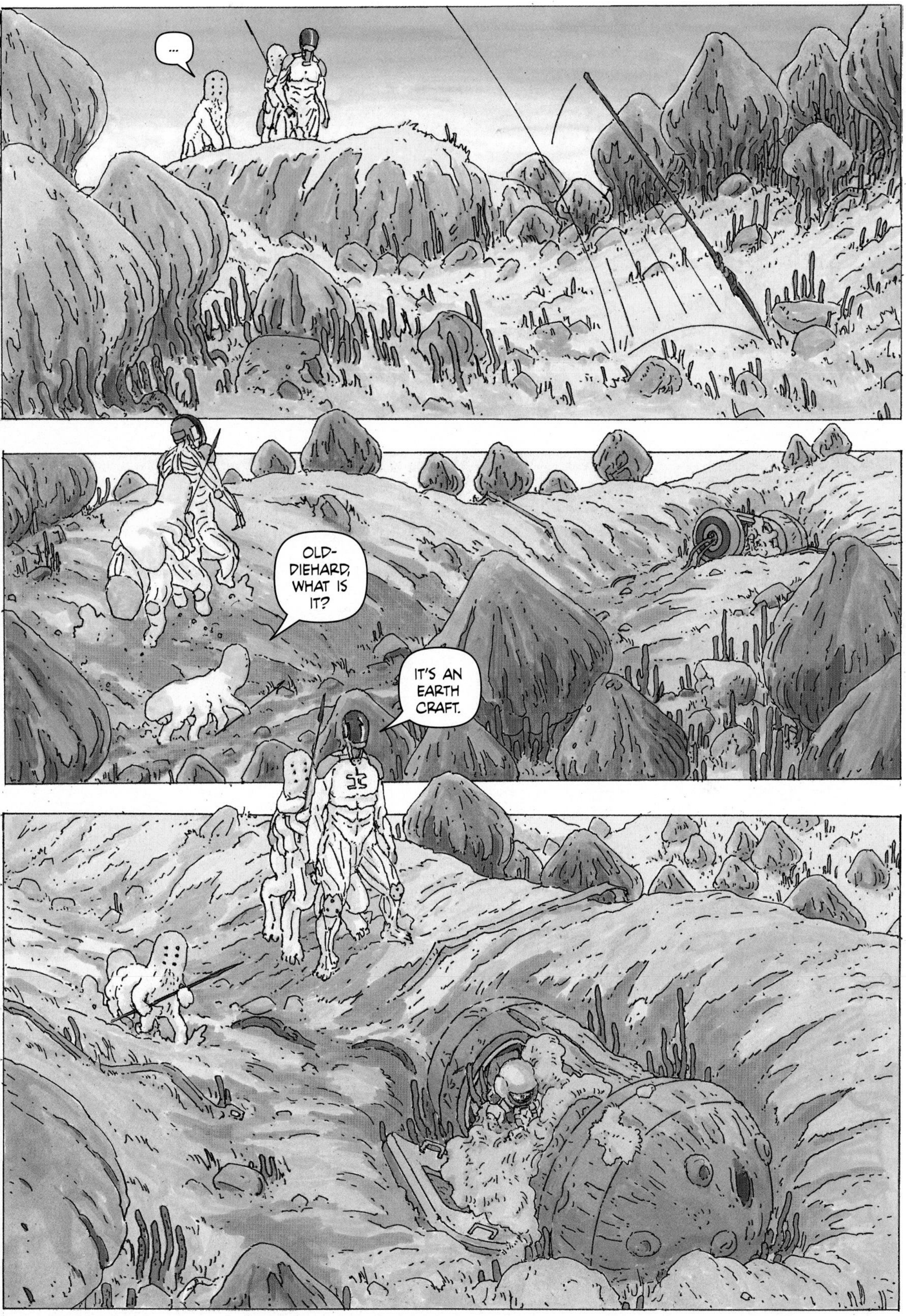
...
OLD-DIEHARD, WHAT IS IT?
IT'S AN EARTH CRAFT.

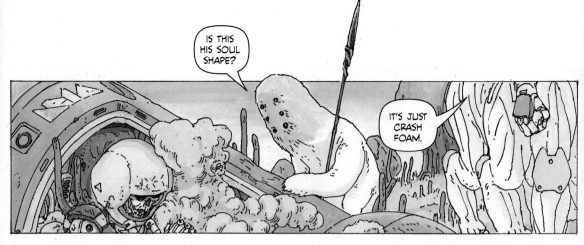

IS THIS HIS SOUL SHAPE?

IT'S JUST CRASH FOAM.

COME. THERE IS NOTHING BUT DEATH HERE.

BUT YOU'RE FROM EARTH.

THE POISON OF THE 7FINGER WAR LEFT HIS CITY TURNED TO BLACK GLASS. HIS FAMILY DEAD.

AGE 6,655.

AGE 6,656.

KYKLOS SHRINKS INTO THE DISTANCE.

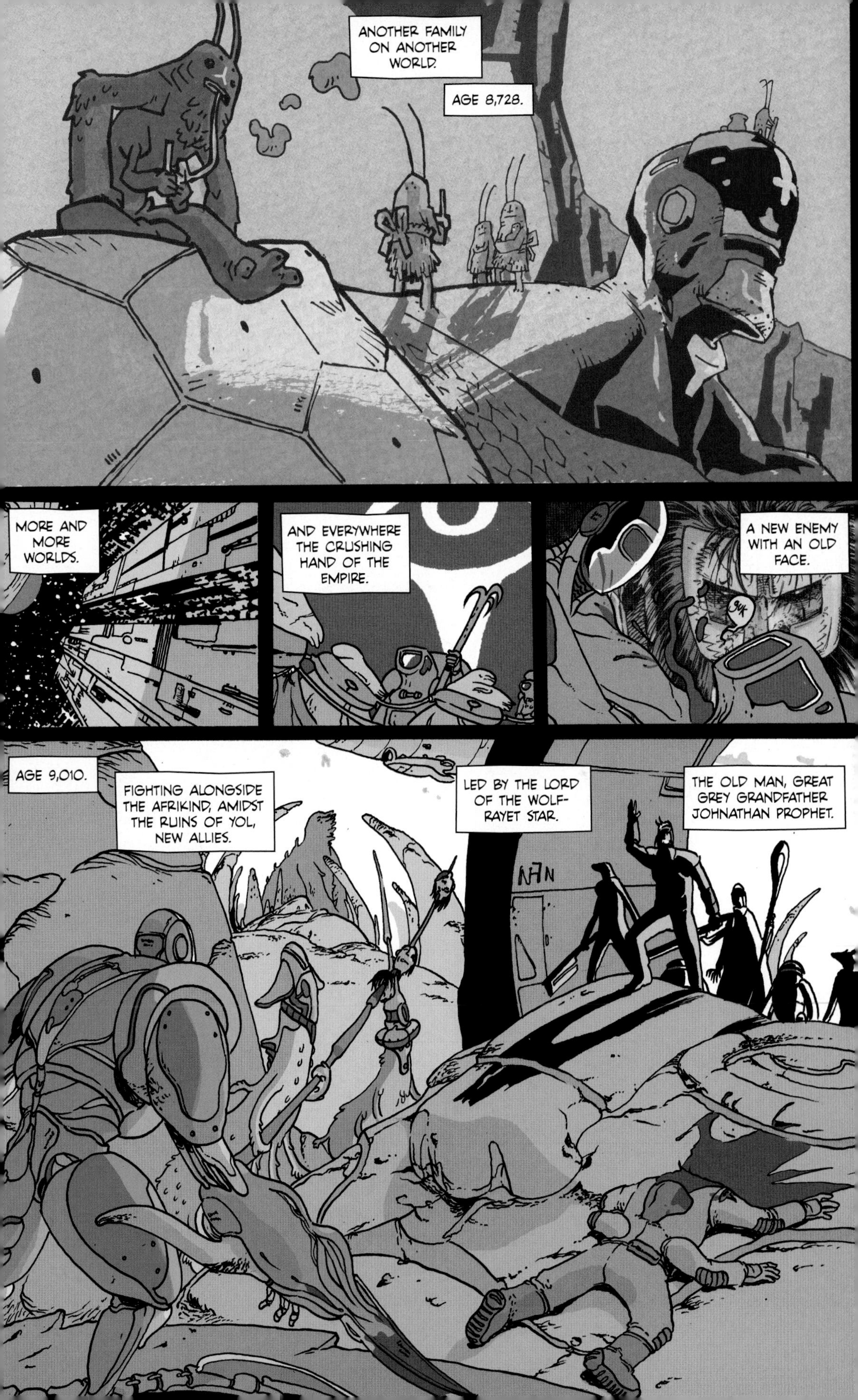
ANOTHER FAMILY ON ANOTHER WORLD.
AGE 8,728.
MORE AND MORE WORLDS.
AND EVERYWHERE THE CRUSHING HAND OF THE EMPIRE.
A NEW ENEMY WITH AN OLD FACE.
GUK
AGE 9,010.
FIGHTING ALONGSIDE THE AFRIKIND, AMIDST THE RUINS OF YOL, NEW ALLIES.
LED BY THE LORD OF THE WOLF-RAYET STAR.
THE OLD MAN, GREAT GREY GRANDFATHER JOHNATHAN PROPHET.

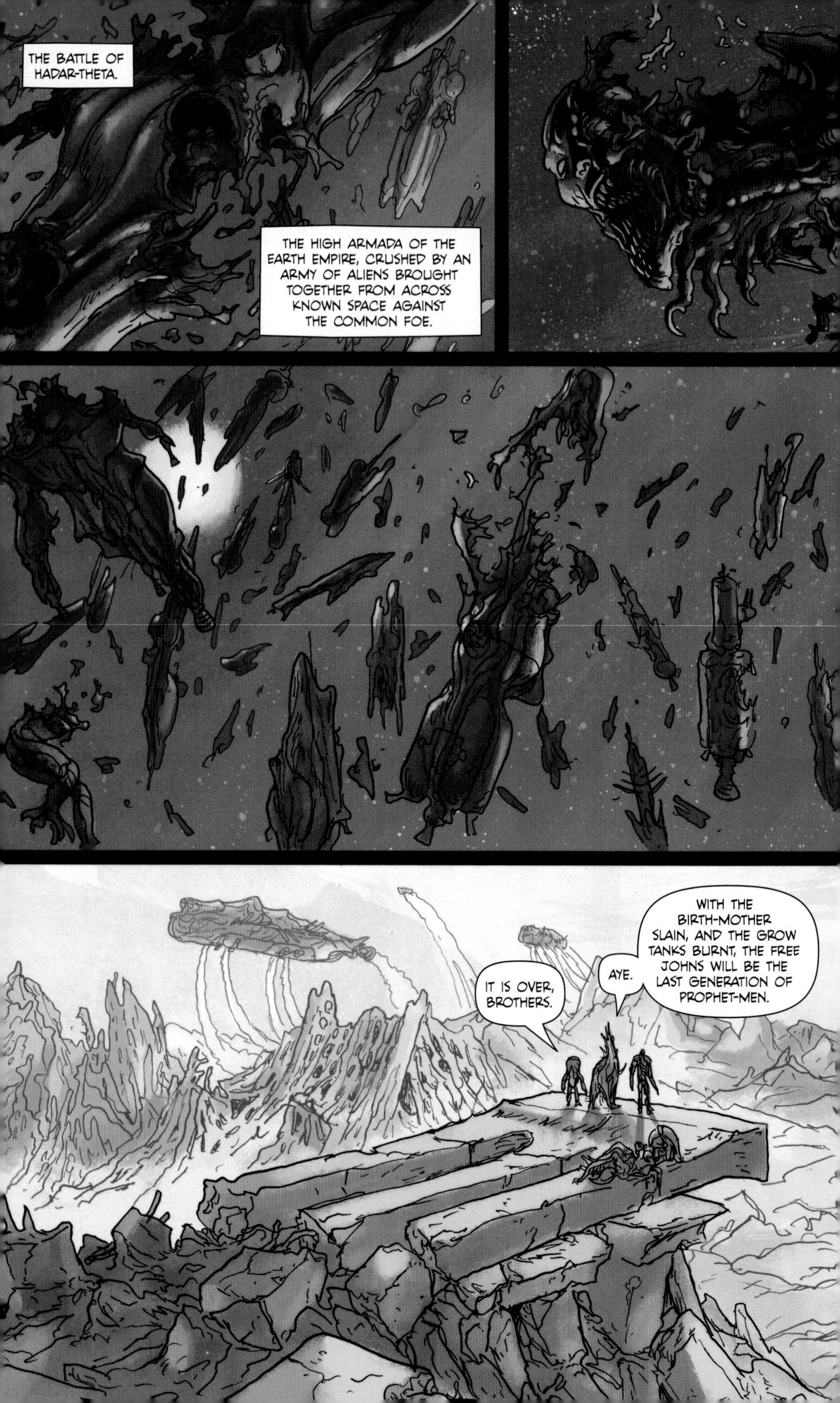
THE BATTLE OF HADAR-THETA.
THE HIGH ARMADA OF THE EARTH EMPIRE, CRUSHED BY AN ARMY OF ALIENS BROUGHT TOGETHER FROM ACROSS KNOWN SPACE AGAINST THE COMMON FOE.
IT IS OVER, BROTHERS.
AYE.
WITH THE BIRTH-MOTHER SLAIN, AND THE GROW TANKS BURNT, THE FREE JOHNS WILL BE THE LAST GENERATION OF PROPHET-MEN.

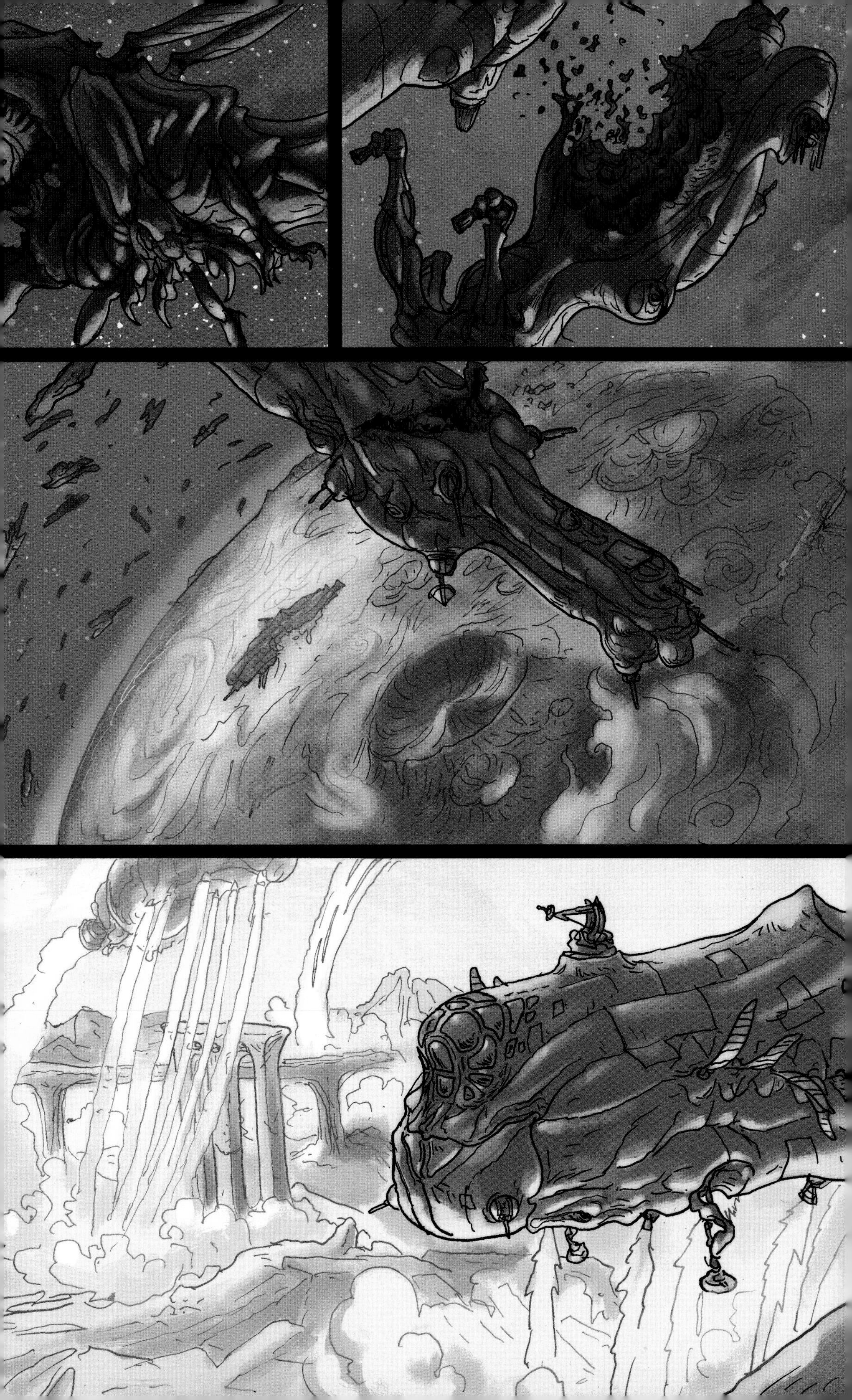

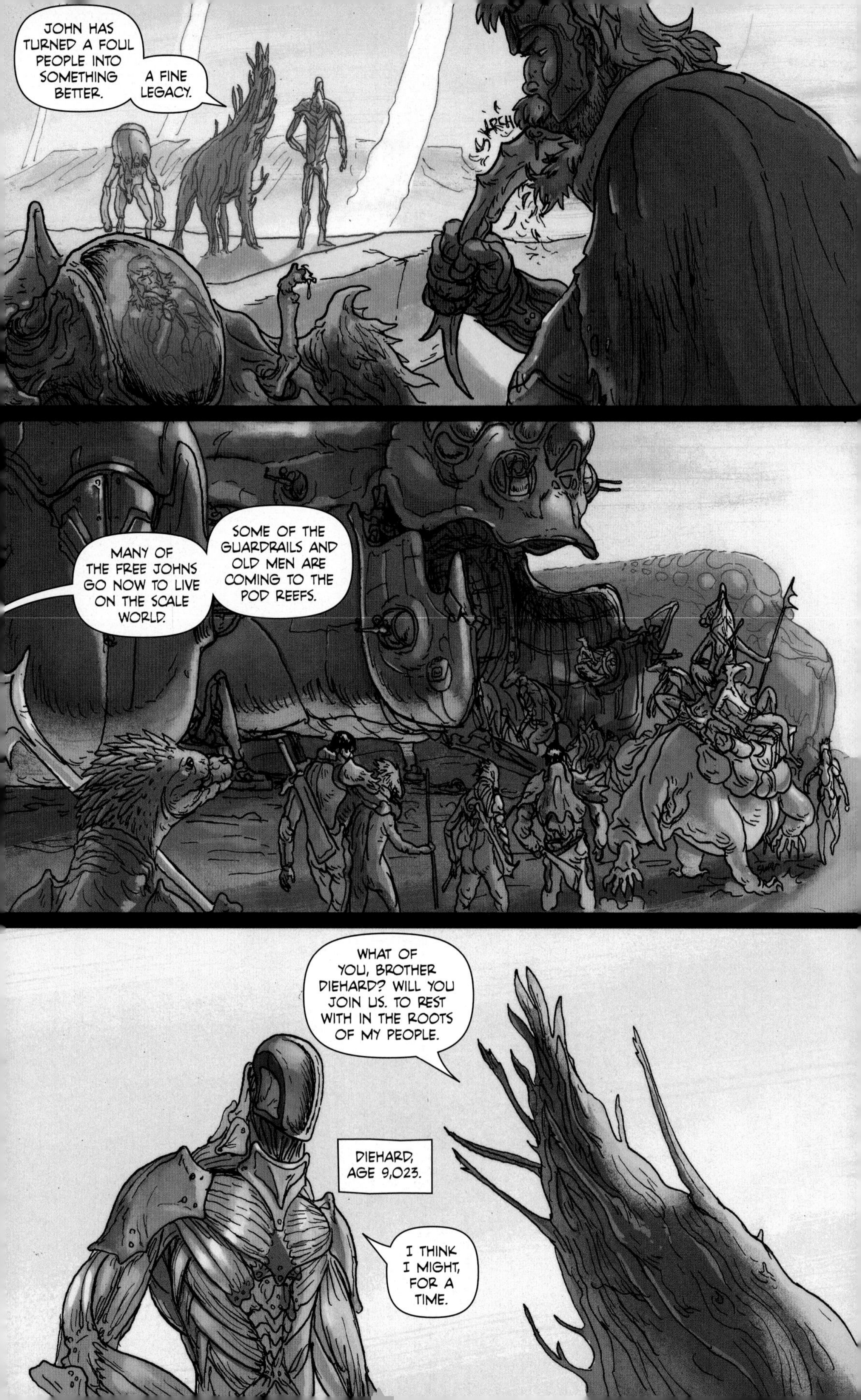
JOHN HAS TURNED A FOUL PEOPLE INTO SOMETHING BETTER.
A FINE LEGACY.
SKRCH
MANY OF THE FREE JOHNS GO NOW TO LIVE ON THE SCALE WORLD.
SOME OF THE GUARDRAILS AND OLD MEN ARE COMING TO THE POD REEFS.
WHAT OF YOU, BROTHER DIEHARD? WILL YOU JOIN US. TO REST WITH IN THE ROOTS OF MY PEOPLE.
DIEHARD, AGE 9,023.
I THINK I MIGHT, FOR A TIME.

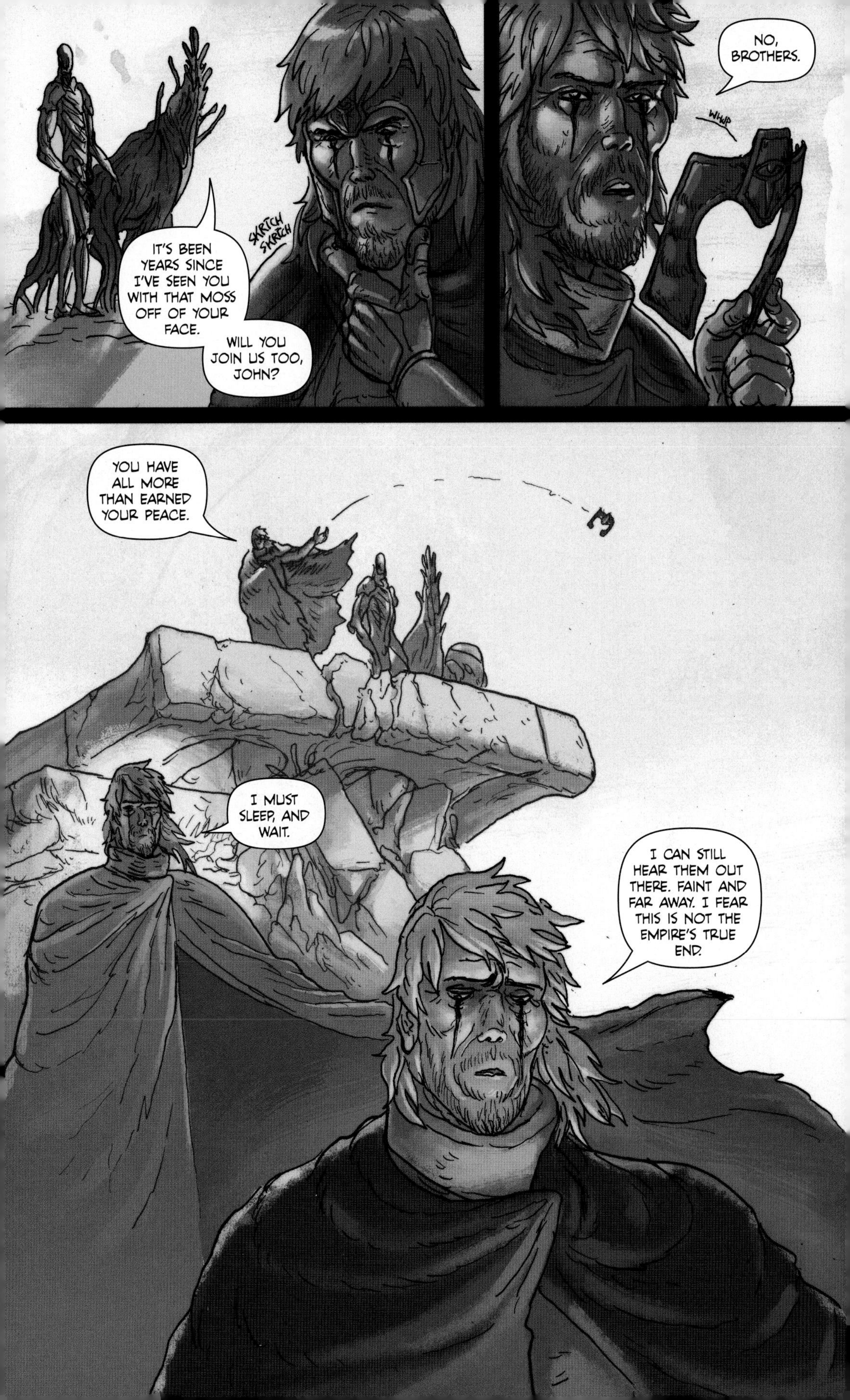
SKRITCH SKRITCH
IT'S BEEN YEARS SINCE I'VE SEEN YOU WITH THAT MOSS OFF OF YOUR FACE.
WILL YOU JOIN US TOO, JOHN?
NO, BROTHERS.
WHIP
YOU HAVE ALL MORE THAN EARNED YOUR PEACE.
I MUST SLEEP, AND WAIT.
I CAN STILL HEAR THEM OUT THERE. FAINT AND FAR AWAY. I FEAR THIS IS NOT THE EMPIRE'S TRUE END.

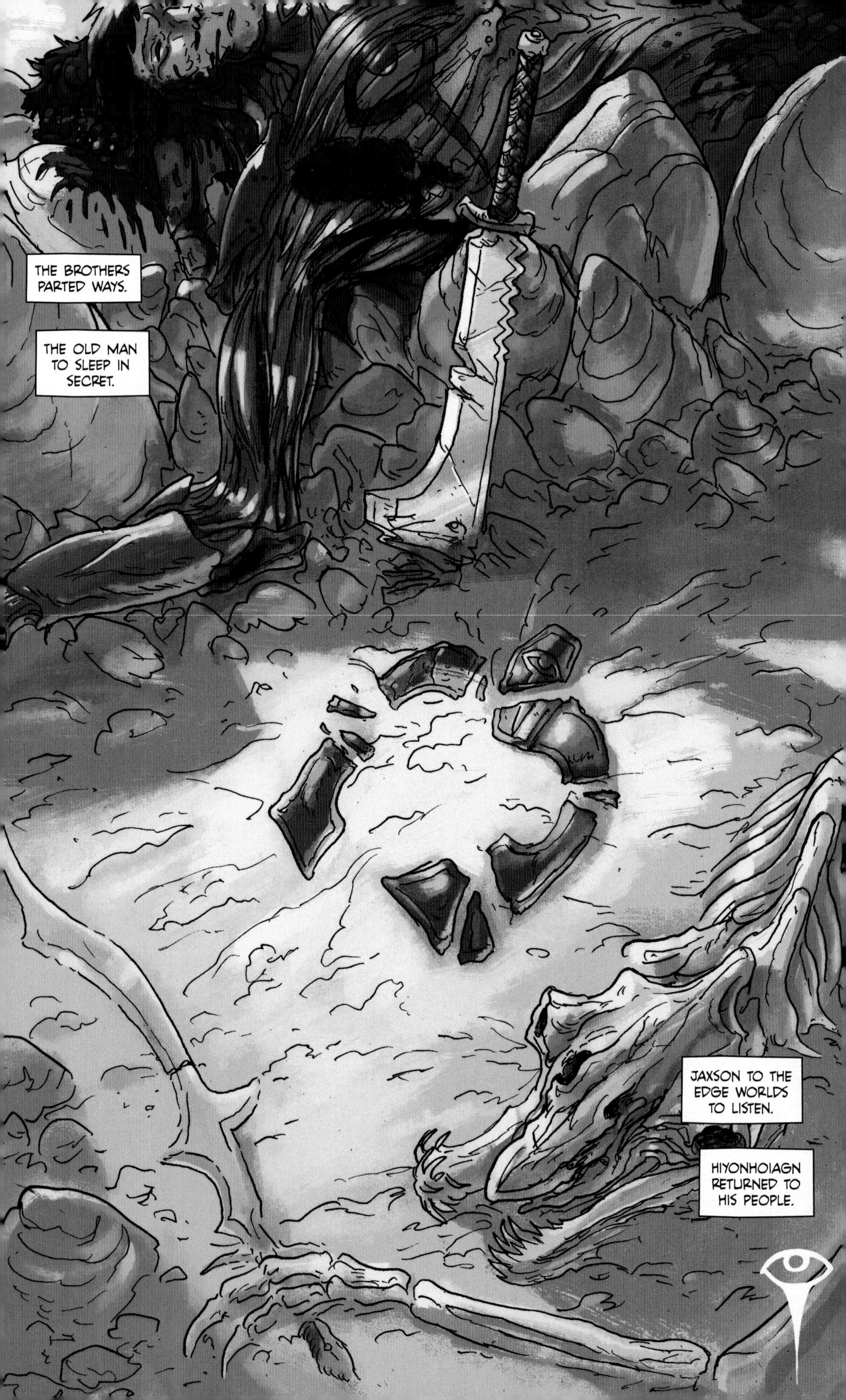
THE BROTHERS PARTED WAYS.
THE OLD MAN TO SLEEP IN SECRET.
JAXSON TO THE EDGE WORLDS TO LISTEN.
HIYONHOIAGN RETURNED TO HIS PEOPLE.

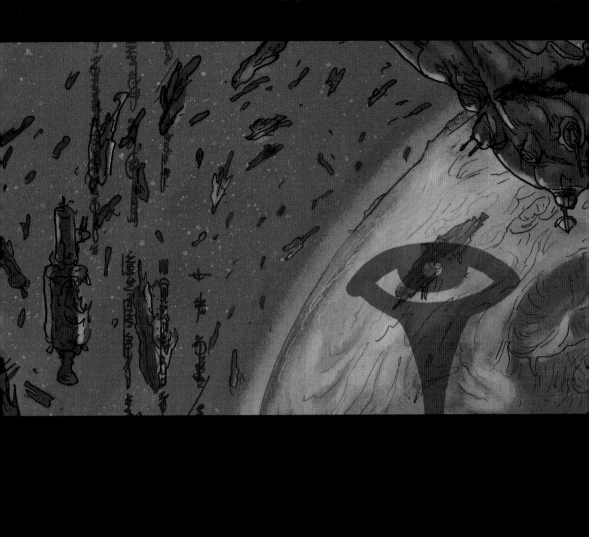

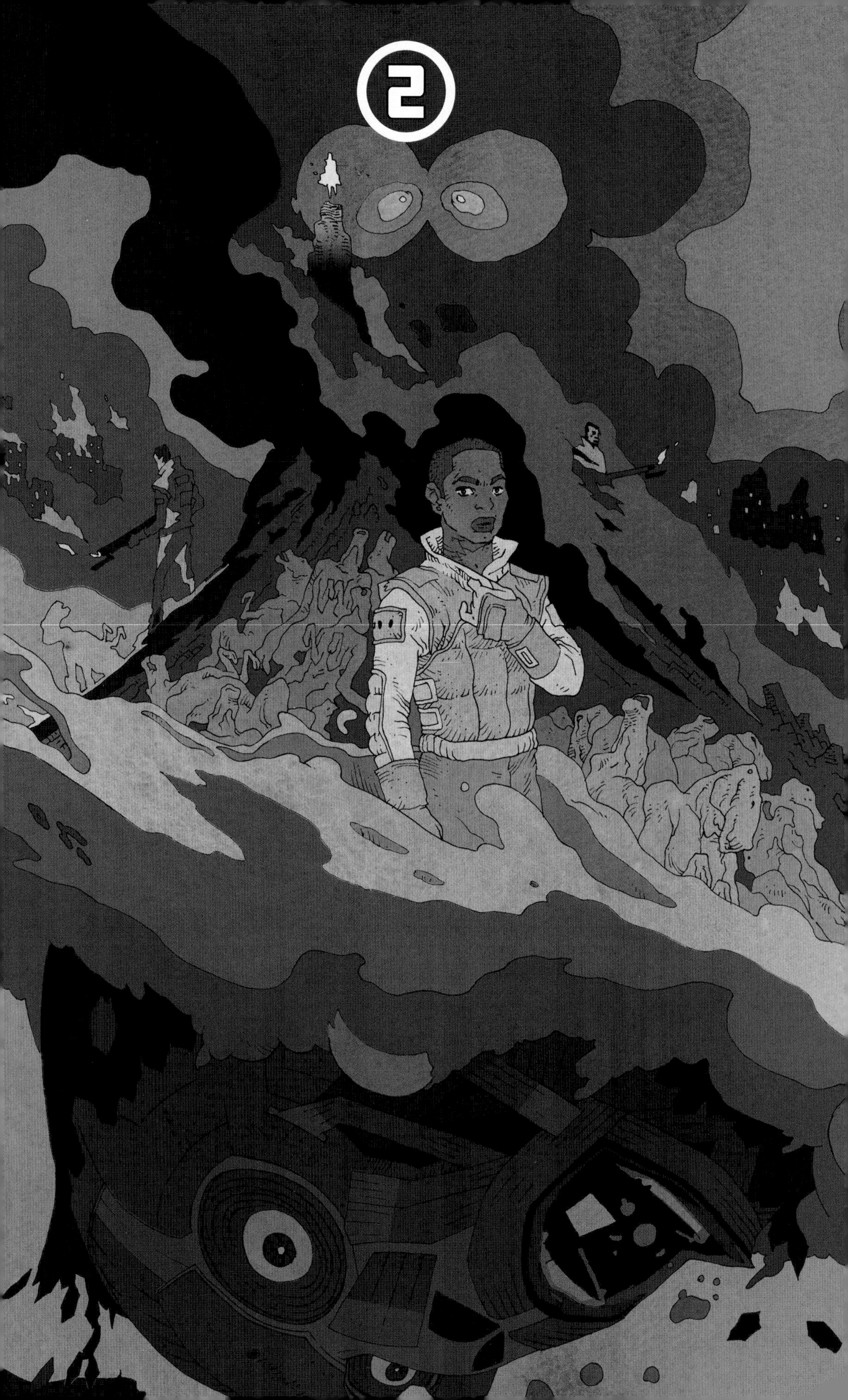
2

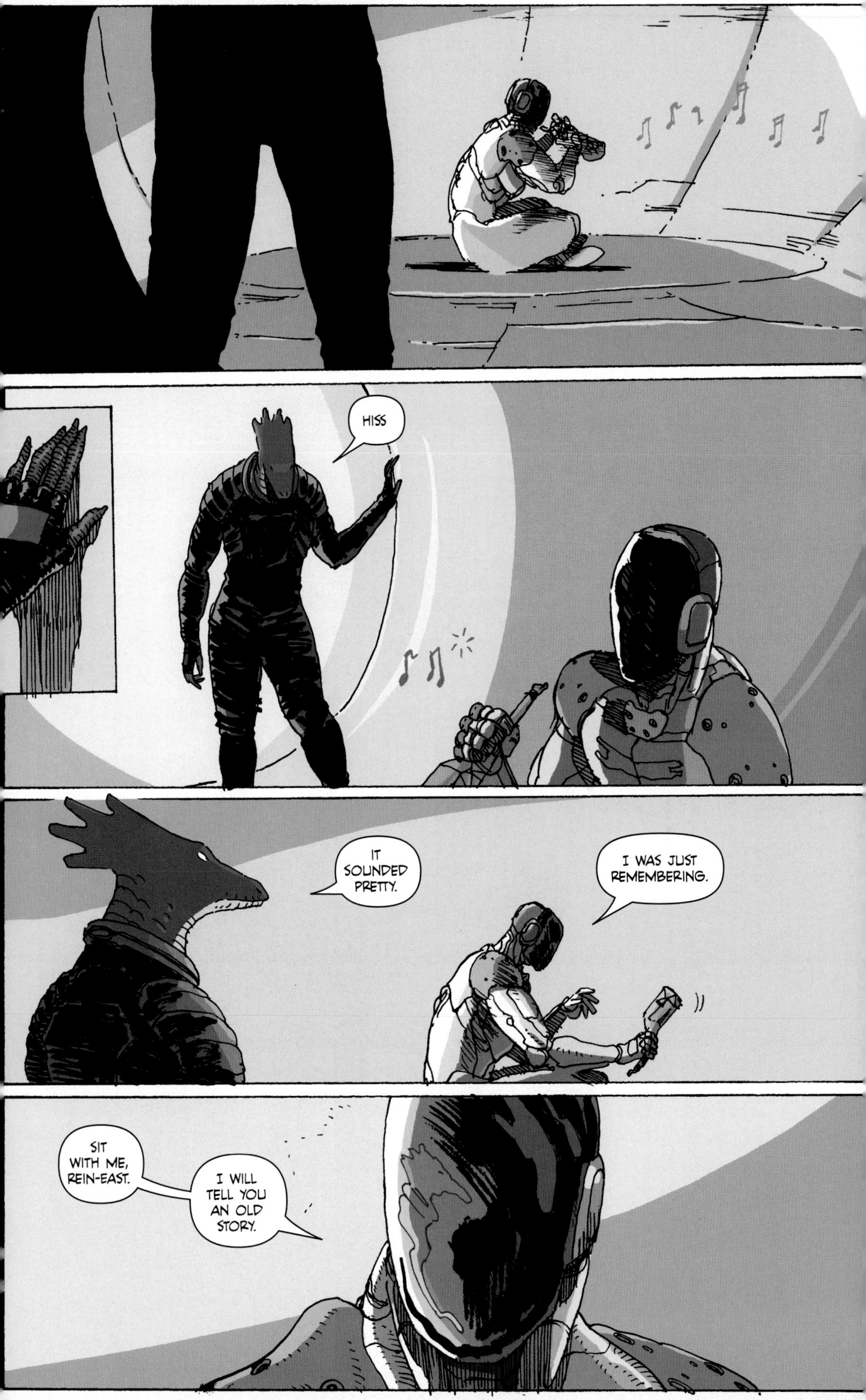
HISS
IT SOUNDED PRETTY.
I WAS JUST REMEMBERING.
SIT WITH ME, REIN-EAST.
I WILL TELL YOU AN OLD STORY.

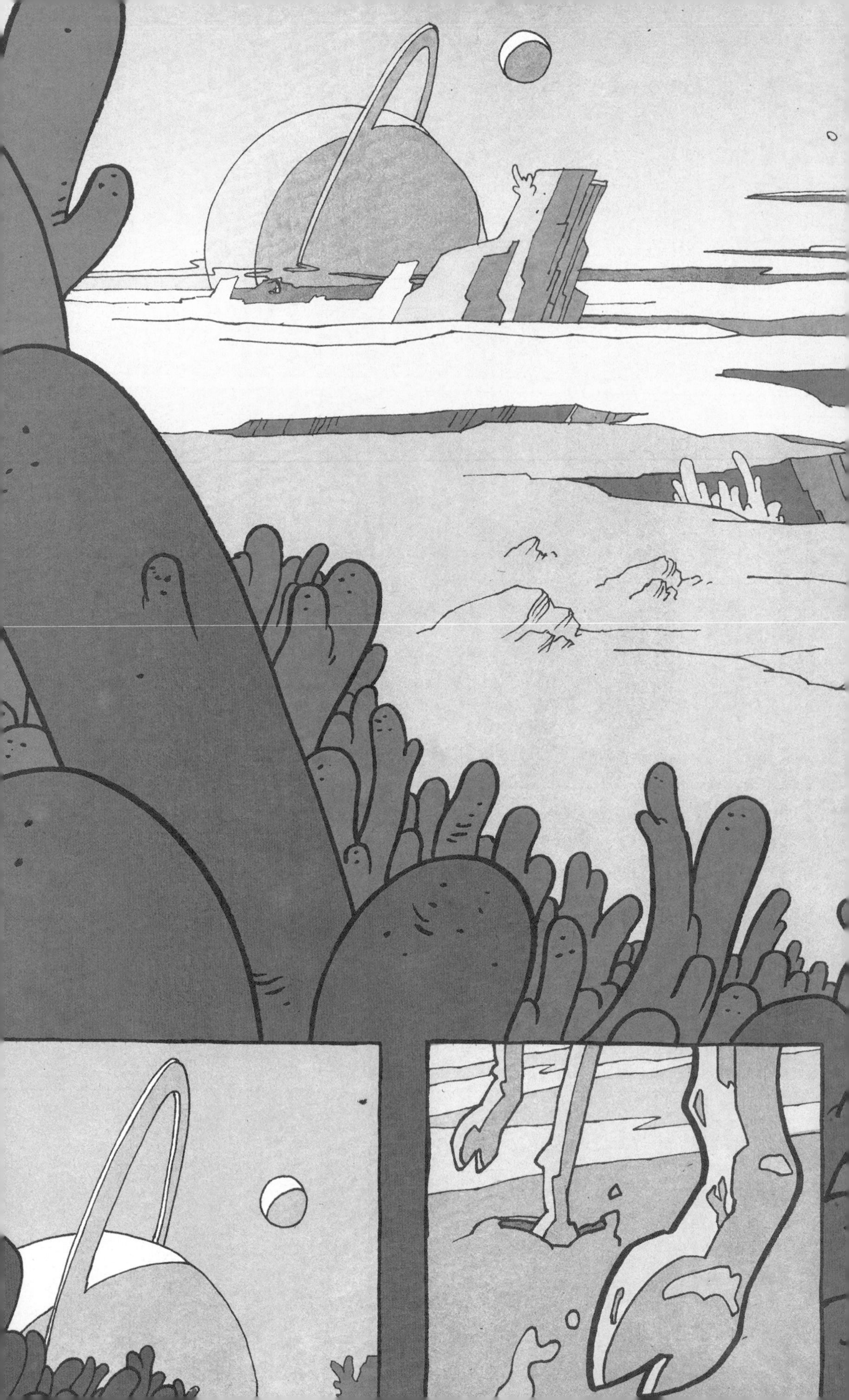

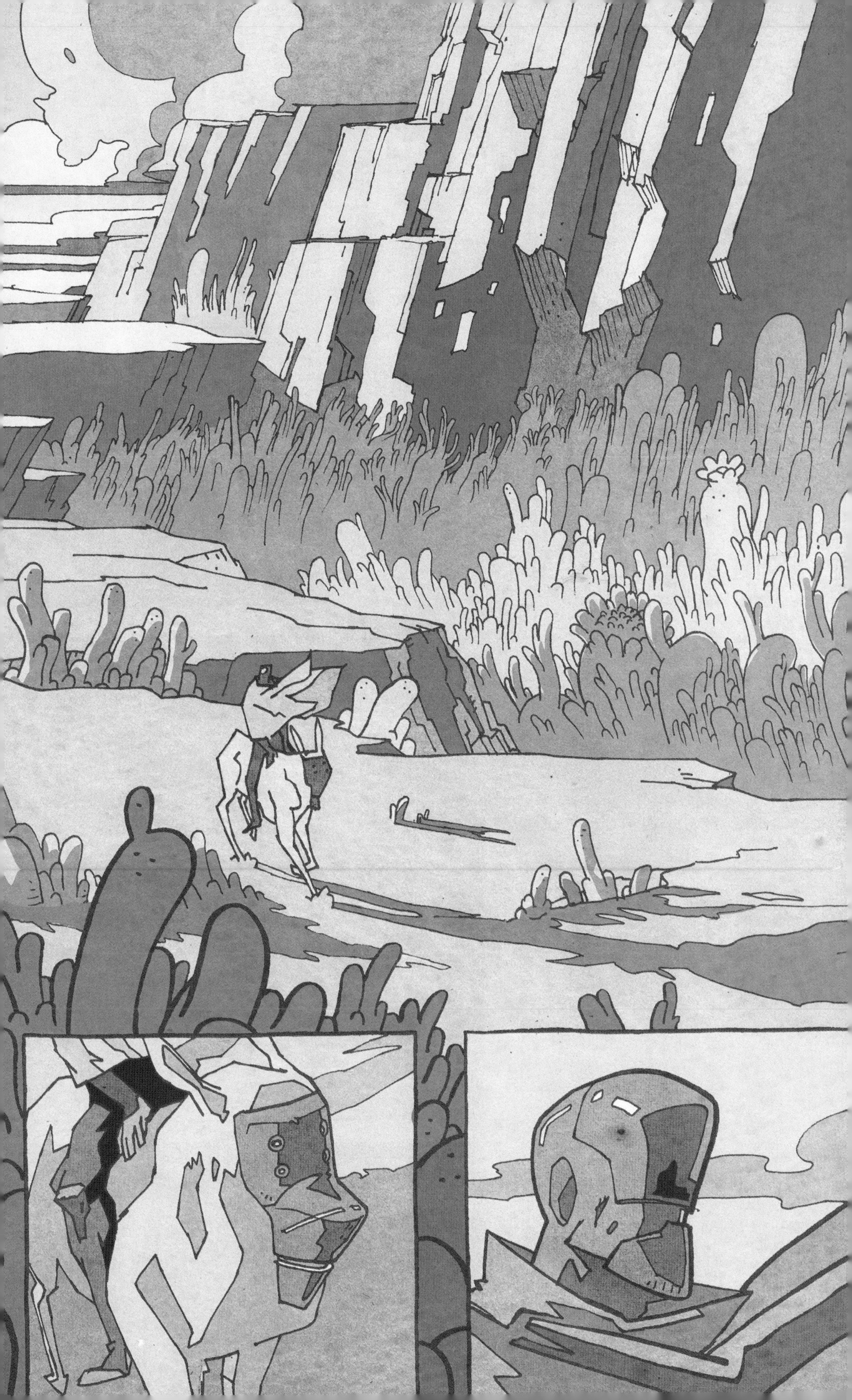

"I'D TAKEN UP WITH THE KOXO PEOPLE IN THE STEPS OF THE RELATIVELY OBSCURE PLANETOID D314159.

"I WAS RETURNING FROM A FAILED VISION QUEST.

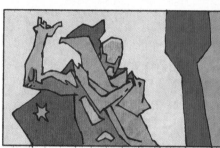

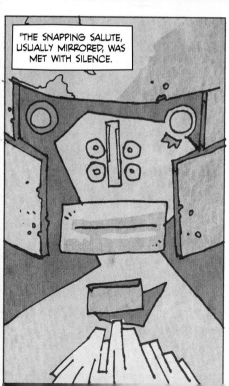

"THE SNAPPING SALUTE, USUALLY MIRRORED, WAS MET WITH SILENCE.

"...THAT'S WHEN I KNEW SOMETHING WAS WRONG."

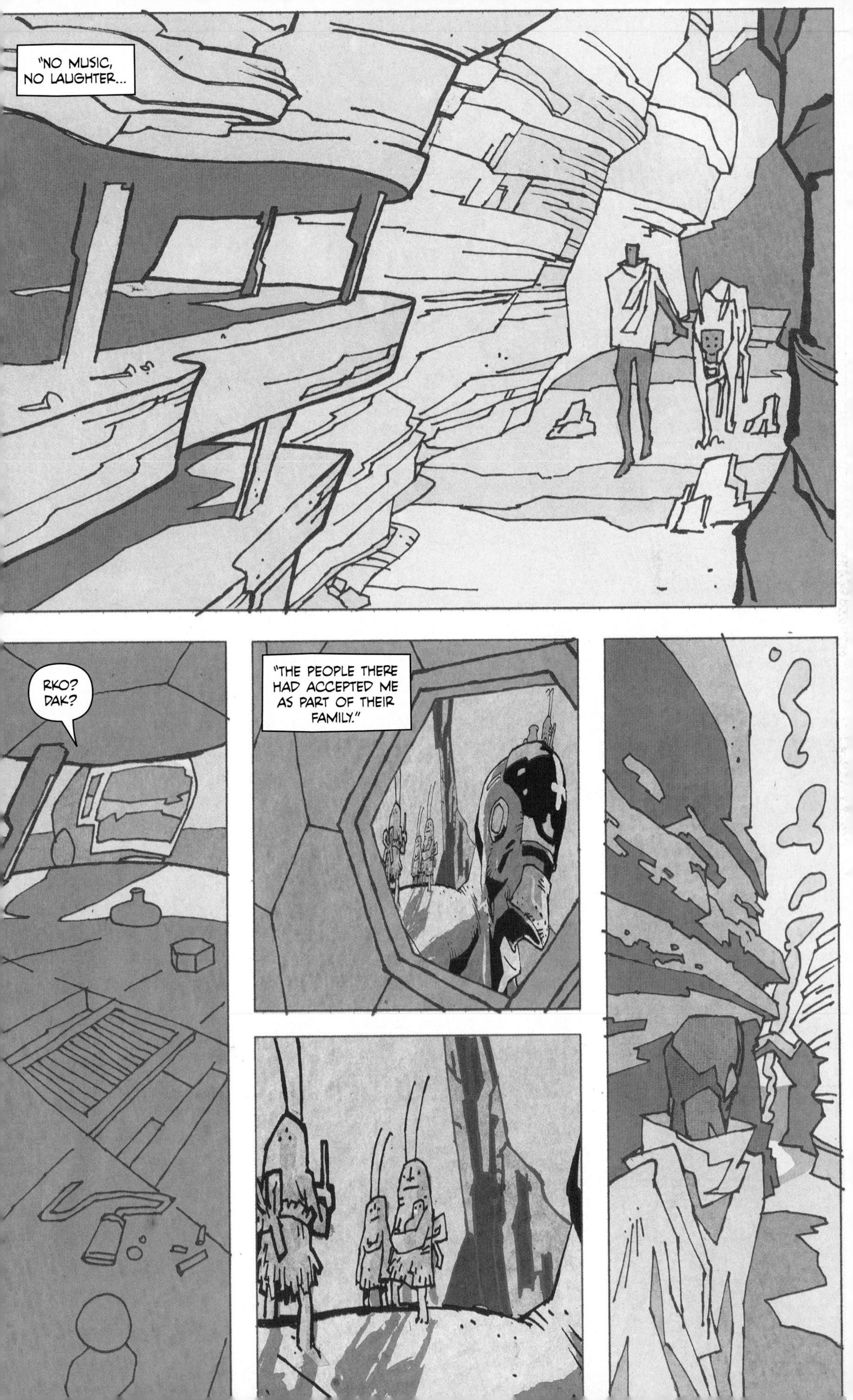
"NO MUSIC,
NO LAUGHTER...
RKO?
DAK?
"THE PEOPLE THERE
HAD ACCEPTED ME
AS PART OF THEIR
FAMILY."

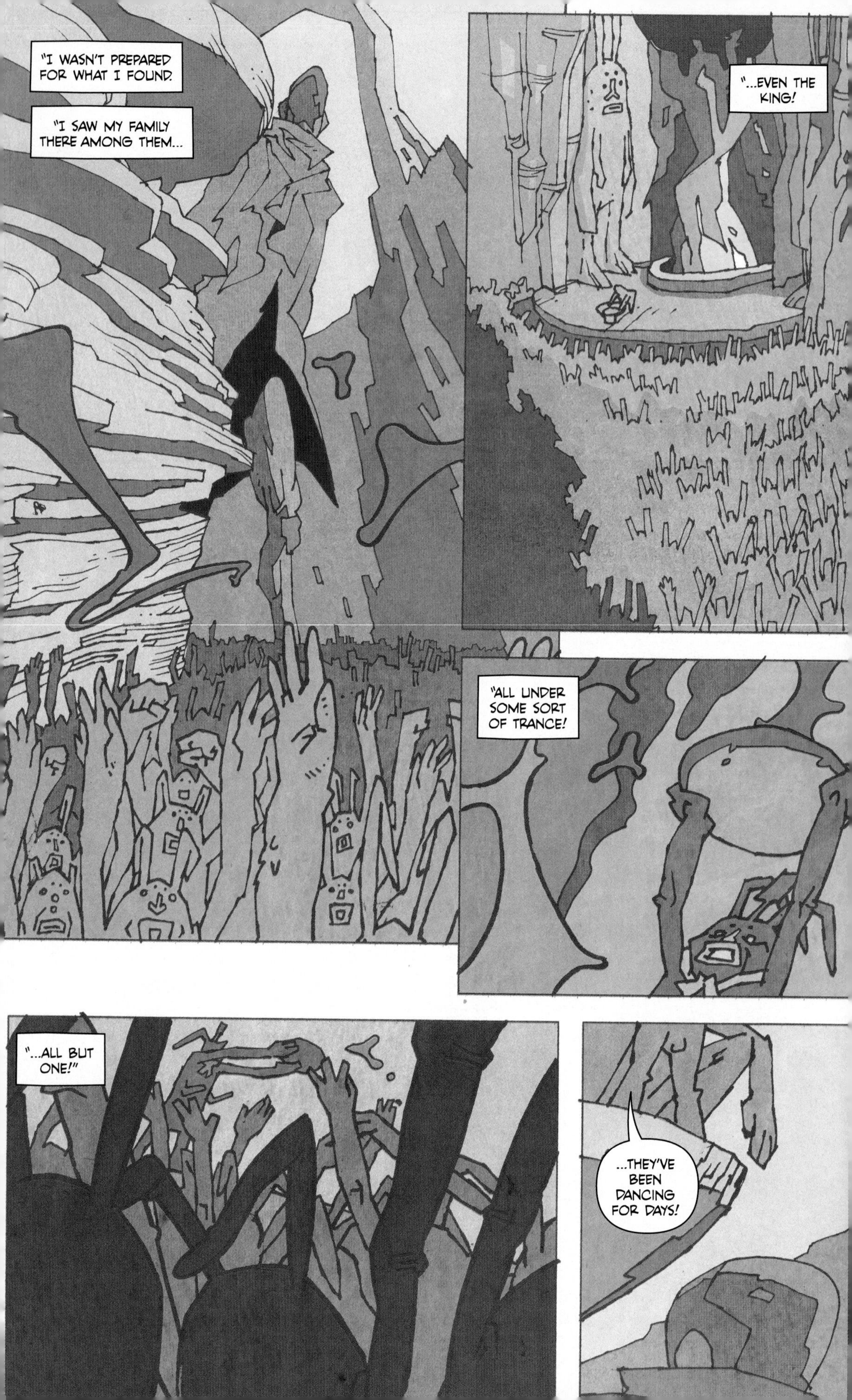
"I WASN'T PREPARED FOR WHAT I FOUND.
"I SAW MY FAMILY THERE AMONG THEM...
"...EVEN THE KING!
"ALL UNDER SOME SORT OF TRANCE!
"...ALL BUT ONE!"
...THEY'VE BEEN DANCING FOR DAYS!

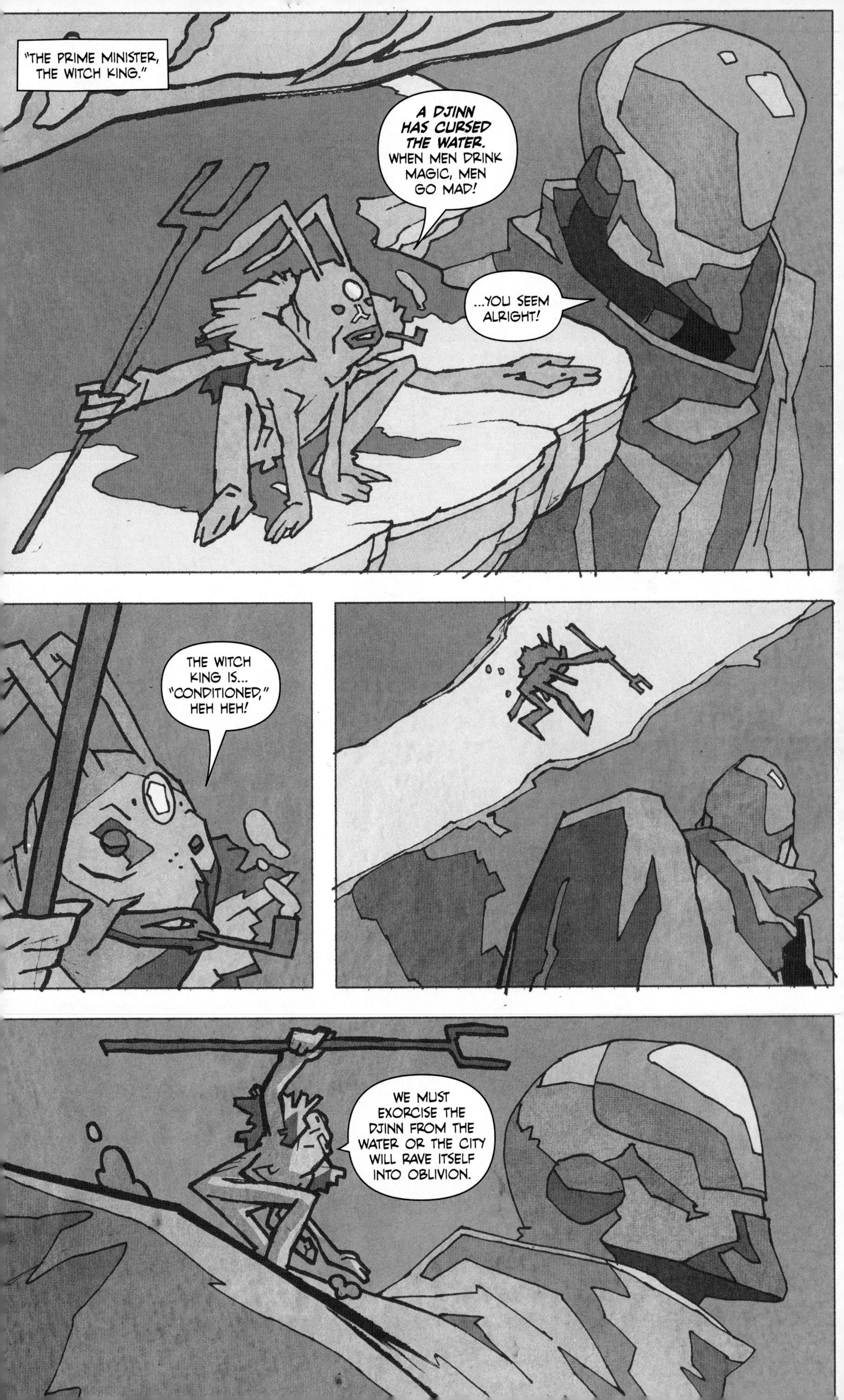
"THE PRIME MINISTER, THE WITCH KING."
A DJINN HAS CURSED THE WATER. WHEN MEN DRINK MAGIC, MEN GO MAD!
...YOU SEEM ALRIGHT!
THE WITCH KING IS... "CONDITIONED," HEH HEH!
WE MUST EXORCISE THE DJINN FROM THE WATER OR THE CITY WILL RAVE ITSELF INTO OBLIVION.

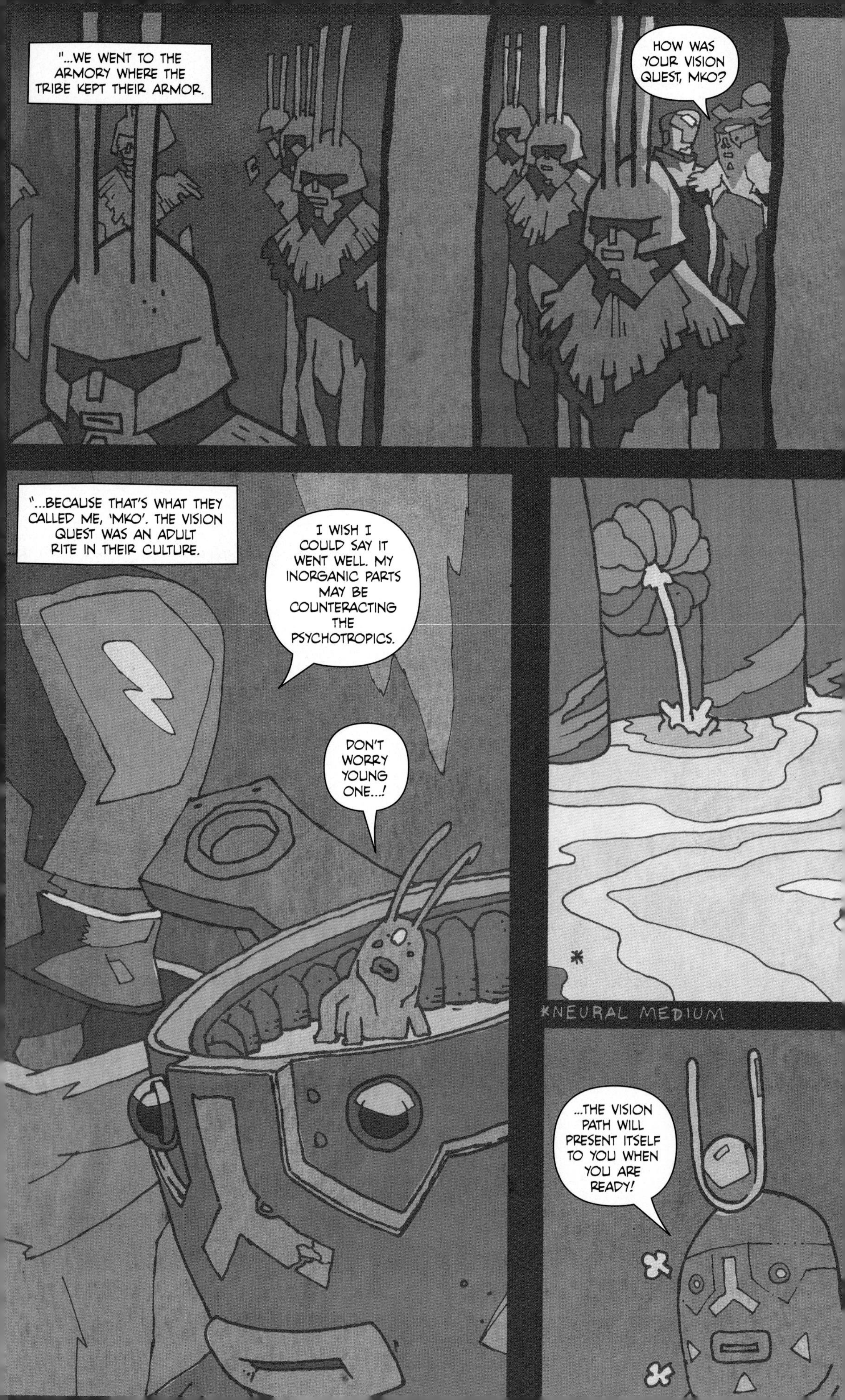
"...WE WENT TO THE ARMORY WHERE THE TRIBE KEPT THEIR ARMOR.
HOW WAS YOUR VISION QUEST, MKO?
"...BECAUSE THAT'S WHAT THEY CALLED ME, 'MKO'. THE VISION QUEST WAS AN ADULT RITE IN THEIR CULTURE.
I WISH I COULD SAY IT WENT WELL. MY INORGANIC PARTS MAY BE COUNTERACTING THE PSYCHOTROPICS.
DON'T WORRY YOUNG ONE...!
*
*NEURAL MEDIUM
...THE VISION PATH WILL PRESENT ITSELF TO YOU WHEN YOU ARE READY!

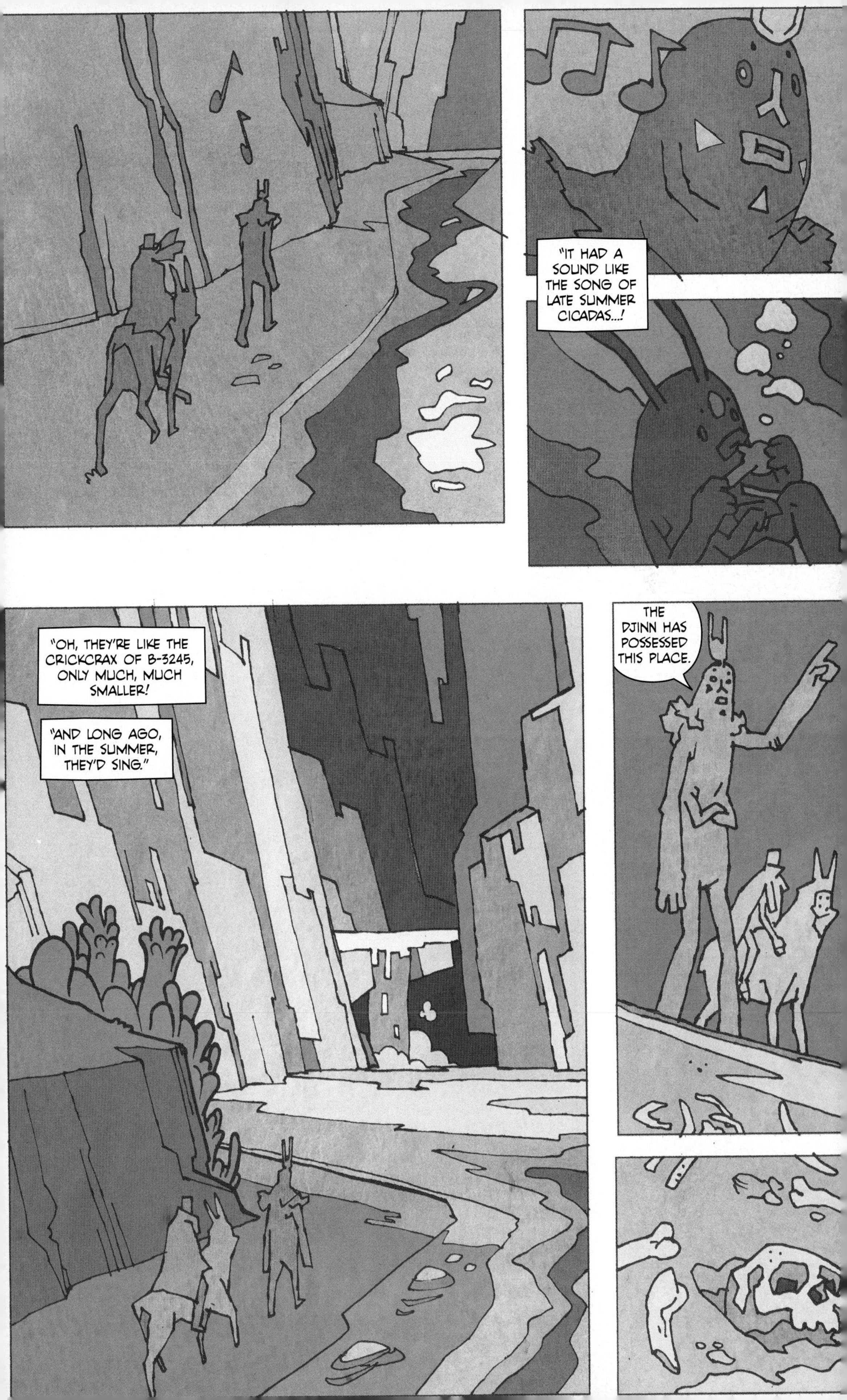
"IT HAD A SOUND LIKE THE SONG OF LATE SUMMER CICADAS...!
"OH, THEY'RE LIKE THE CRICKCRAX OF B-3245, ONLY MUCH, MUCH SMALLER!
"AND LONG AGO, IN THE SUMMER, THEY'D SING."
THE DJINN HAS POSSESSED THIS PLACE.

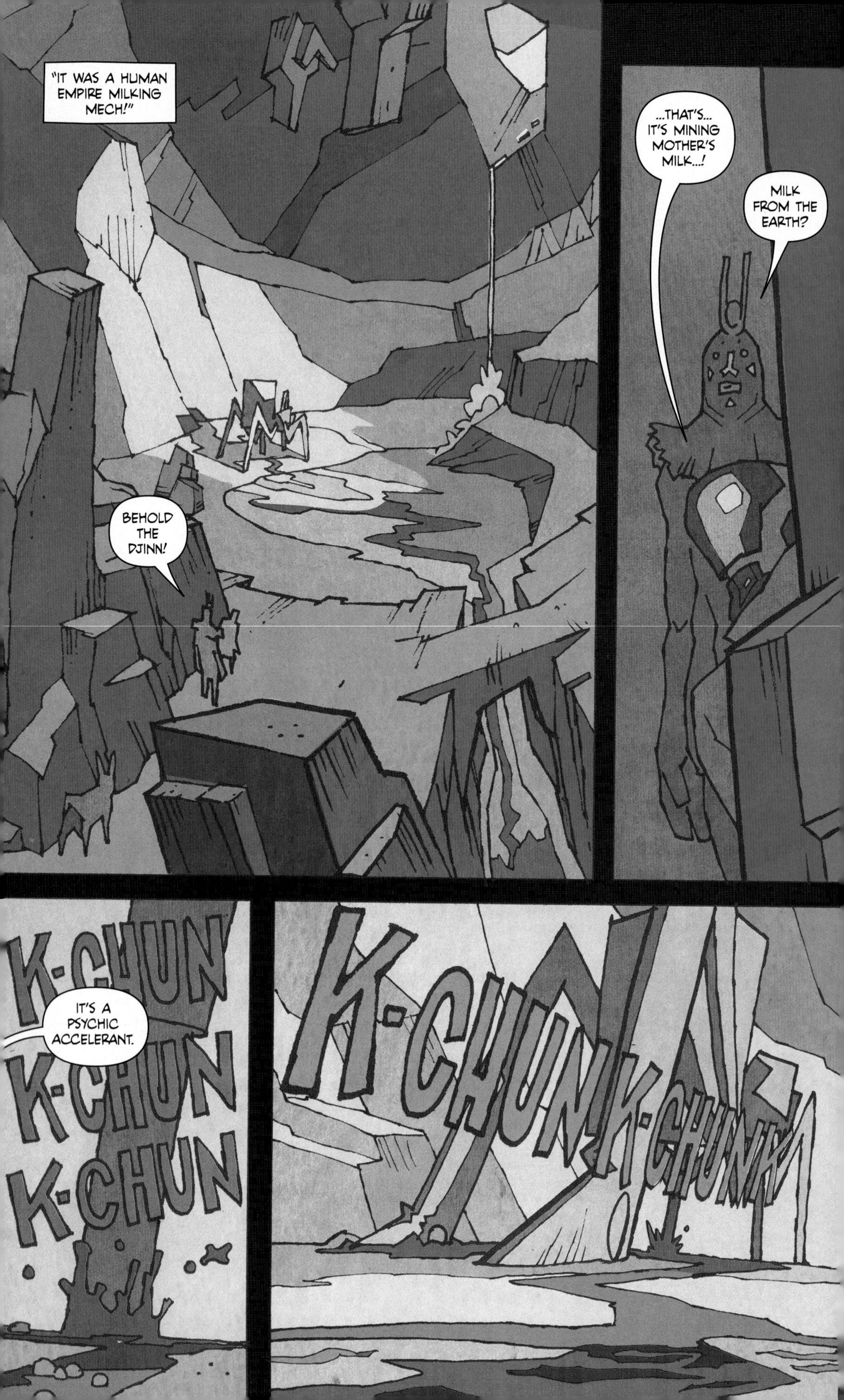
"IT WAS A HUMAN EMPIRE MILKING MECH!"
BEHOLD THE DJINN!
...THAT'S... IT'S MINING MOTHER'S MILK...!
MILK FROM THE EARTH?
K-CHUN
IT'S A PSYCHIC ACCELERANT.
K-CHUN
K-CHUN
K-CHUNK-CHUNK

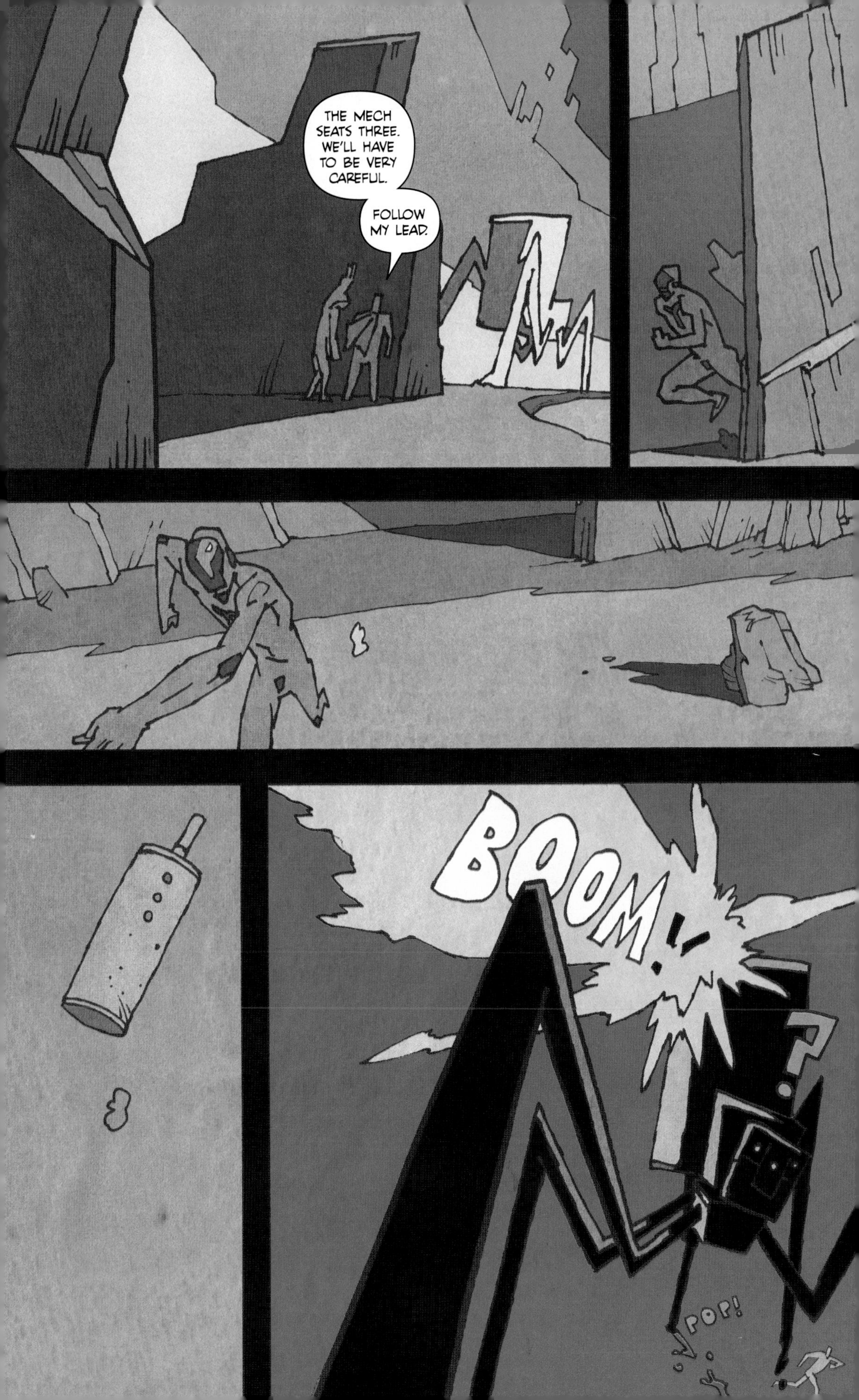
THE MECH SEATS THREE. WE'LL HAVE TO BE VERY CAREFUL.
FOLLOW MY LEAD.
BOOM!
?
POP!

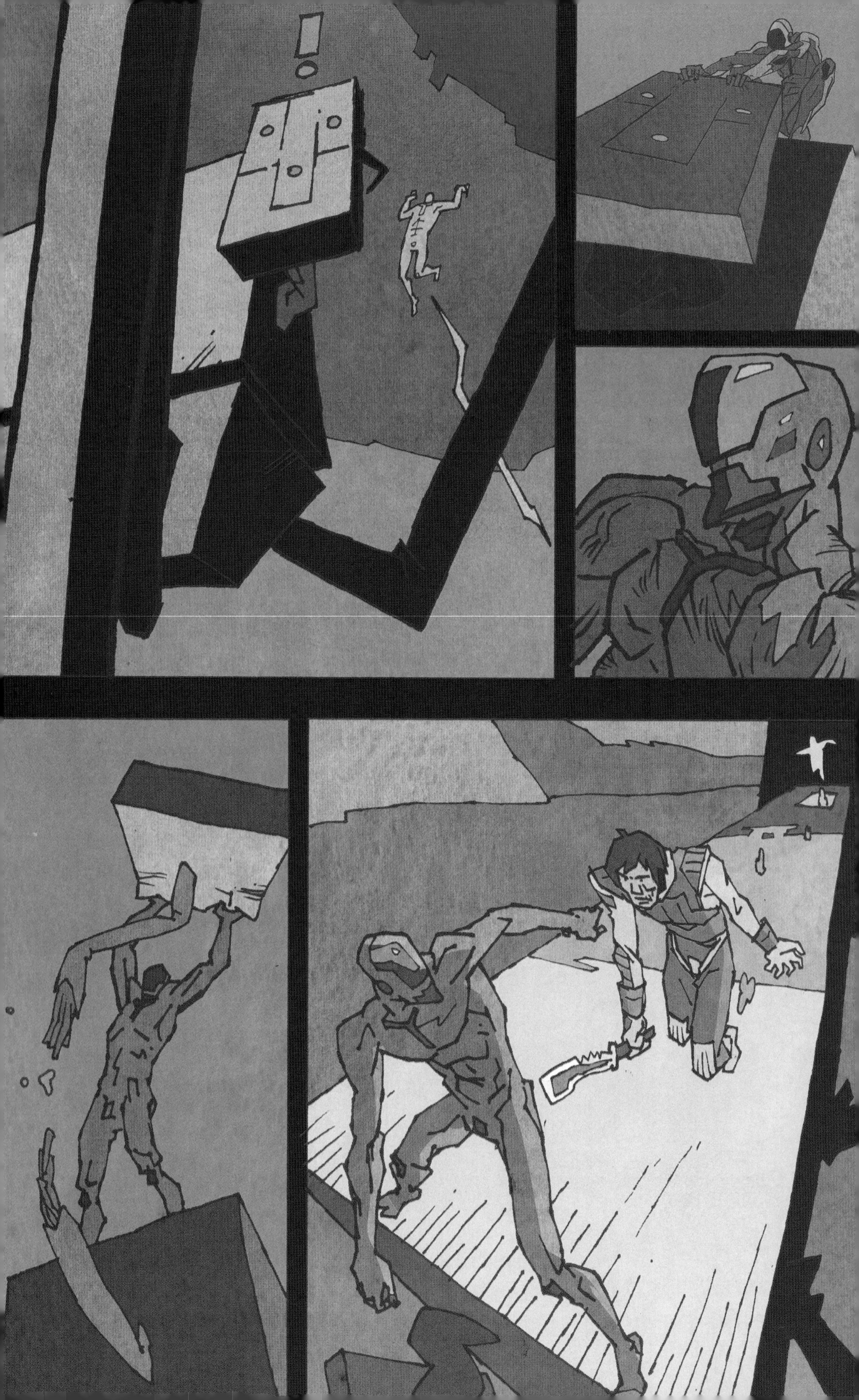

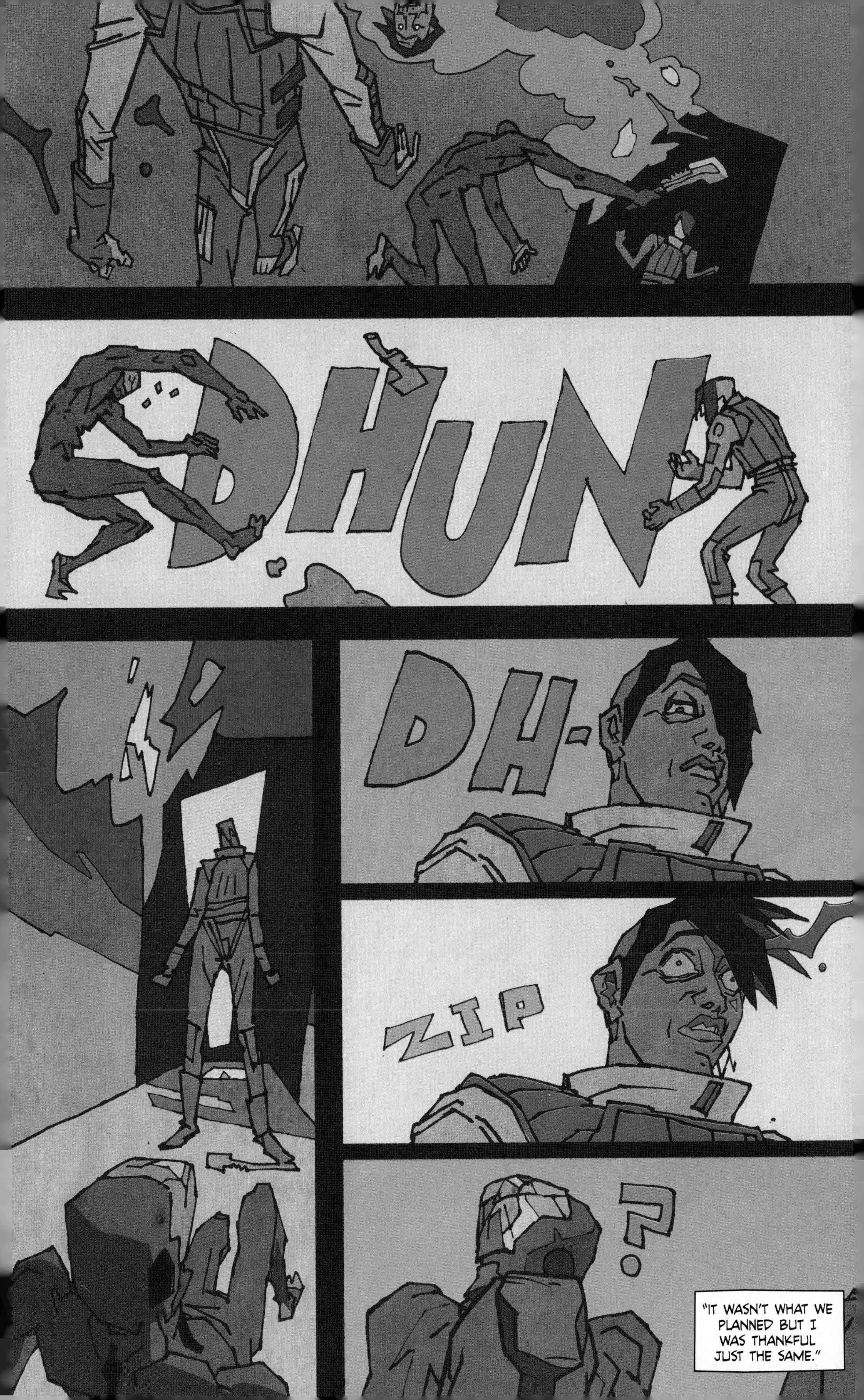
DHUN
DH-
ZIP
?
"IT WASN'T WHAT WE PLANNED BUT I WAS THANKFUL JUST THE SAME."

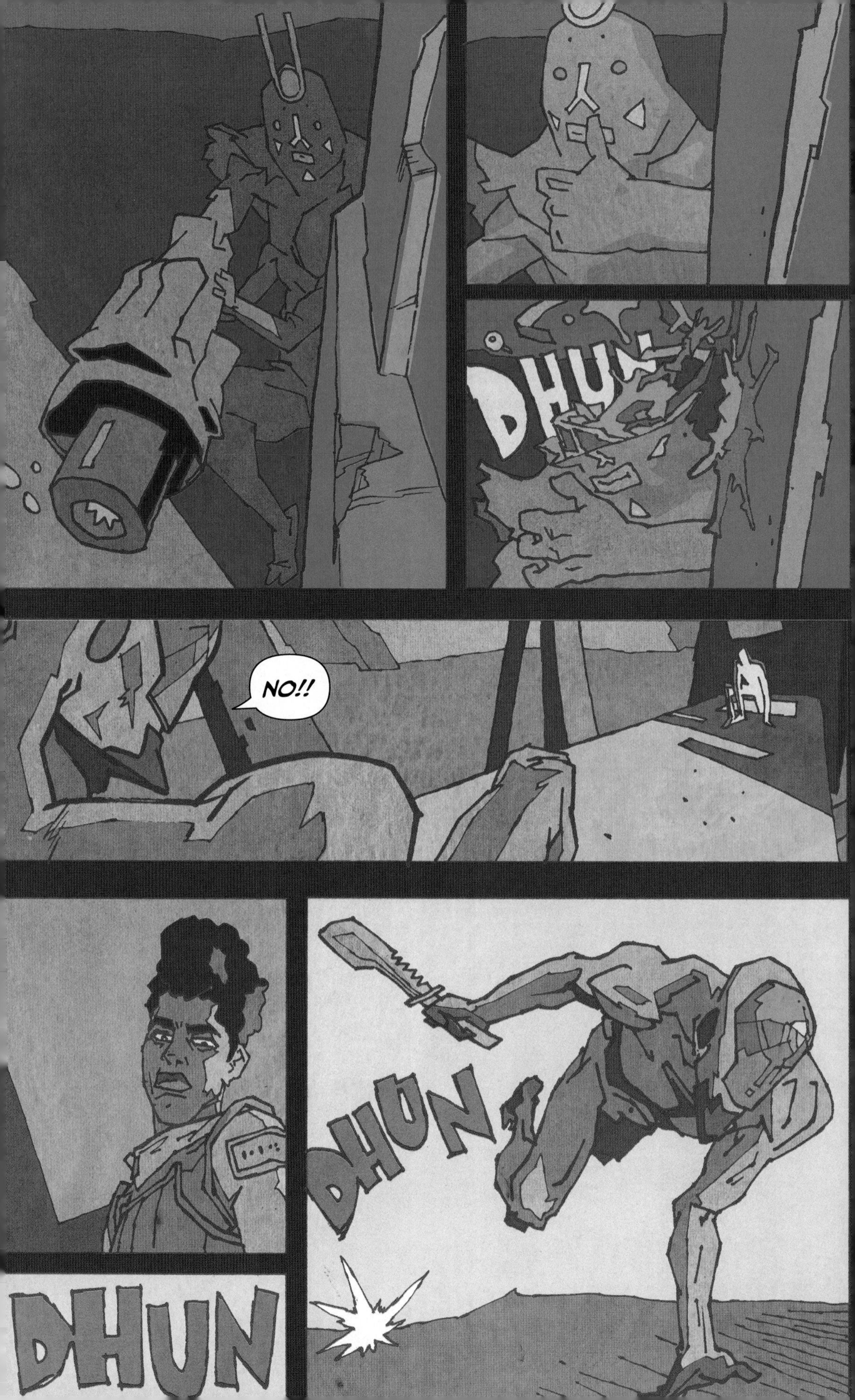
DHUN
NO!!
DHUN
DHUN

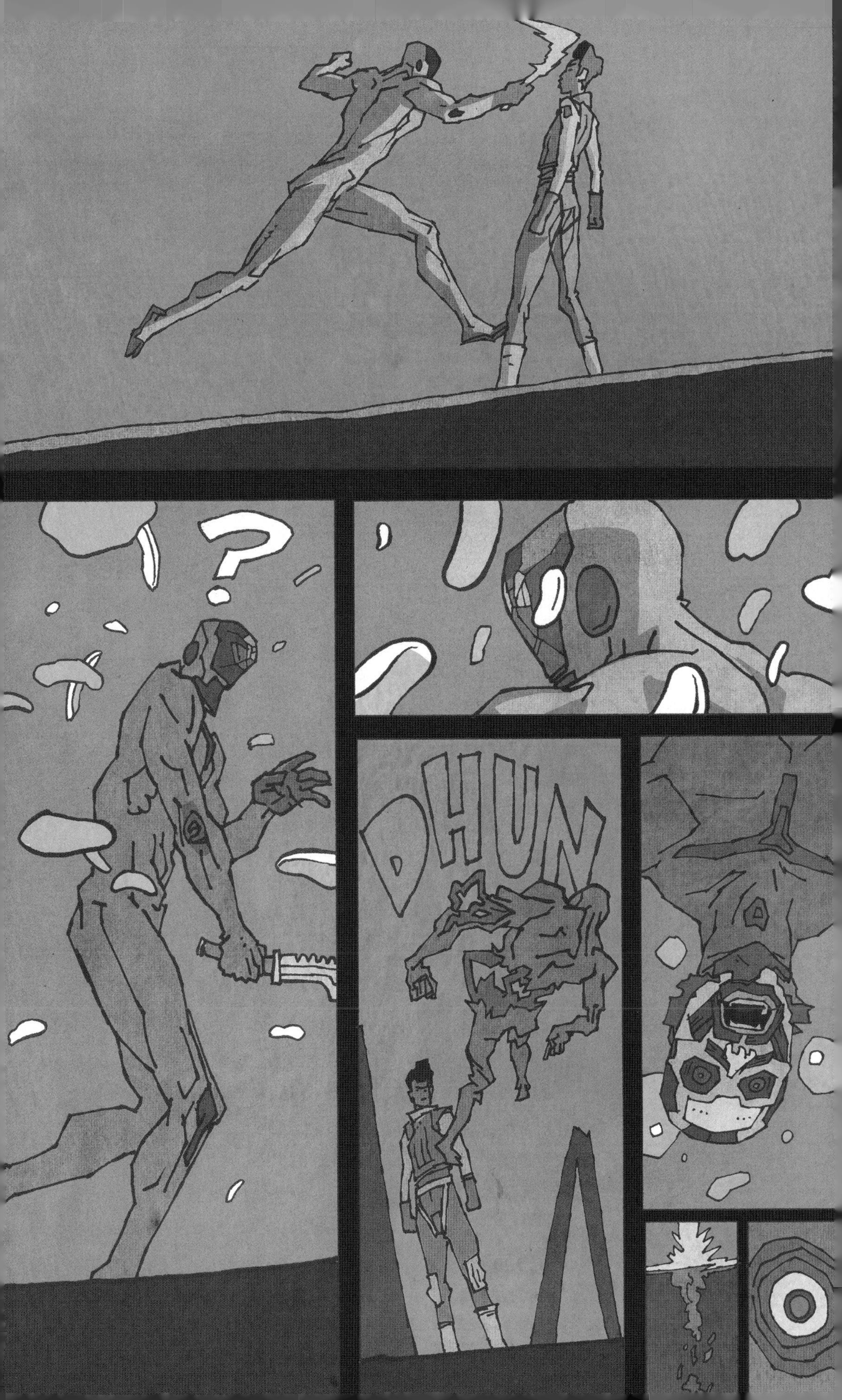
?
DHUN

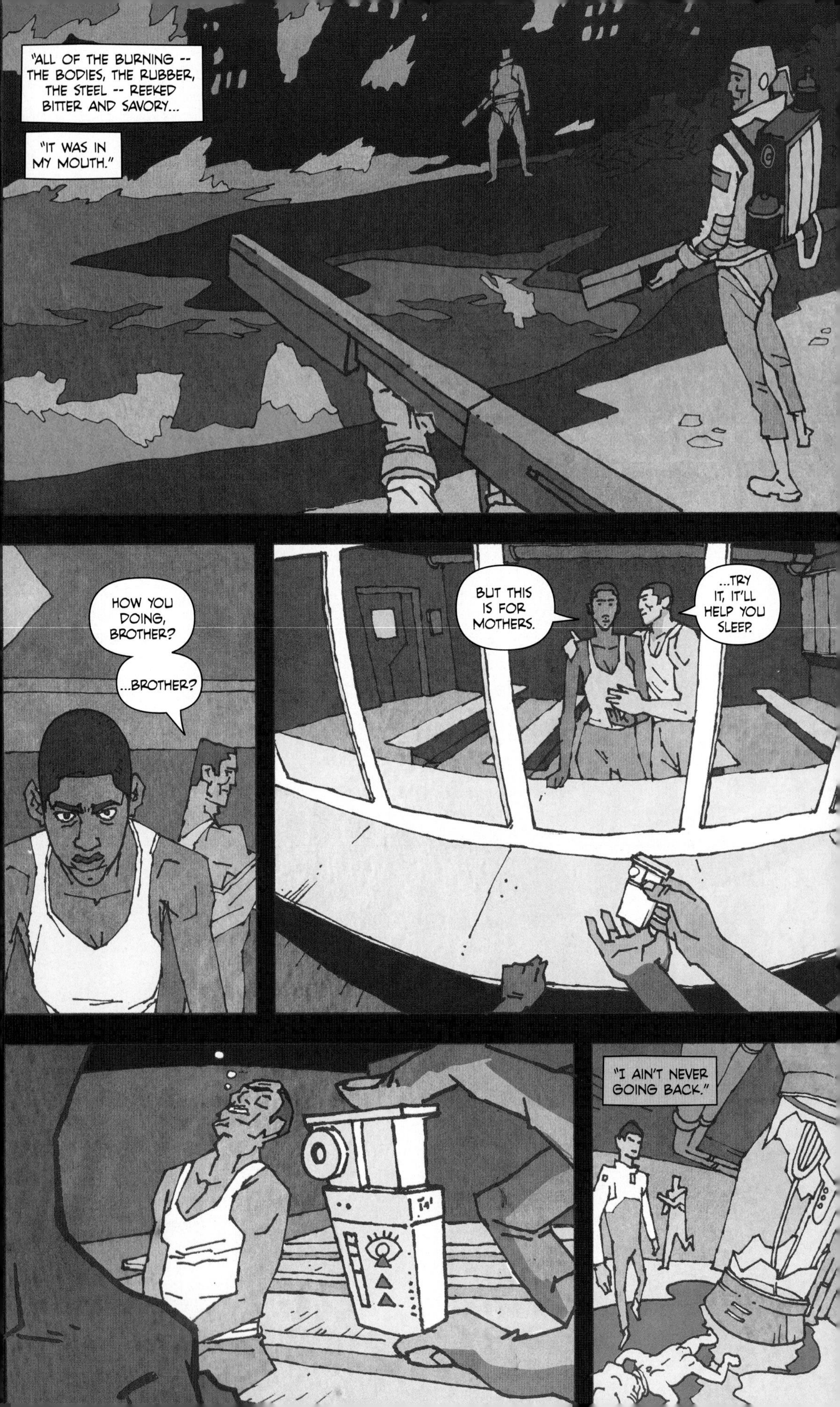
"ALL OF THE BURNING -- THE BODIES, THE RUBBER, THE STEEL -- REEKED BITTER AND SAVORY...
"IT WAS IN MY MOUTH."
HOW YOU DOING, BROTHER?
...BROTHER?
BUT THIS IS FOR MOTHERS.
...TRY IT, IT'LL HELP YOU SLEEP.
"I AIN'T NEVER GOING BACK."

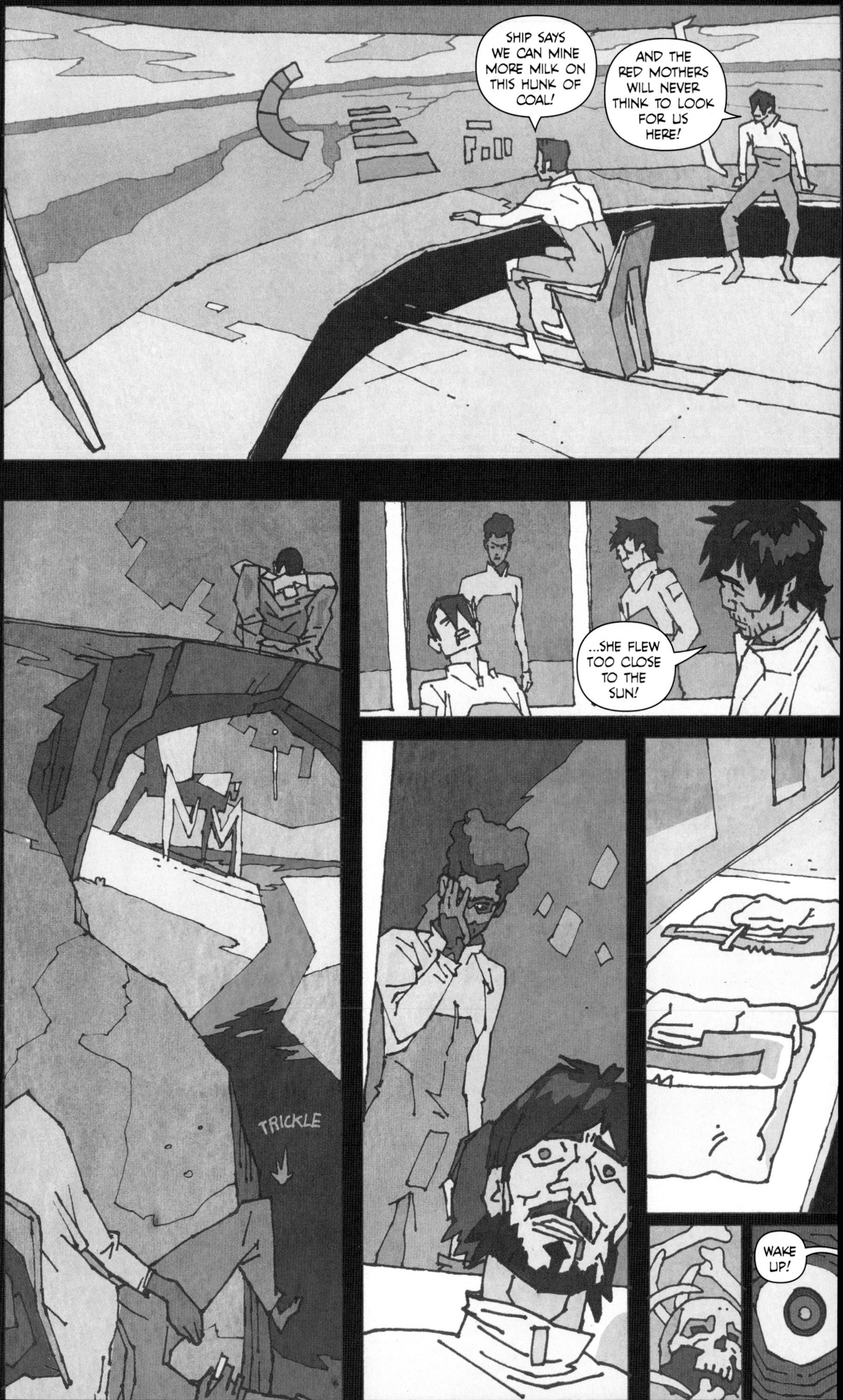
SHIP SAYS WE CAN MINE MORE MILK ON THIS HUNK OF COAL!
AND THE RED MOTHERS WILL NEVER THINK TO LOOK FOR US HERE!
TRICKLE
...SHE FLEW TOO CLOSE TO THE SUN!
WAKE UP!

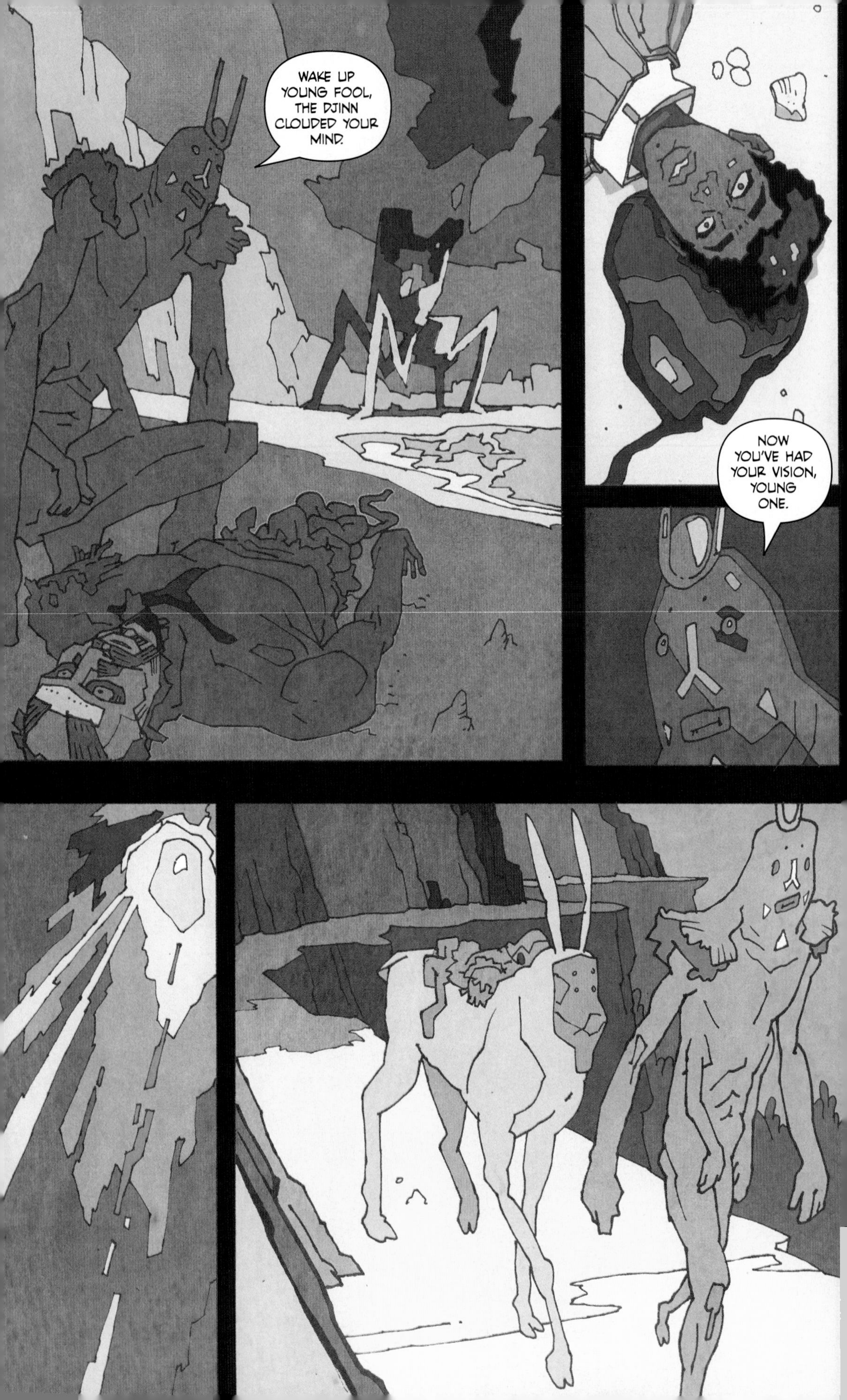
WAKE UP YOUNG FOOL, THE DJINN CLOUDED YOUR MIND.
NOW YOU'VE HAD YOUR VISION, YOUNG ONE.

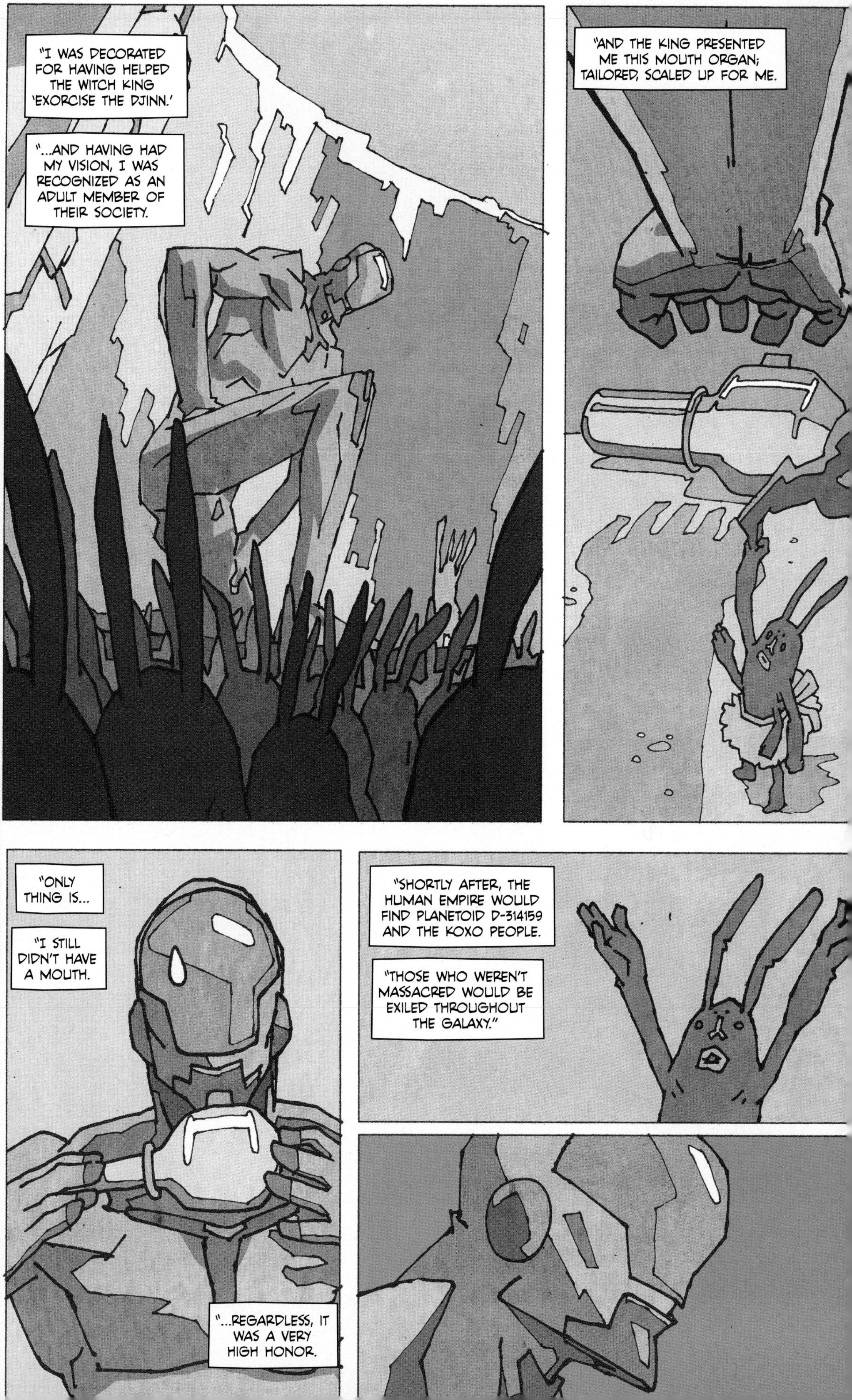
"I WAS DECORATED FOR HAVING HELPED THE WITCH KING 'EXORCISE THE DJINN.'
"...AND HAVING HAD MY VISION, I WAS RECOGNIZED AS AN ADULT MEMBER OF THEIR SOCIETY.
"AND THE KING PRESENTED ME THIS MOUTH ORGAN; TAILORED, SCALED UP FOR ME.
"ONLY THING IS...
"I STILL DIDN'T HAVE A MOUTH.
"...REGARDLESS, IT WAS A VERY HIGH HONOR.
"SHORTLY AFTER, THE HUMAN EMPIRE WOULD FIND PLANETOID D-314159 AND THE KOXO PEOPLE.
"THOSE WHO WEREN'T MASSACRED WOULD BE EXILED THROUGHOUT THE GALAXY."

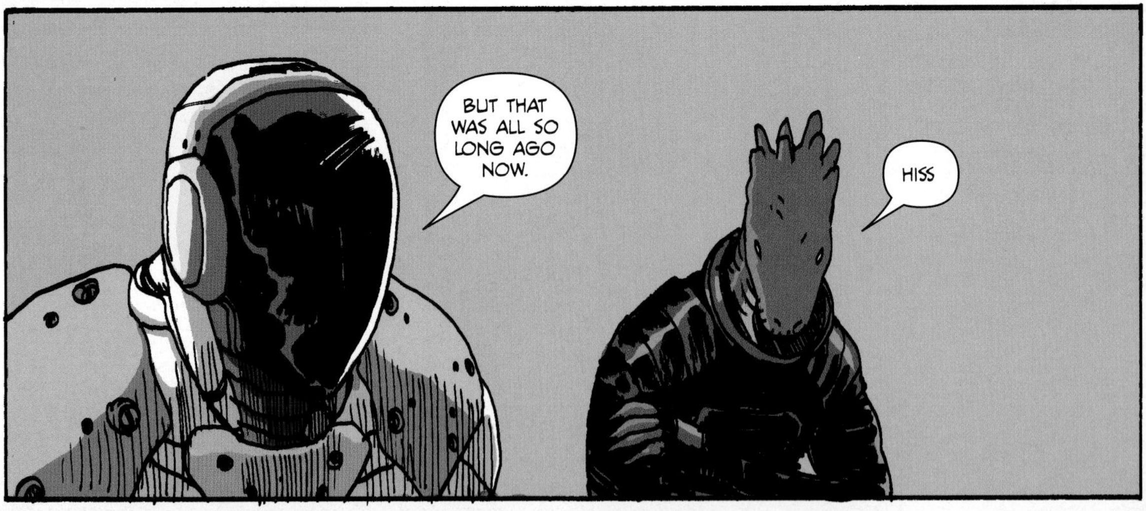
BUT THAT WAS ALL SO LONG AGO NOW.
HISS

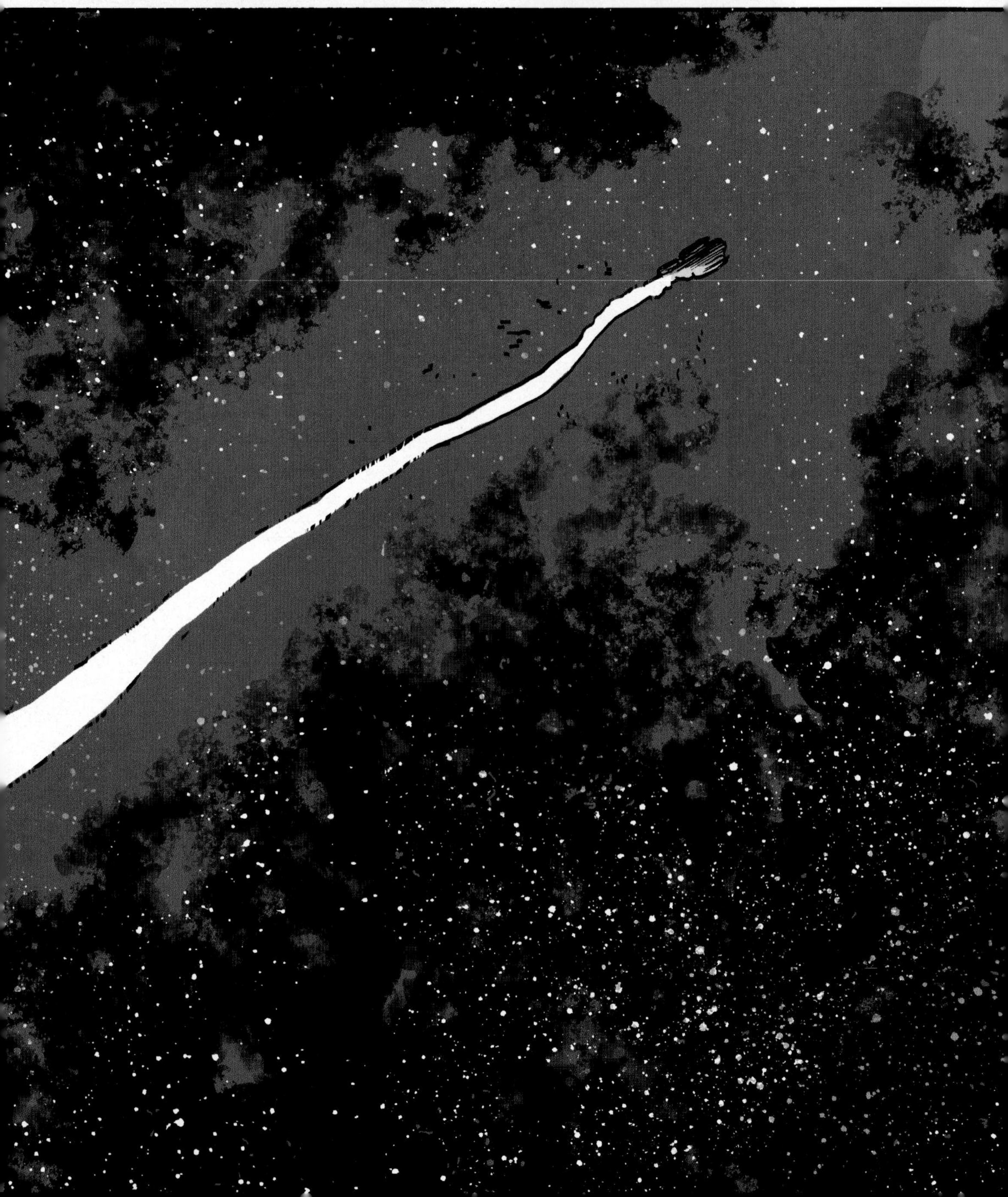

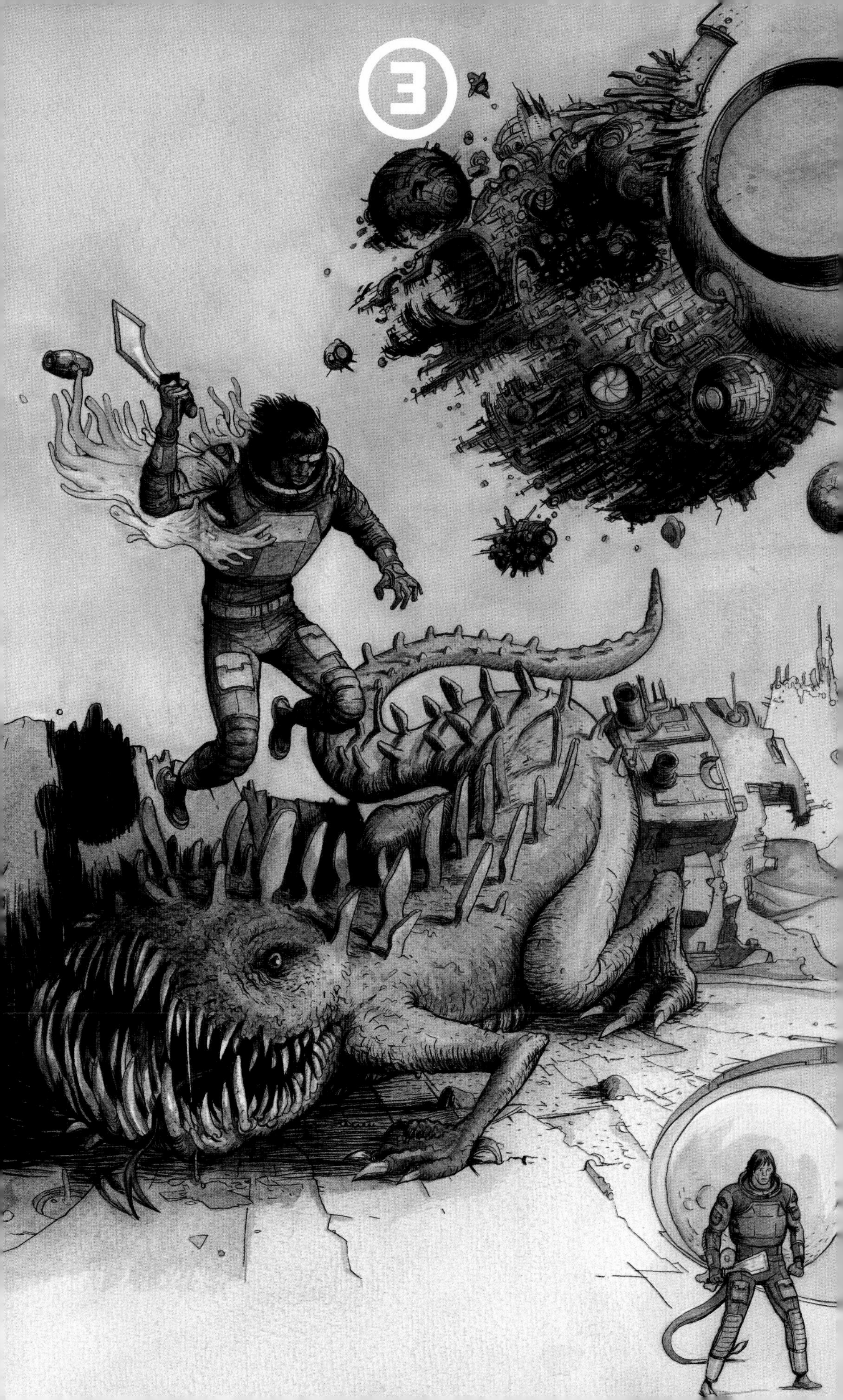
3

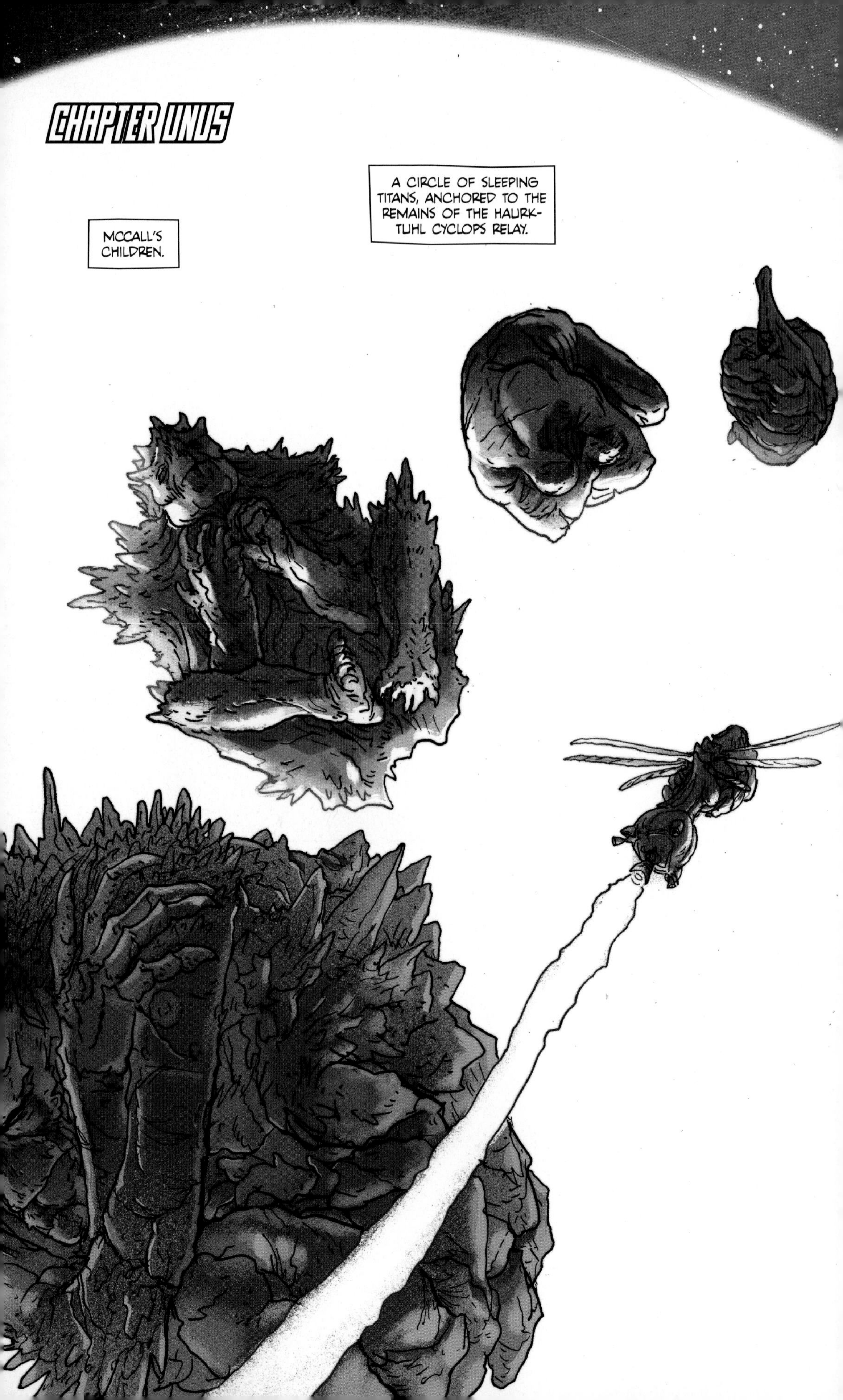
CHAPTER UNUS
A CIRCLE OF SLEEPING TITANS, ANCHORED TO THE REMAINS OF THE HAURK-TUHL CYCLOPS RELAY.
MCCALL'S CHILDREN.

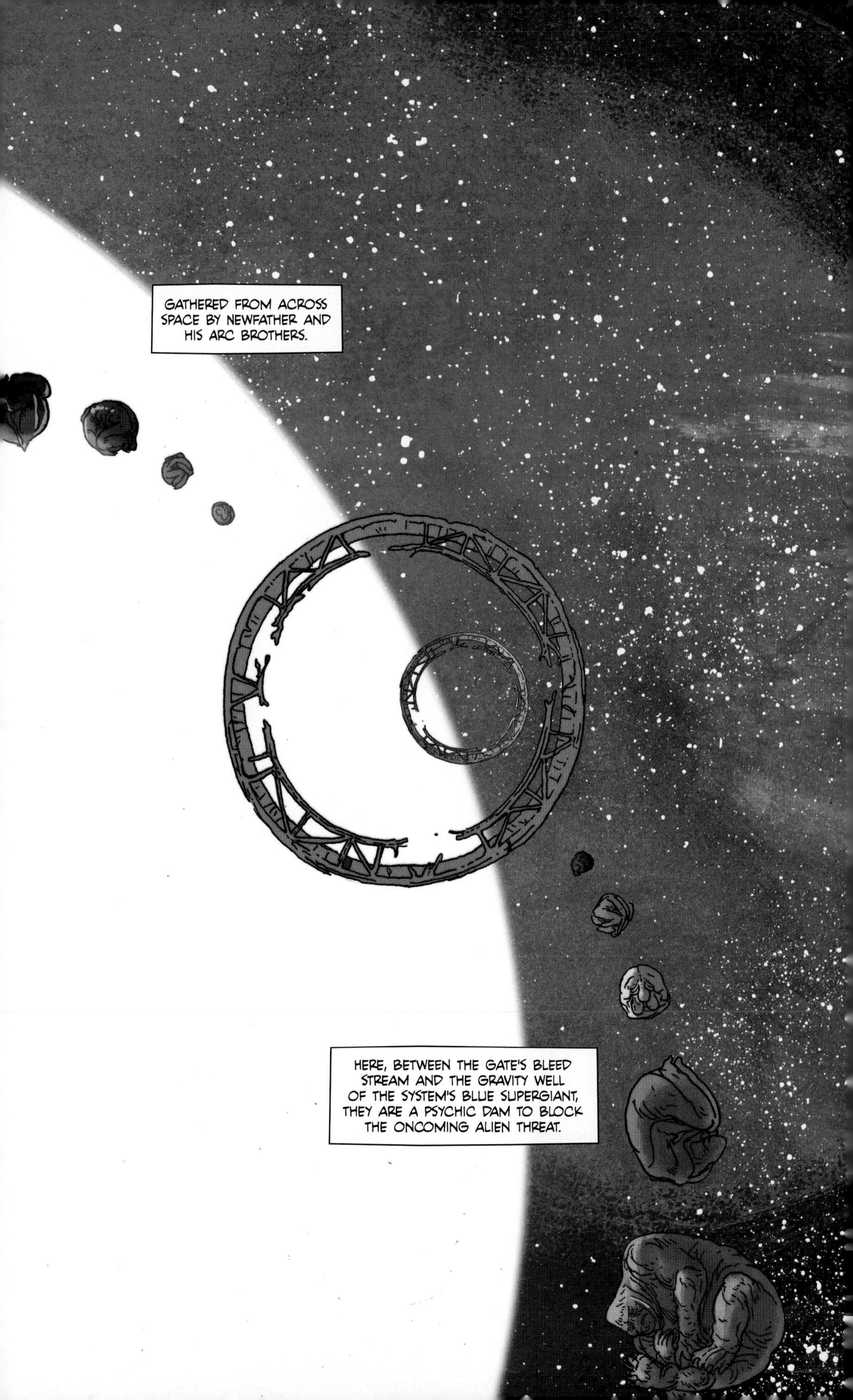
GATHERED FROM ACROSS SPACE BY NEWFATHER AND HIS ARC BROTHERS.
HERE, BETWEEN THE GATE'S BLEED STREAM AND THE GRAVITY WELL OF THE SYSTEM'S BLUE SUPERGIANT, THEY ARE A PSYCHIC DAM TO BLOCK THE ONCOMING ALIEN THREAT.

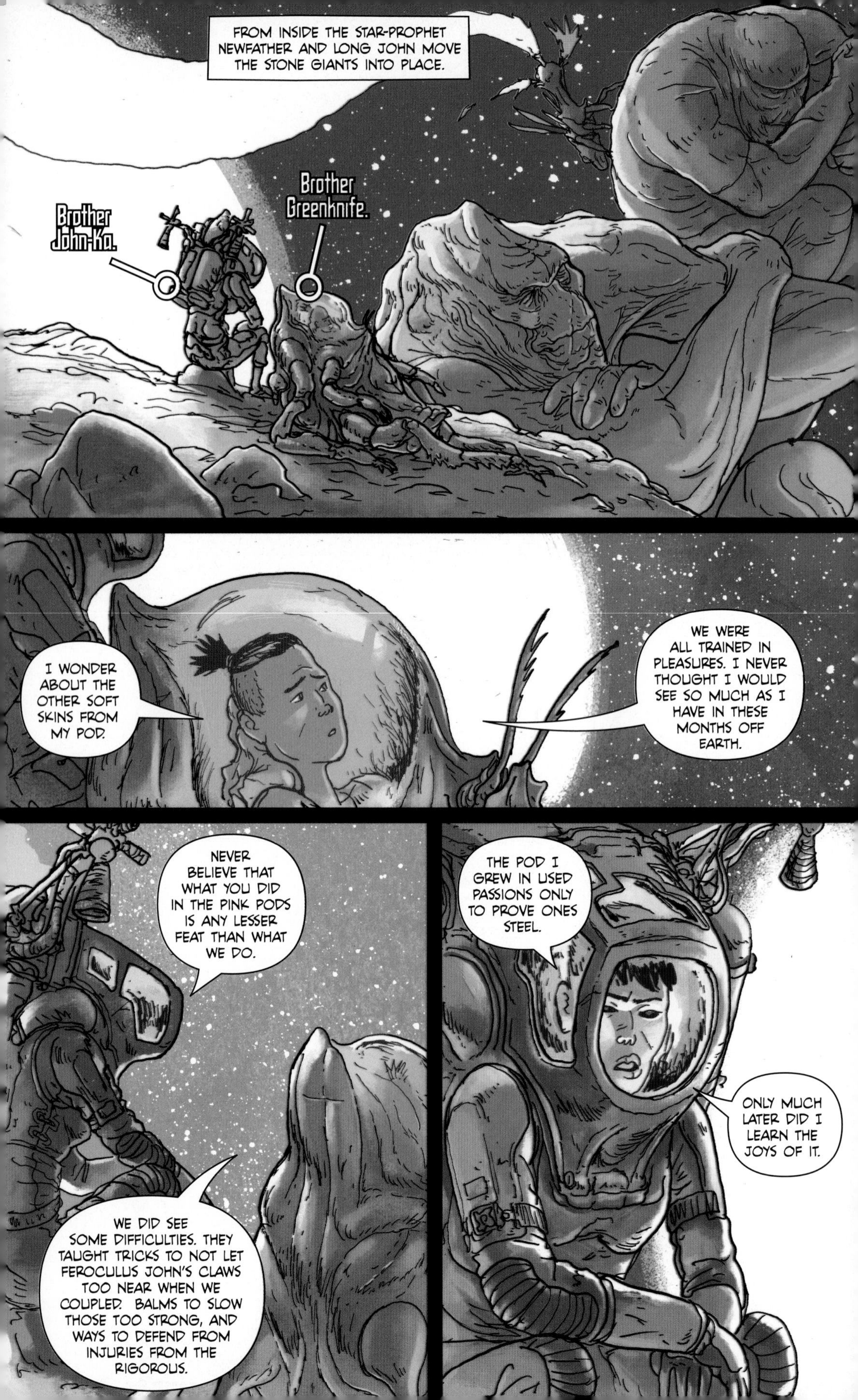
FROM INSIDE THE STAR-PROPHET NEWFATHER AND LONG JOHN MOVE THE STONE GIANTS INTO PLACE.
Brother John-Ka.
Brother Greenknife.
I WONDER ABOUT THE OTHER SOFT SKINS FROM MY POD.
WE WERE ALL TRAINED IN PLEASURES. I NEVER THOUGHT I WOULD SEE SO MUCH AS I HAVE IN THESE MONTHS OFF EARTH.
NEVER BELIEVE THAT WHAT YOU DID IN THE PINK PODS IS ANY LESSER FEAT THAN WHAT WE DO.
WE DID SEE SOME DIFFICULTIES. THEY TAUGHT TRICKS TO NOT LET FEROCULUS JOHN'S CLAWS TOO NEAR WHEN WE COUPLED. BALMS TO SLOW THOSE TOO STRONG, AND WAYS TO DEFEND FROM INJURIES FROM THE RIGOROUS.
THE POD I GREW IN USED PASSIONS ONLY TO PROVE ONES STEEL.
ONLY MUCH LATER DID I LEARN THE JOYS OF IT.

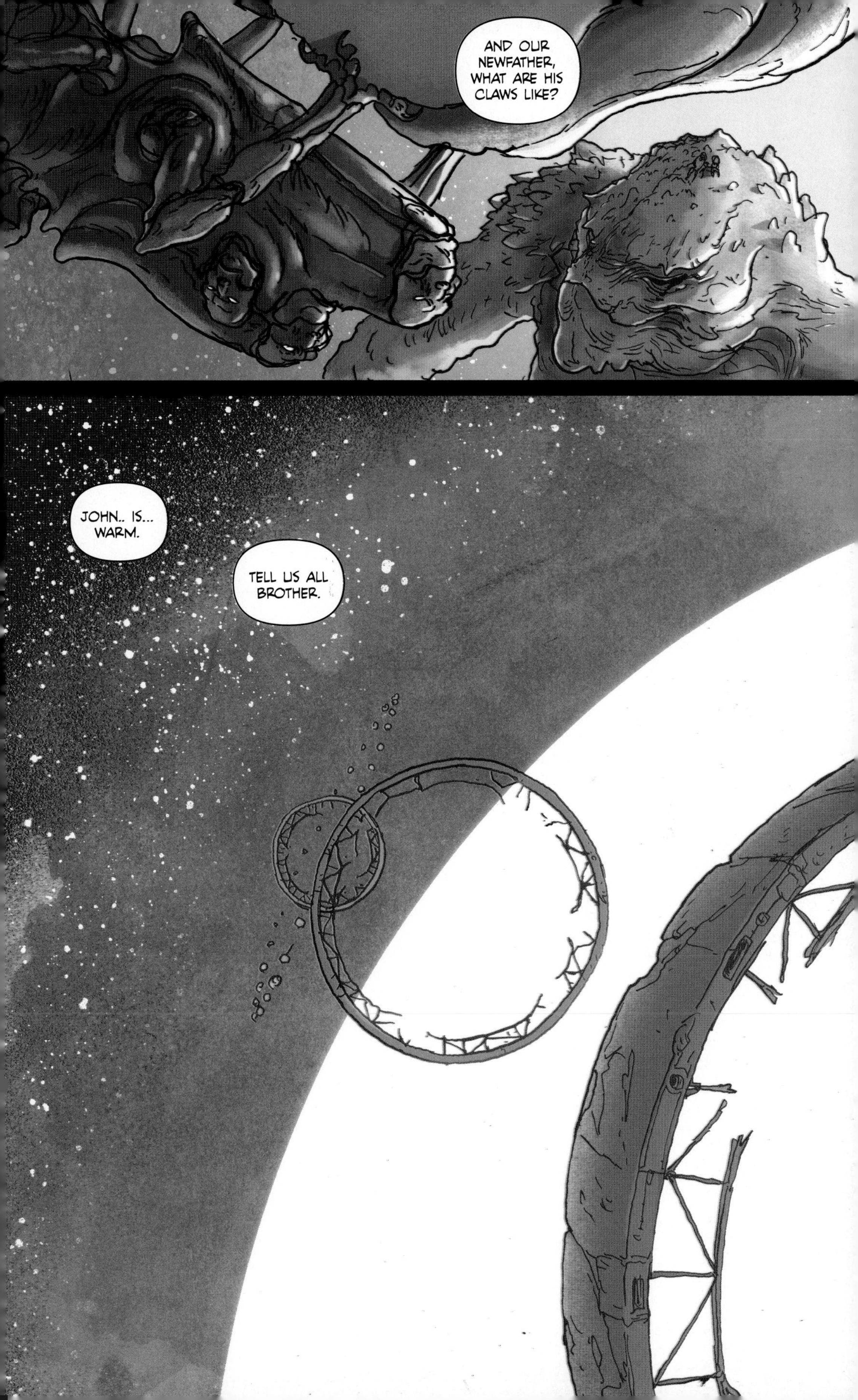
AND OUR NEWFATHER, WHAT ARE HIS CLAWS LIKE?
JOHN.. IS... WARM.
TELL US ALL BROTHER.

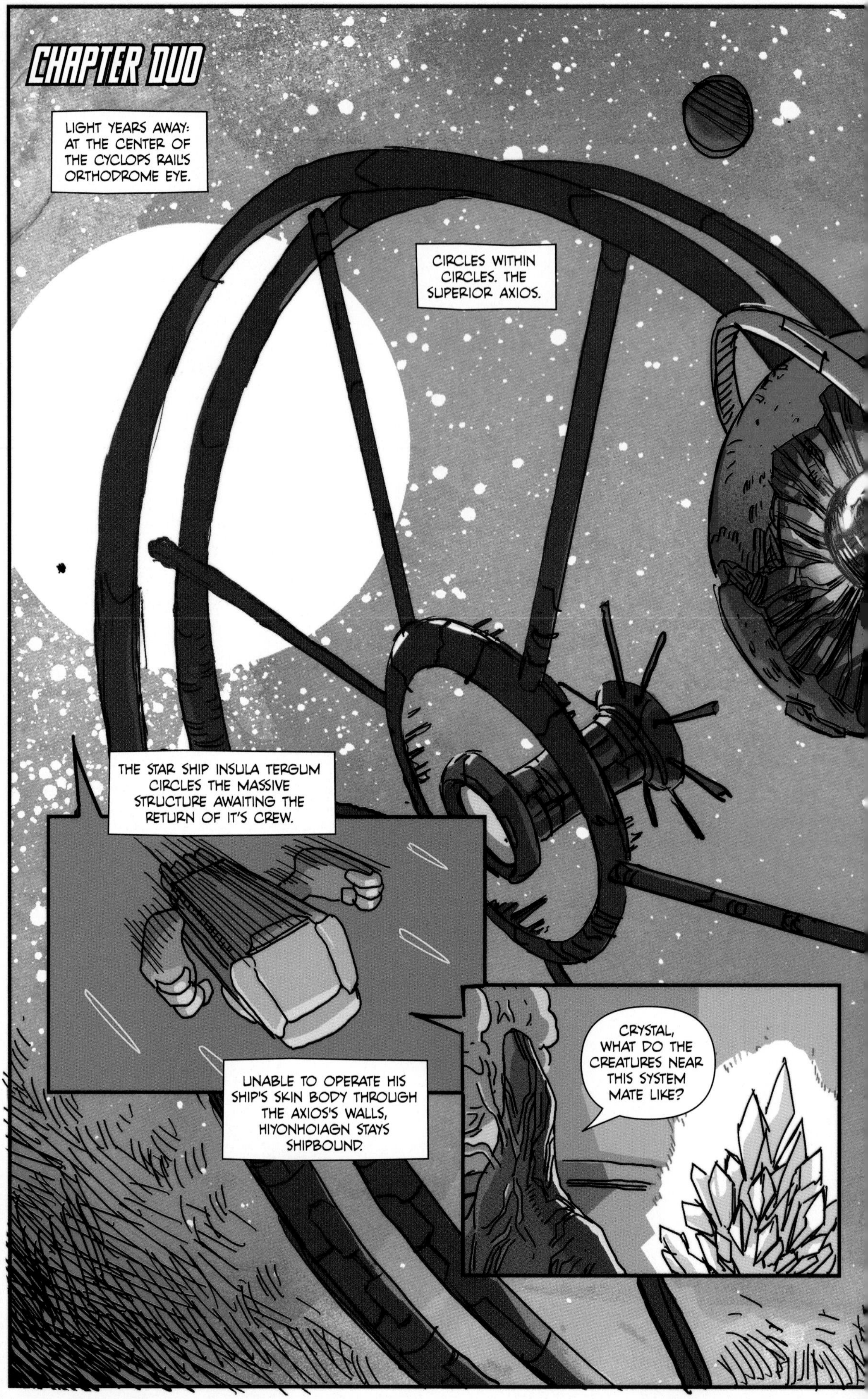
CHAPTER DUO
LIGHT YEARS AWAY: AT THE CENTER OF THE CYCLOPS RAIL'S ORTHODROME EYE.
CIRCLES WITHIN CIRCLES. THE SUPERIOR AXIOS.
THE STAR SHIP INSULA TERGUM CIRCLES THE MASSIVE STRUCTURE AWAITING THE RETURN OF IT'S CREW.
UNABLE TO OPERATE HIS SHIP'S SKIN BODY THROUGH THE AXIOS'S WALLS, HIYONHOIAGN STAYS SHIPBOUND.
CRYSTAL, WHAT DO THE CREATURES NEAR THIS SYSTEM MATE LIKE?

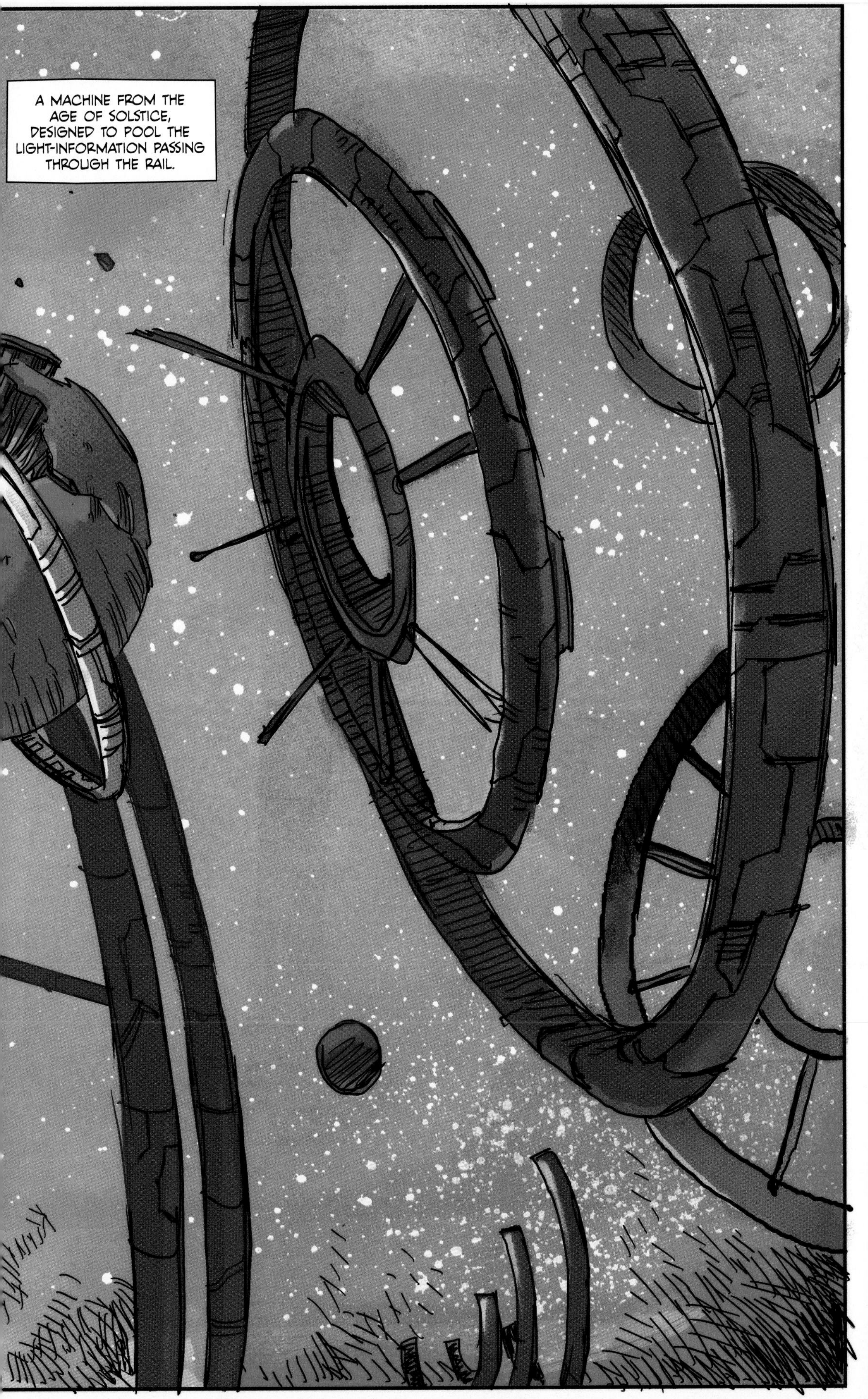
A MACHINE FROM THE AGE OF SOLSTICE, DESIGNED TO POOL THE LIGHT-INFORMATION PASSING THROUGH THE RAIL.

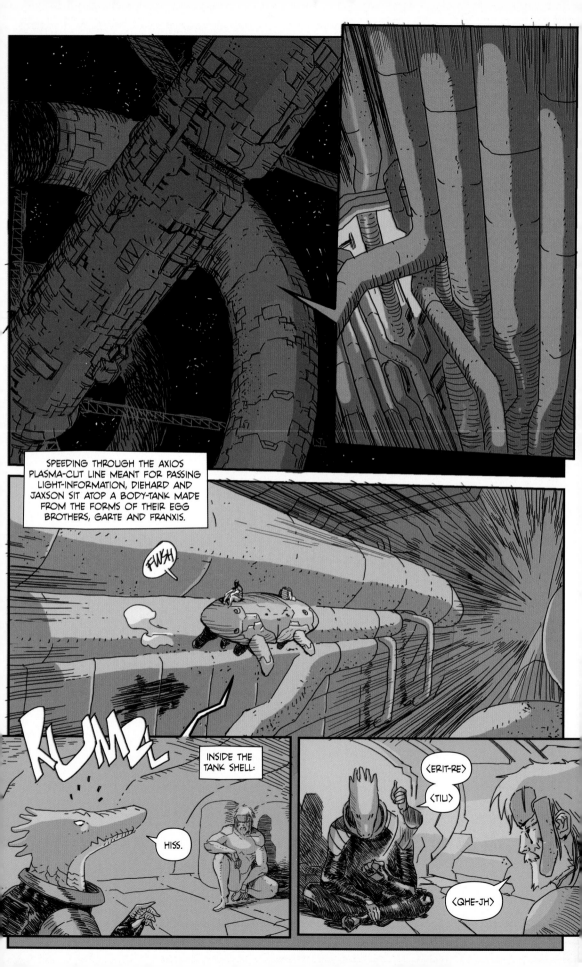

SPEEDING THROUGH THE AXIOS PLASMA-CUT LINE MEANT FOR PASSING LIGHT-INFORMATION, DIEHARD AND JAXSON SIT ATOP A BODY-TANK MADE FROM THE FORMS OF THEIR EGG BROTHERS, GARTE AND FRANXIS.

FWSH

KUMZ

INSIDE THE TANK SHELL:

HISS.

⟨ERIT-RE⟩

⟨TIU⟩

⟨QHE-JH⟩

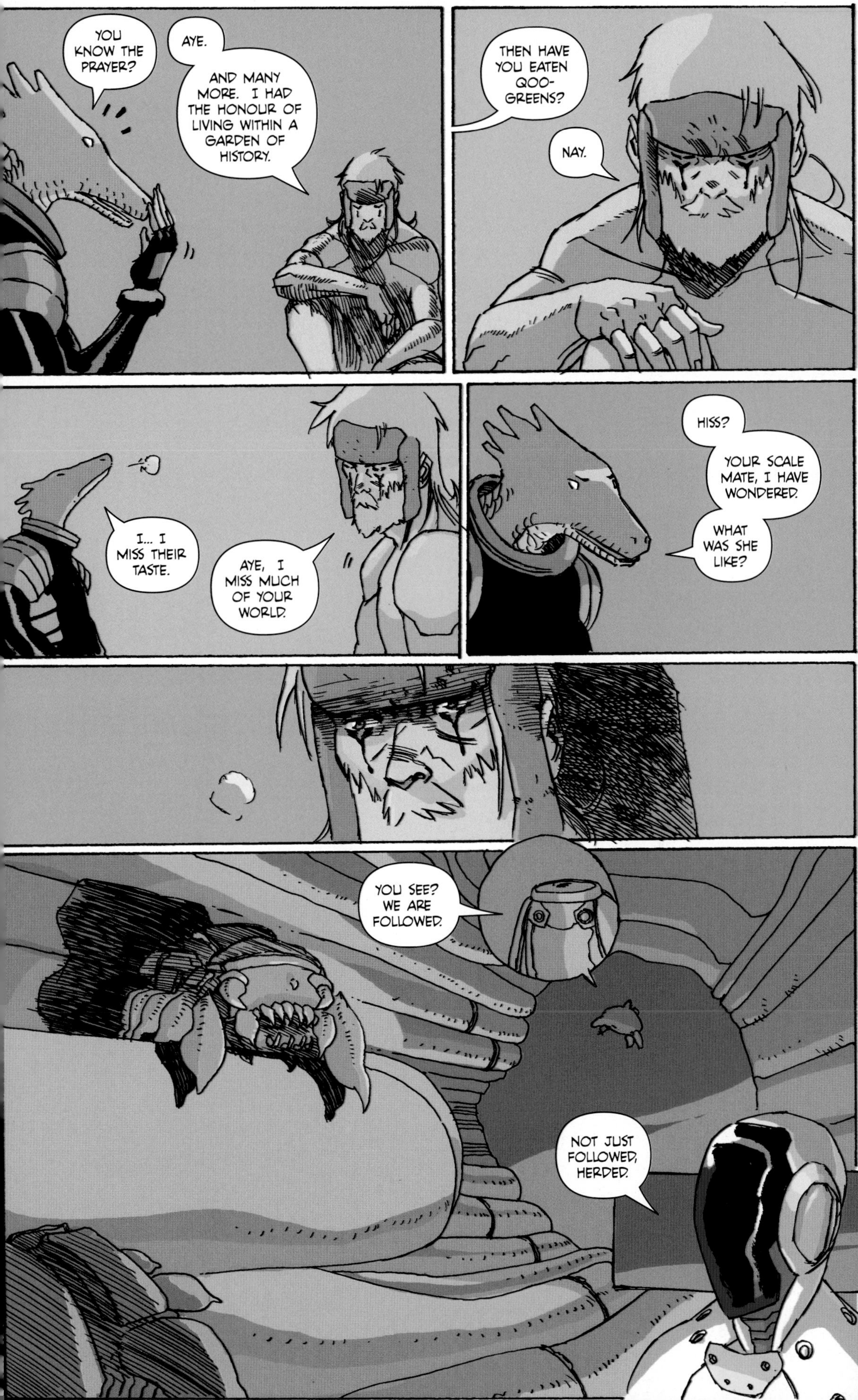
YOU KNOW THE PRAYER?
AYE.
AND MANY MORE. I HAD THE HONOUR OF LIVING WITHIN A GARDEN OF HISTORY.
THEN HAVE YOU EATEN QOO-GREENS?
NAY.
I... I MISS THEIR TASTE.
AYE, I MISS MUCH OF YOUR WORLD.
HISS?
YOUR SCALE MATE, I HAVE WONDERED.
WHAT WAS SHE LIKE?
YOU SEE? WE ARE FOLLOWED.
NOT JUST FOLLOWED, HERDED.

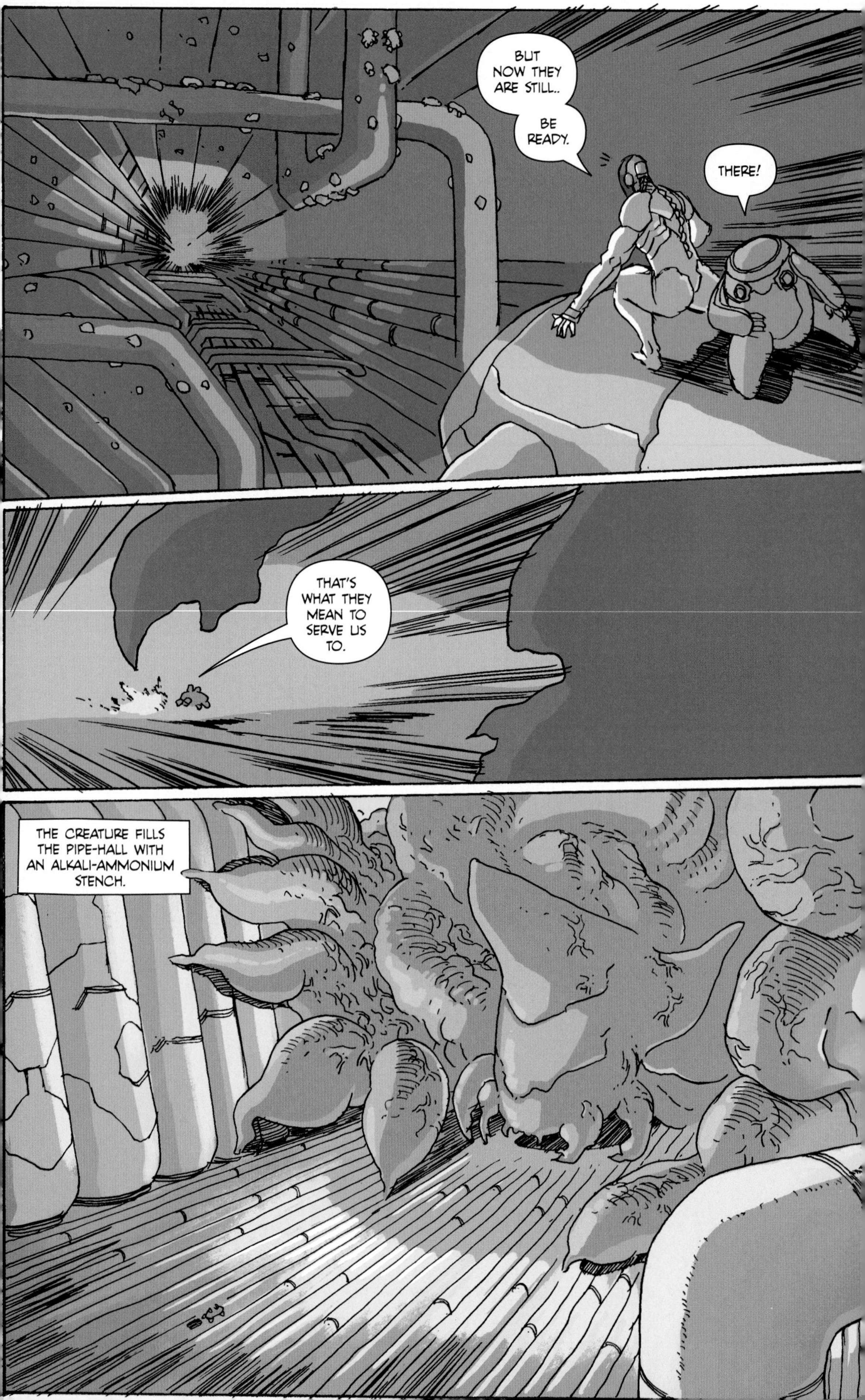
BUT NOW THEY ARE STILL..
BE READY.
THERE!
THAT'S WHAT THEY MEAN TO SERVE US TO.
THE CREATURE FILLS THE PIPE-HALL WITH AN ALKALI-AMMONIUM STENCH.

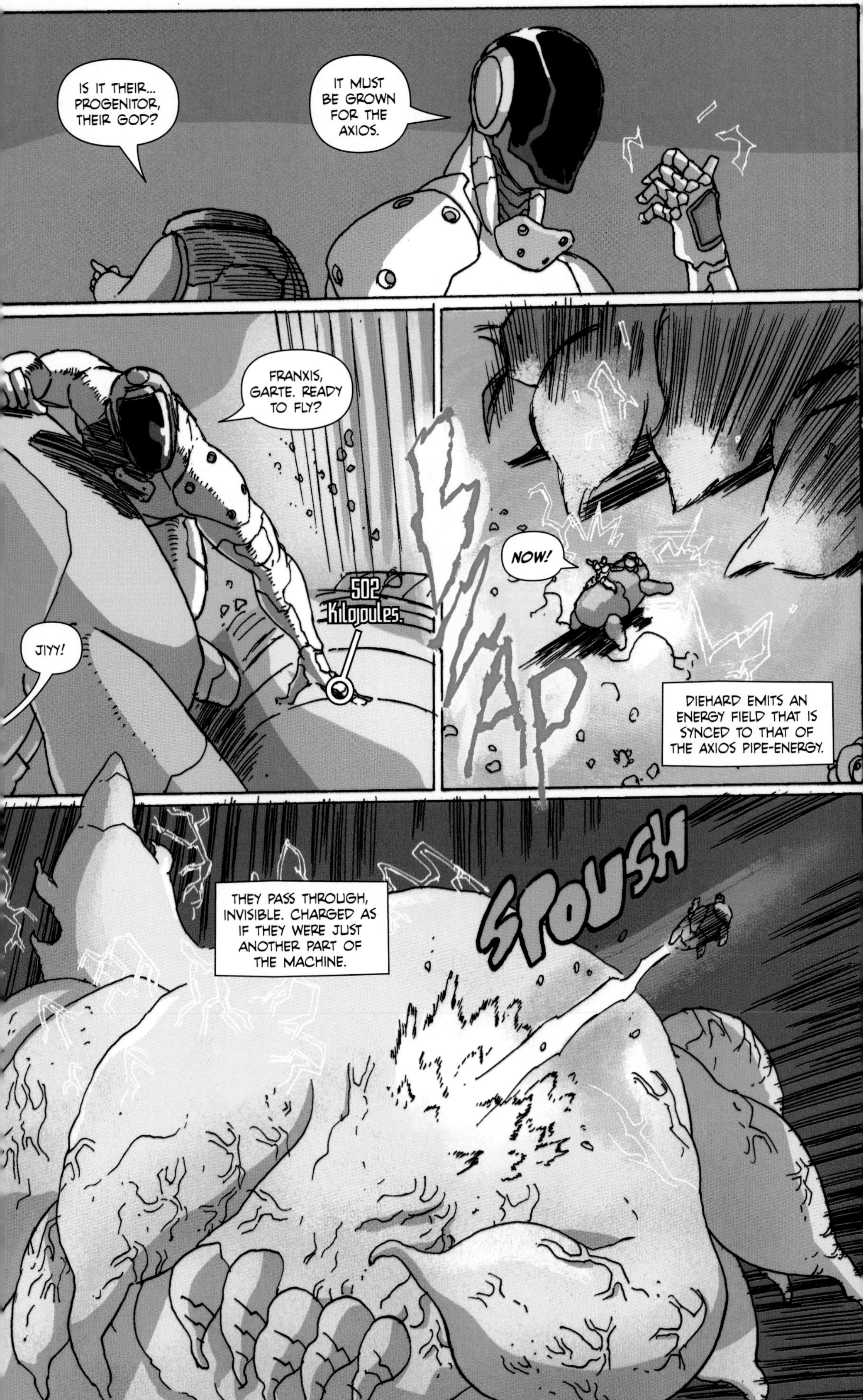
IS IT THEIR... PROGENITOR, THEIR GOD?
IT MUST BE GROWN FOR THE AXIOS.
FRANXIS, GARTE. READY TO FLY?
502 Kilojoules.
JIYY!
ZAP
NOW!
DIEHARD EMITS AN ENERGY FIELD THAT IS SYNCED TO THAT OF THE AXIOS PIPE-ENERGY.
THEY PASS THROUGH, INVISIBLE. CHARGED AS IF THEY WERE JUST ANOTHER PART OF THE MACHINE.
SPOUSH

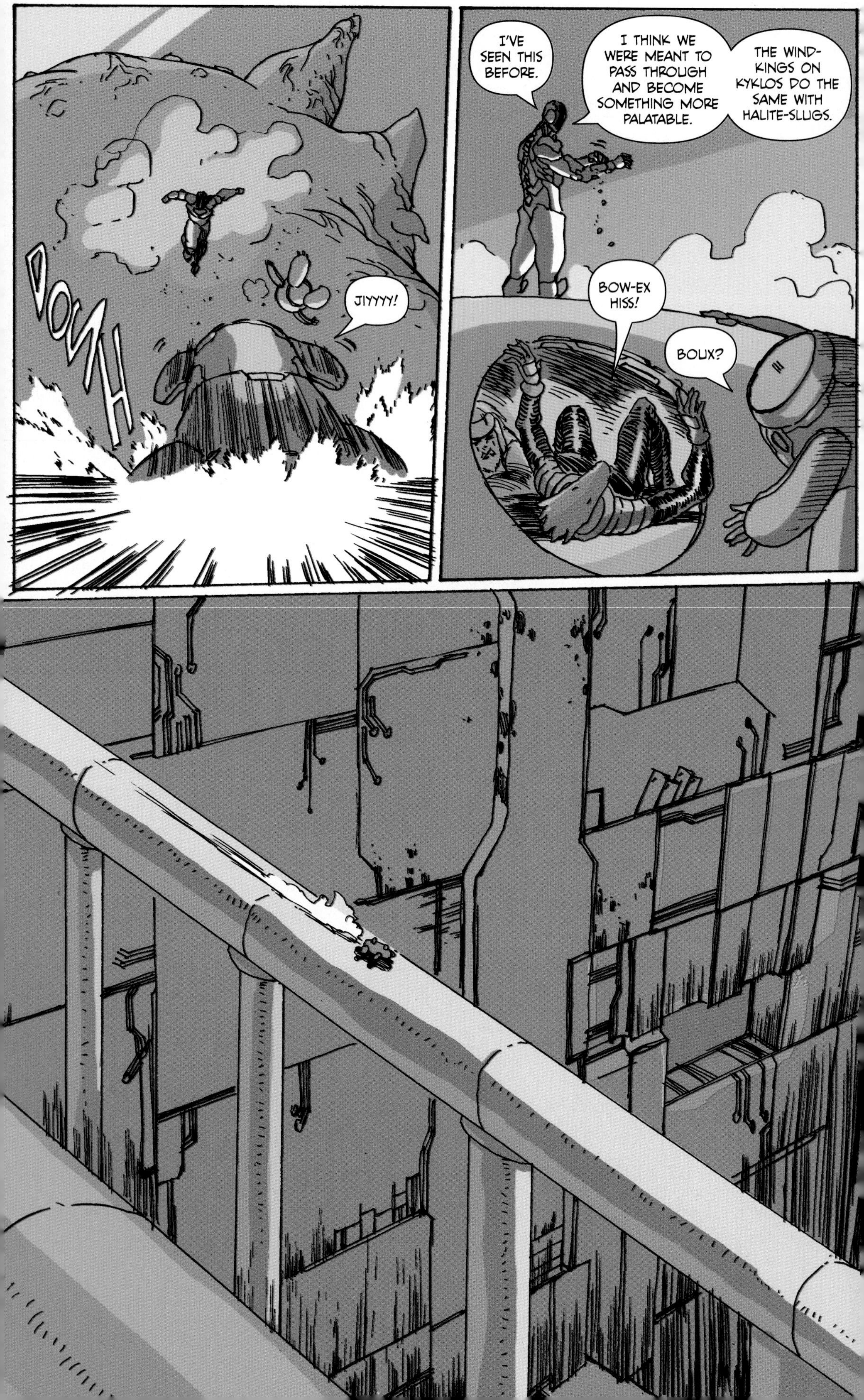
DOUNH
JIYYYY!
I'VE SEEN THIS BEFORE.
I THINK WE WERE MEANT TO PASS THROUGH AND BECOME SOMETHING MORE PALATABLE.
THE WIND-KINGS ON KYKLOS DO THE SAME WITH HALITE-SLUGS.
BOW-EX HISS!
BOUX?

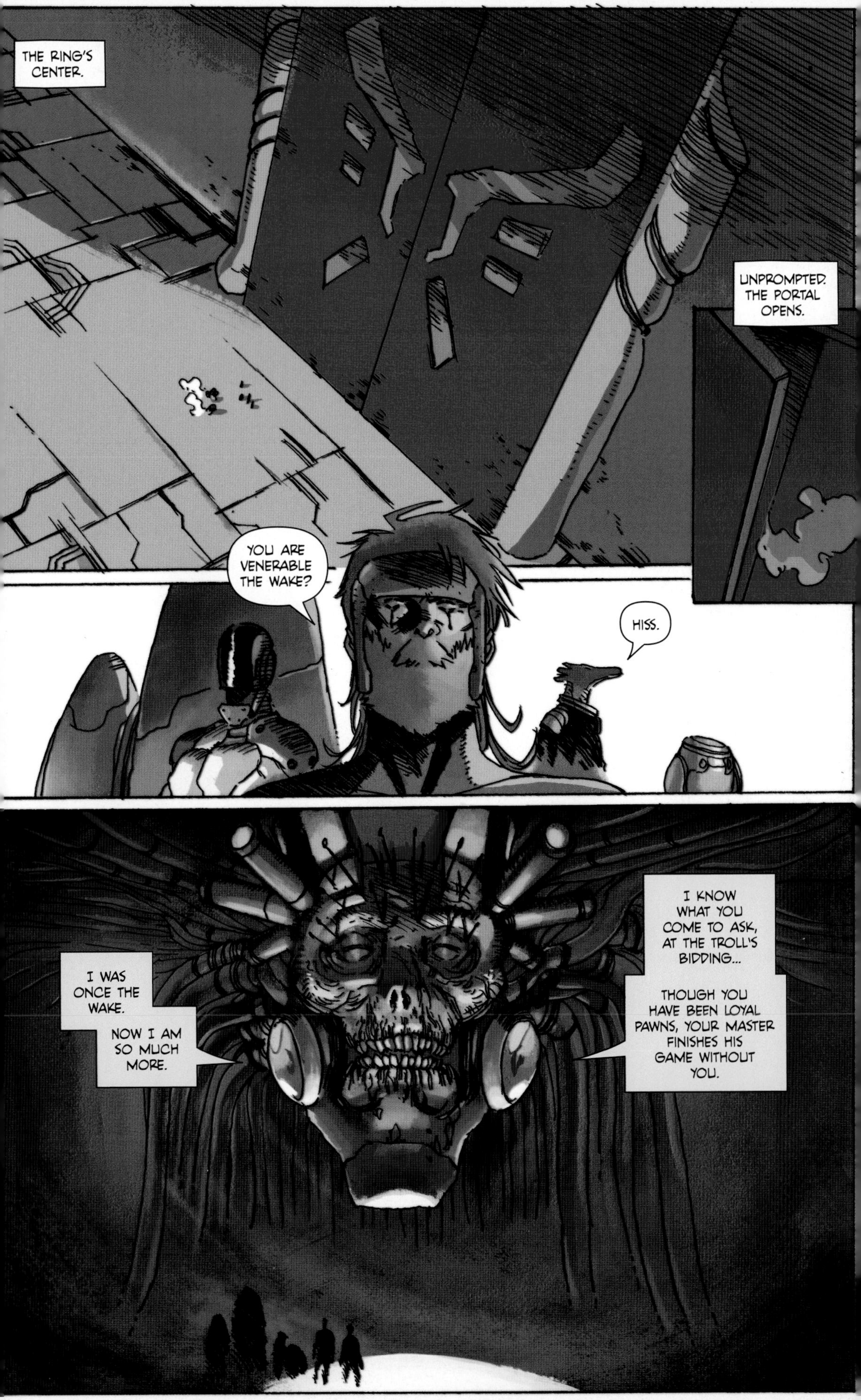
THE RING'S CENTER.
UNPROMPTED. THE PORTAL OPENS.
YOU ARE VENERABLE THE WAKE?
HISS.
I KNOW WHAT YOU COME TO ASK, AT THE TROLL'S BIDDING...
THOUGH YOU HAVE BEEN LOYAL PAWNS, YOUR MASTER FINISHES HIS GAME WITHOUT YOU.
I WAS ONCE THE WAKE.
NOW I AM SO MUCH MORE.

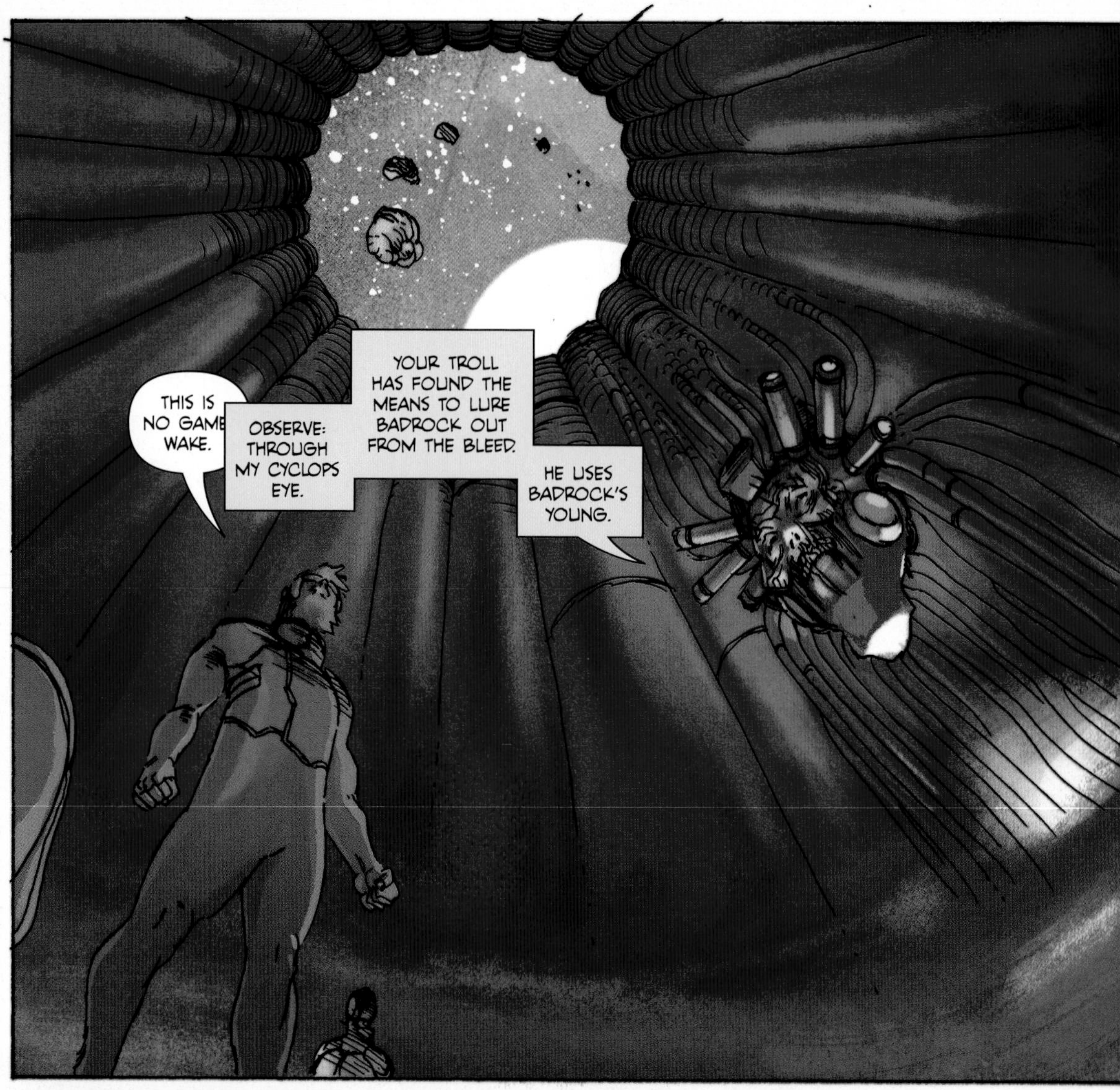
THIS IS NO GAME WAKE.
OBSERVE: THROUGH MY CYCLOPS EYE.
YOUR TROLL HAS FOUND THE MEANS TO LURE BADROCK OUT FROM THE BLEED.
HE USES BADROCK'S YOUNG.

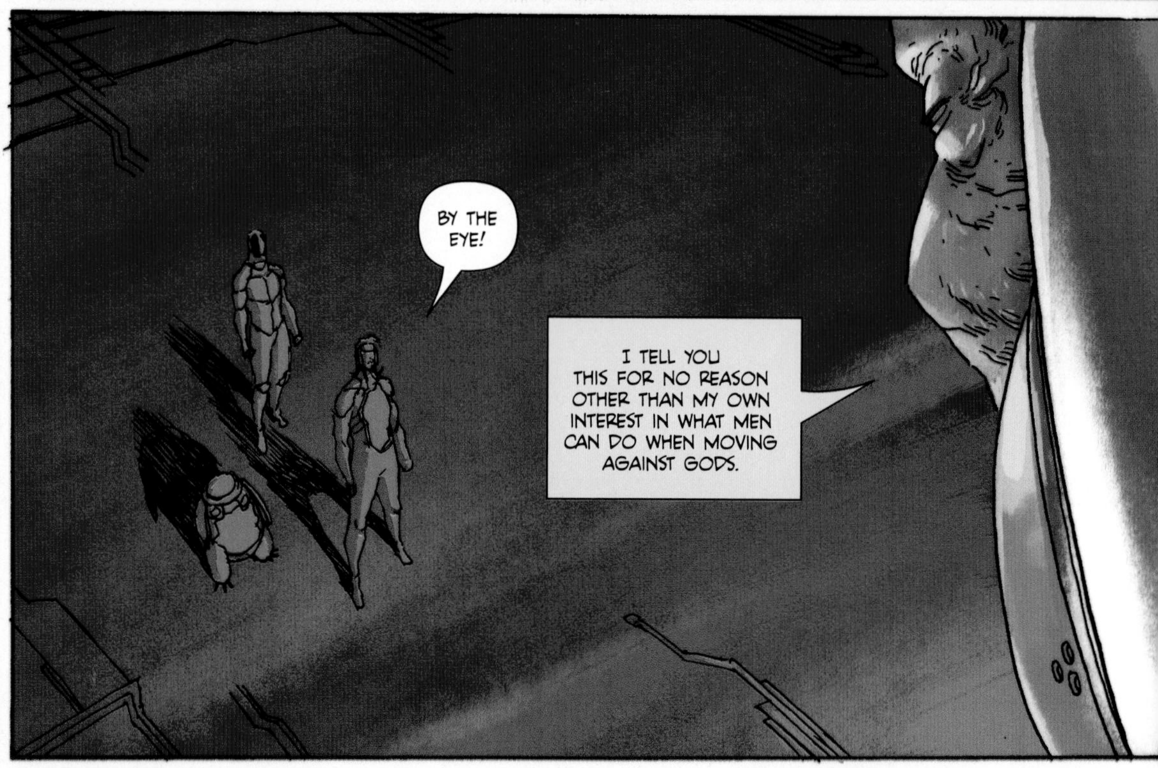
BY THE EYE!
I TELL YOU THIS FOR NO REASON OTHER THAN MY OWN INTEREST IN WHAT MEN CAN DO WHEN MOVING AGAINST GODS.

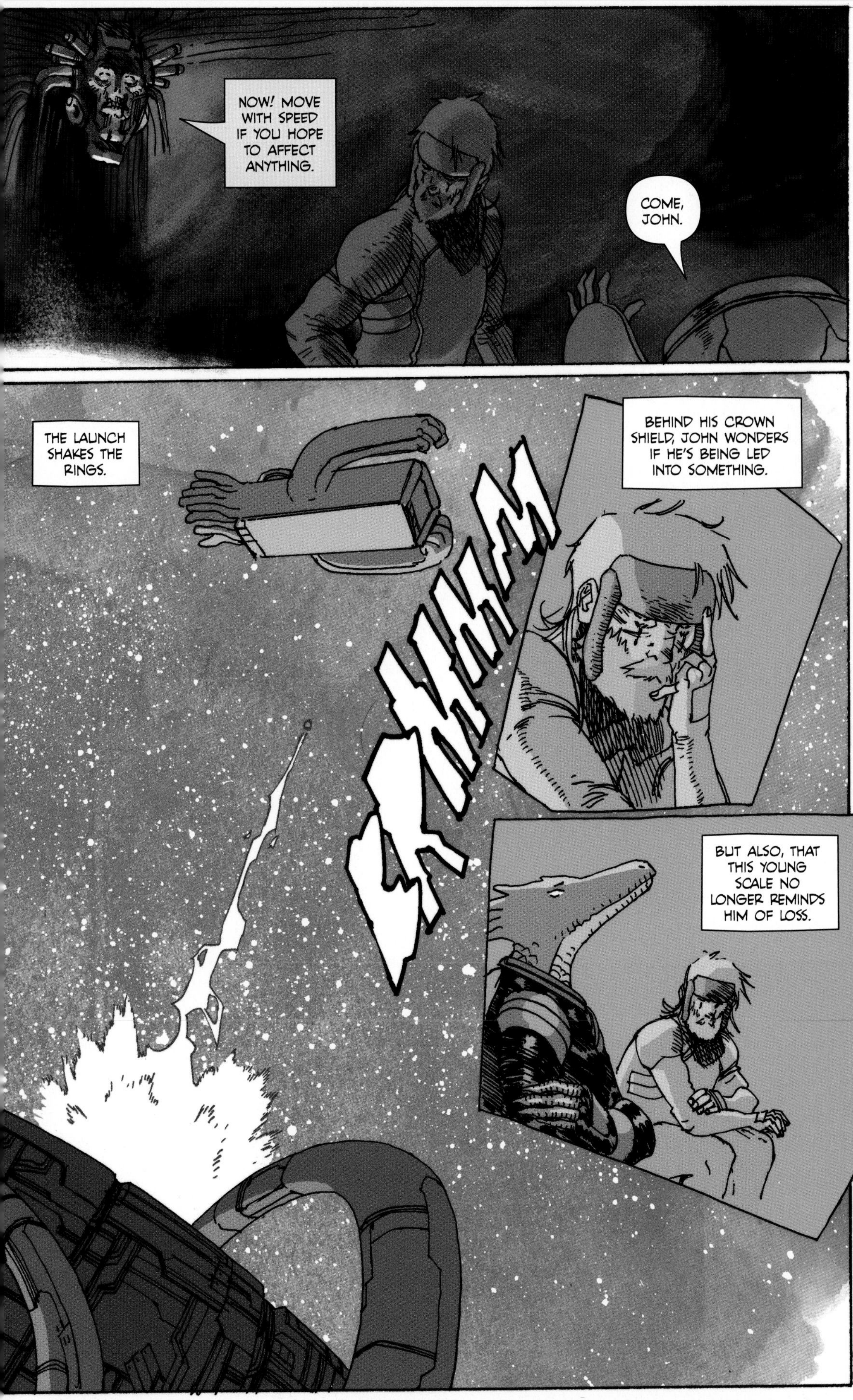
NOW! MOVE WITH SPEED IF YOU HOPE TO AFFECT ANYTHING.
COME, JOHN.
THE LAUNCH SHAKES THE RINGS.
BEHIND HIS CROWN SHIELD, JOHN WONDERS IF HE'S BEING LED INTO SOMETHING.
BUT ALSO, THAT THIS YOUNG SCALE NO LONGER REMINDS HIM OF LOSS.

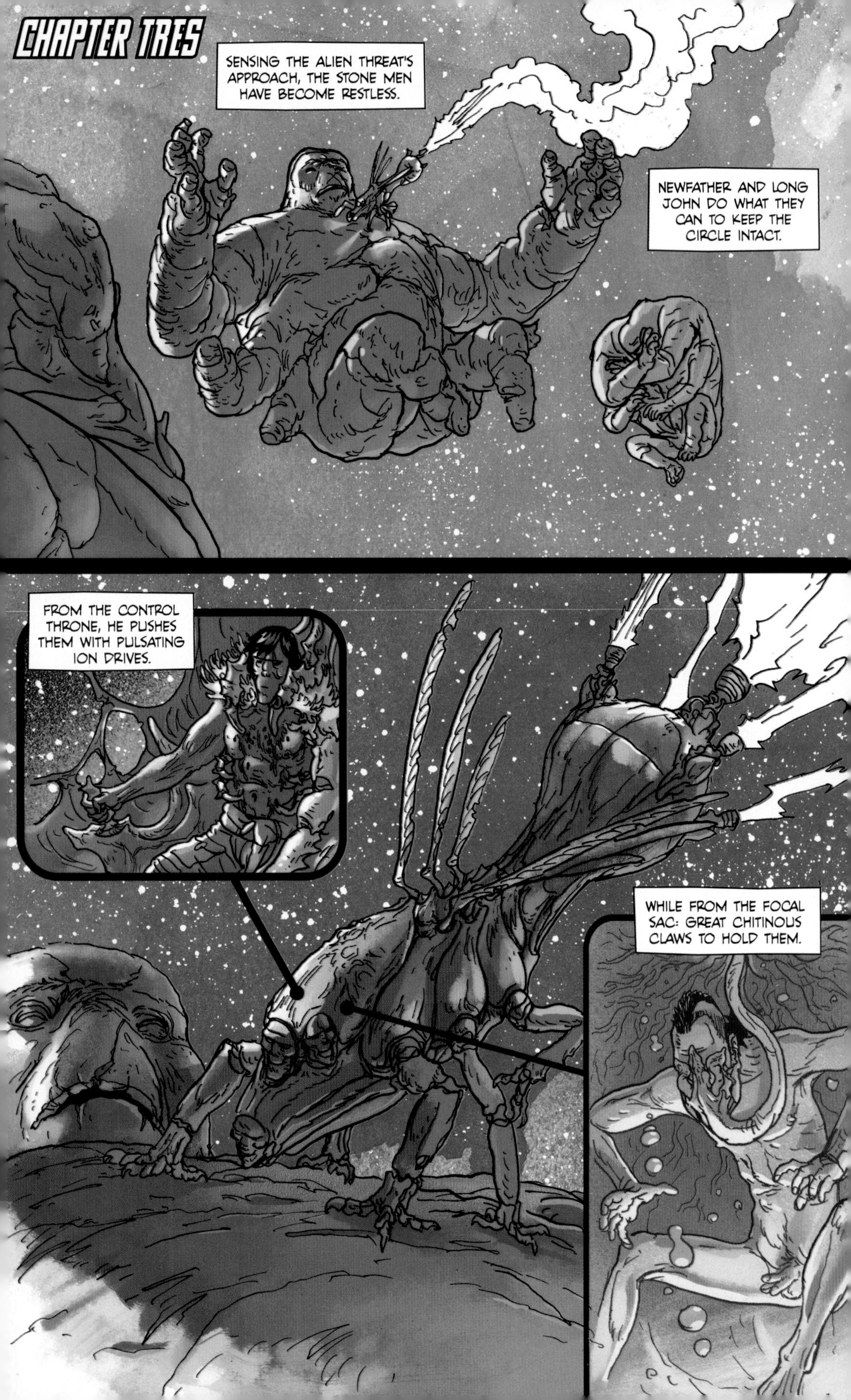
CHAPTER TRES
SENSING THE ALIEN THREAT'S APPROACH, THE STONE MEN HAVE BECOME RESTLESS.
NEWFATHER AND LONG JOHN DO WHAT THEY CAN TO KEEP THE CIRCLE INTACT.
FROM THE CONTROL THRONE, HE PUSHES THEM WITH PULSATING ION DRIVES.
WHILE FROM THE FOCAL SAC: GREAT CHITINOUS CLAWS TO HOLD THEM.

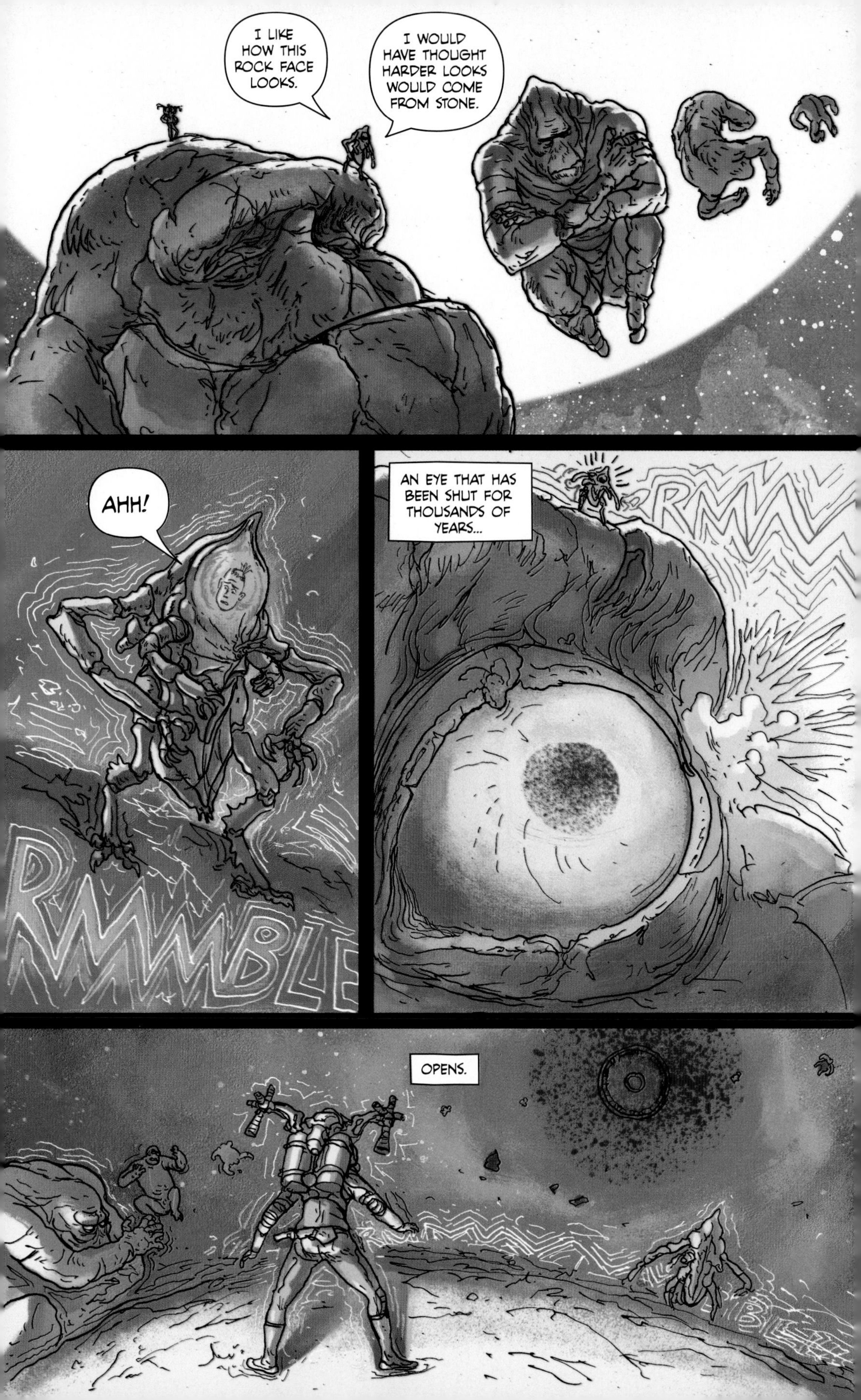
I LIKE HOW THIS ROCK FACE LOOKS.
I WOULD HAVE THOUGHT HARDER LOOKS WOULD COME FROM STONE.
AHH!
RMMBLE
AN EYE THAT HAS BEEN SHUT FOR THOUSANDS OF YEARS...
RMM
OPENS.

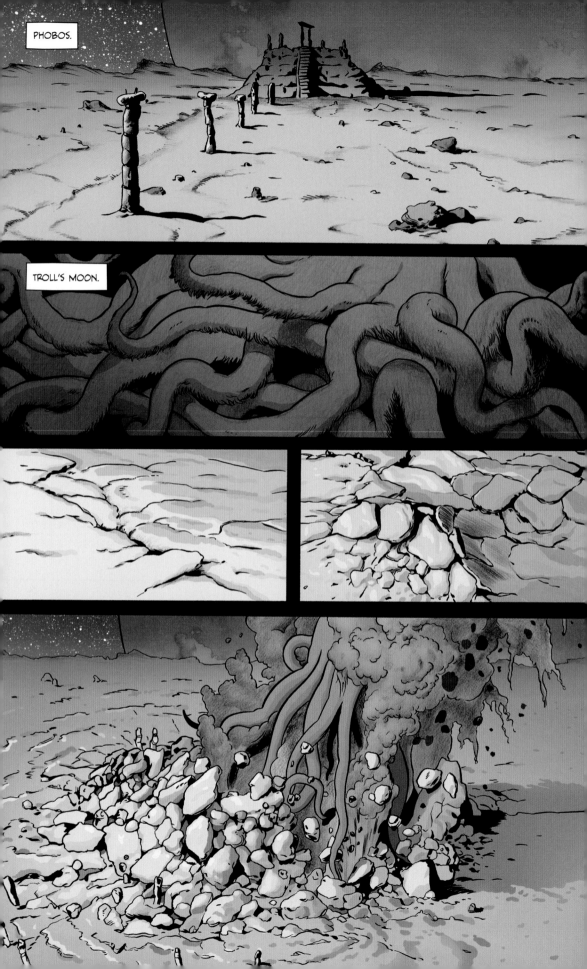

PHOBOS.

TROLL'S MOON.

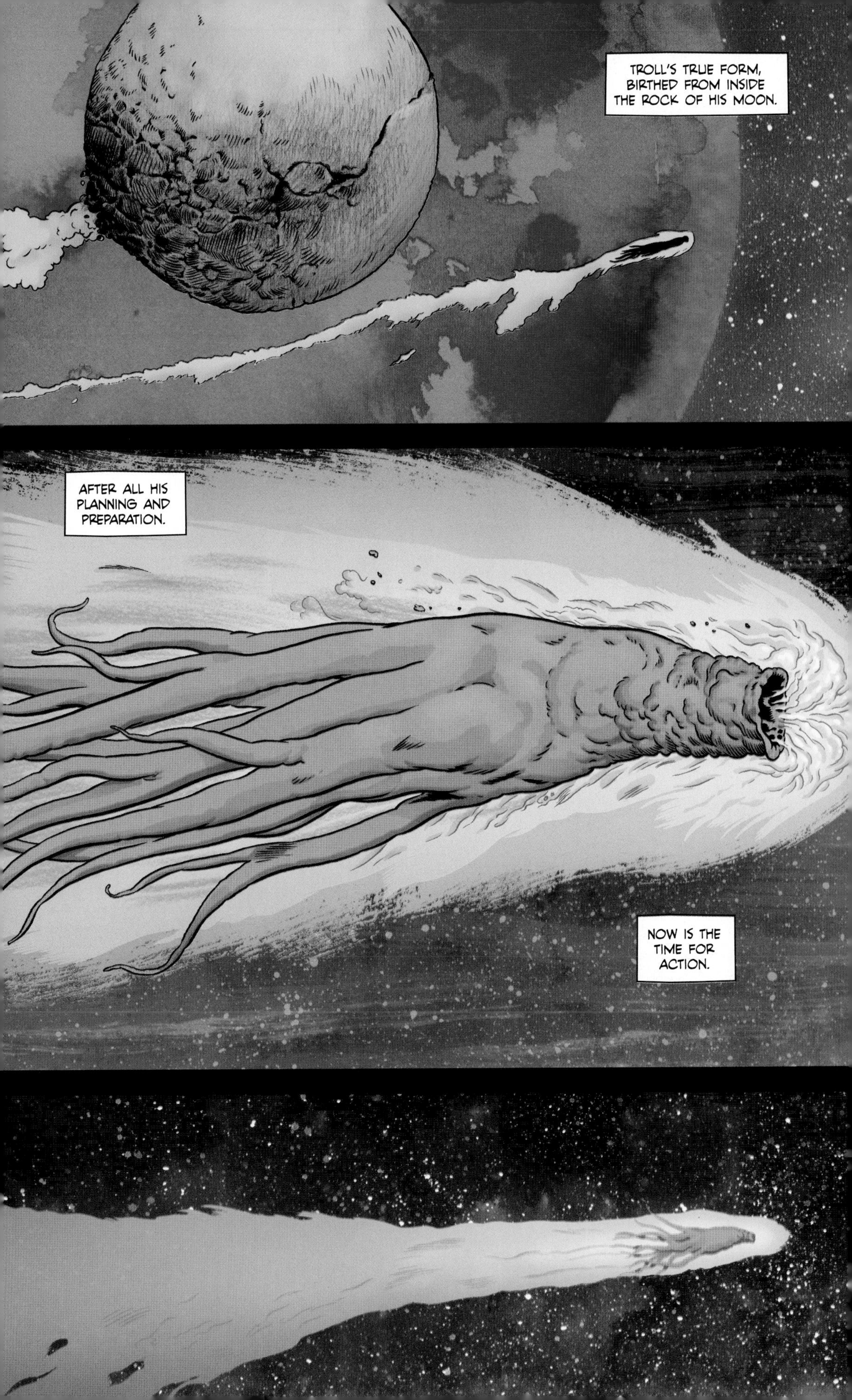
TROLL'S TRUE FORM, BIRTHED FROM INSIDE THE ROCK OF HIS MOON.
AFTER ALL HIS PLANNING AND PREPARATION.
NOW IS THE TIME FOR ACTION.

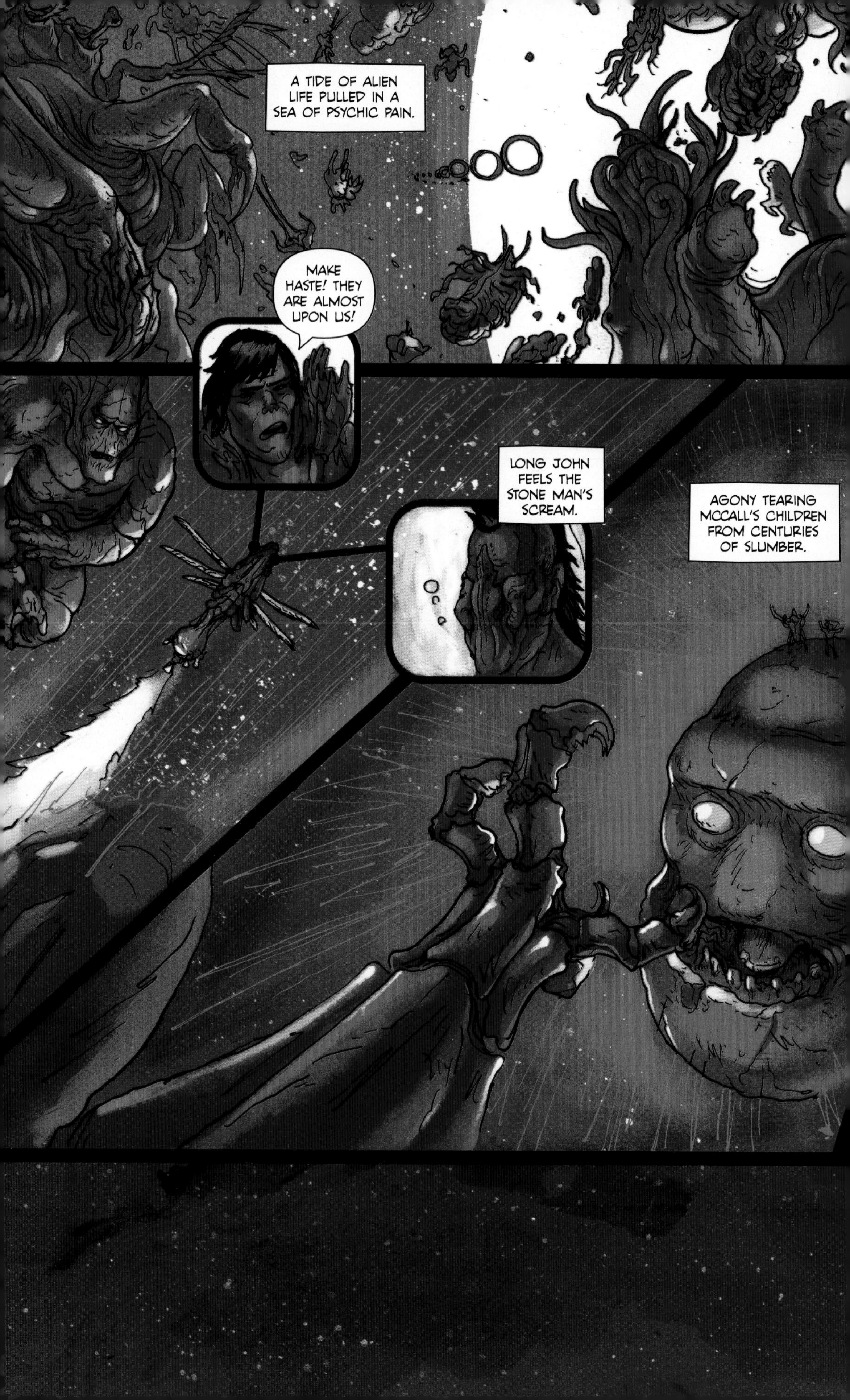
A TIDE OF ALIEN LIFE PULLED IN A SEA OF PSYCHIC PAIN.
MAKE HASTE! THEY ARE ALMOST UPON US!
LONG JOHN FEELS THE STONE MAN'S SCREAM.
AGONY TEARING MCCALL'S CHILDREN FROM CENTURIES OF SLUMBER.

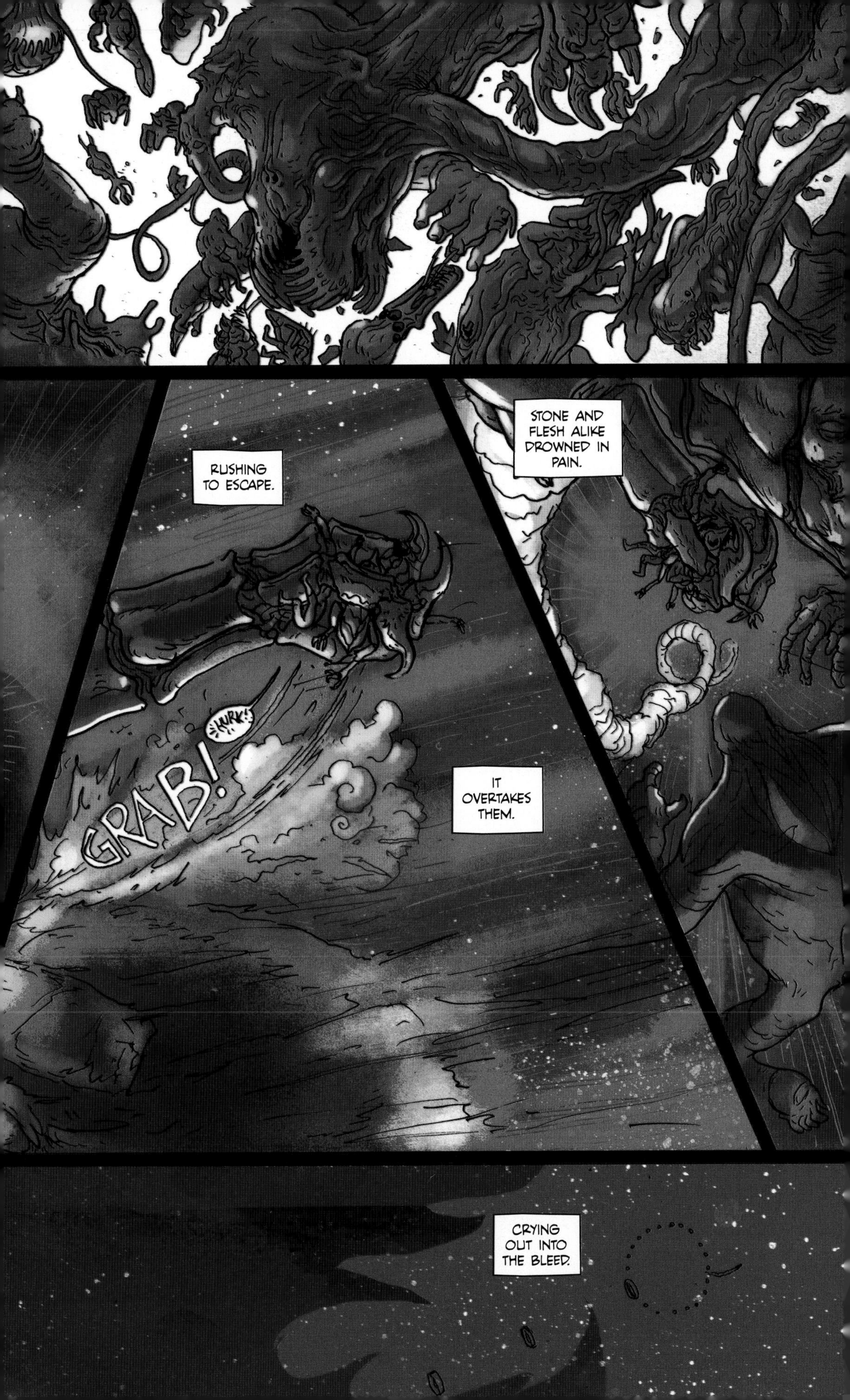
RUSHING TO ESCAPE.
STONE AND FLESH ALIKE DROWNED IN PAIN.
GRAB!
HURK!
IT OVERTAKES THEM.
CRYING OUT INTO THE BLEED.

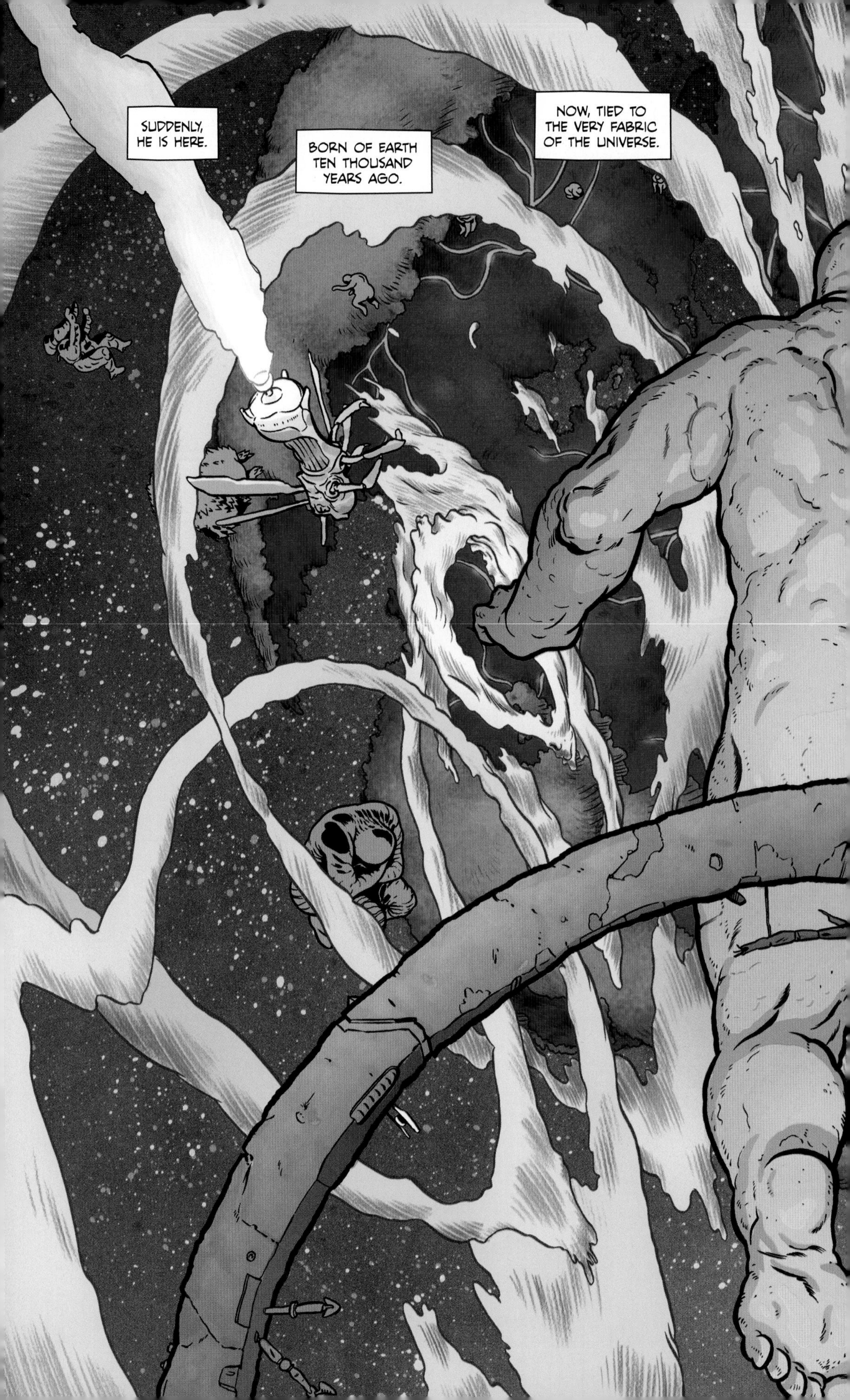
SUDDENLY, HE IS HERE.
BORN OF EARTH TEN THOUSAND YEARS AGO.
NOW, TIED TO THE VERY FABRIC OF THE UNIVERSE.

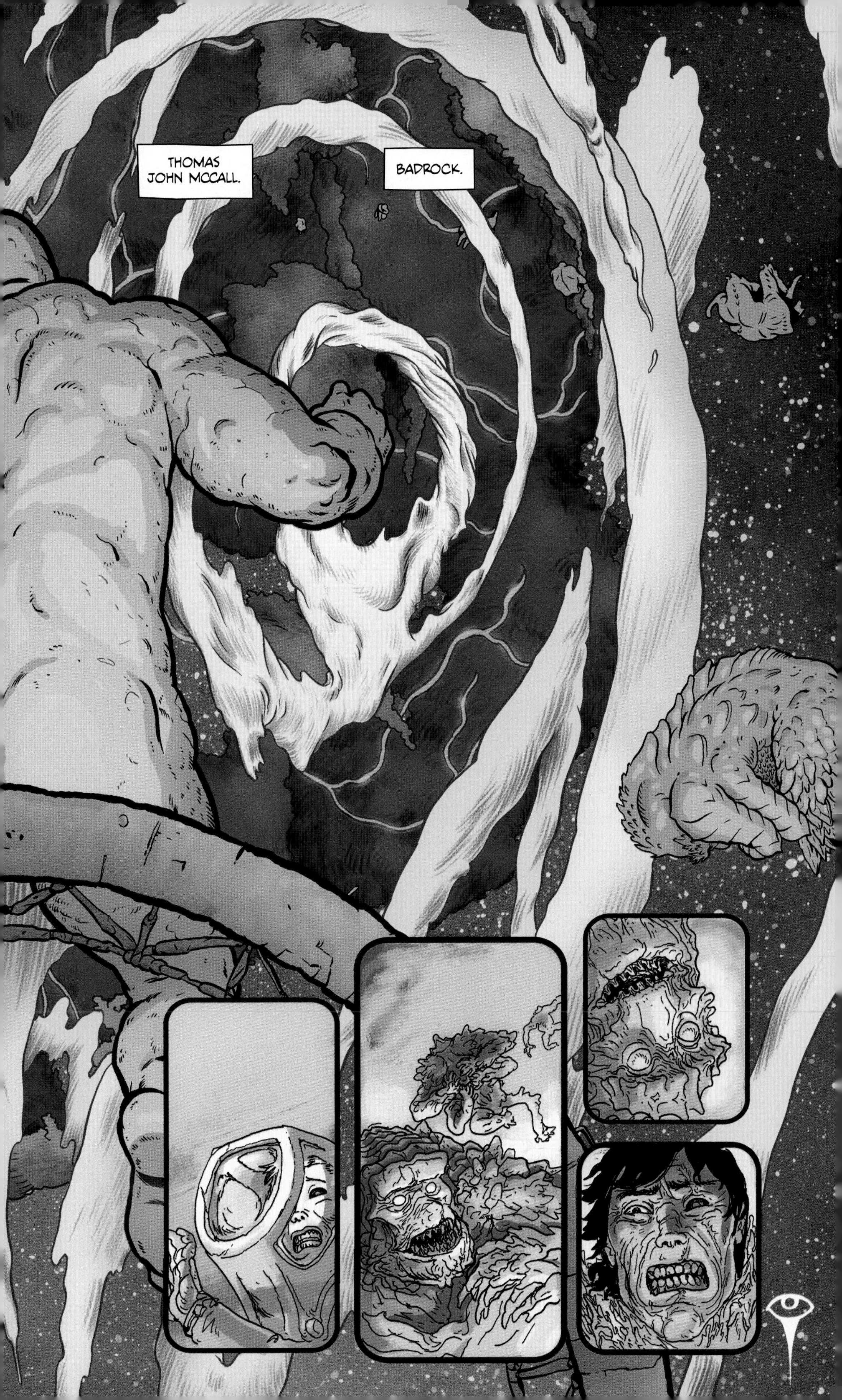
THOMAS JOHN MCCALL.
BADROCK.

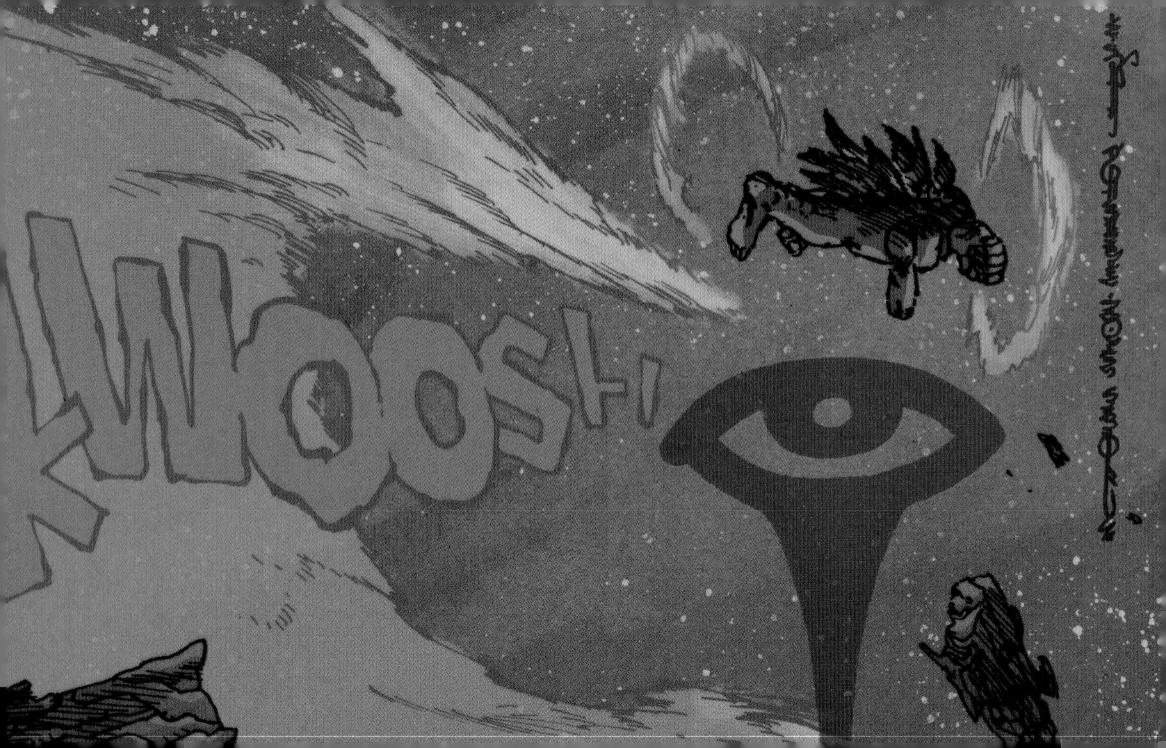
WOOSH!

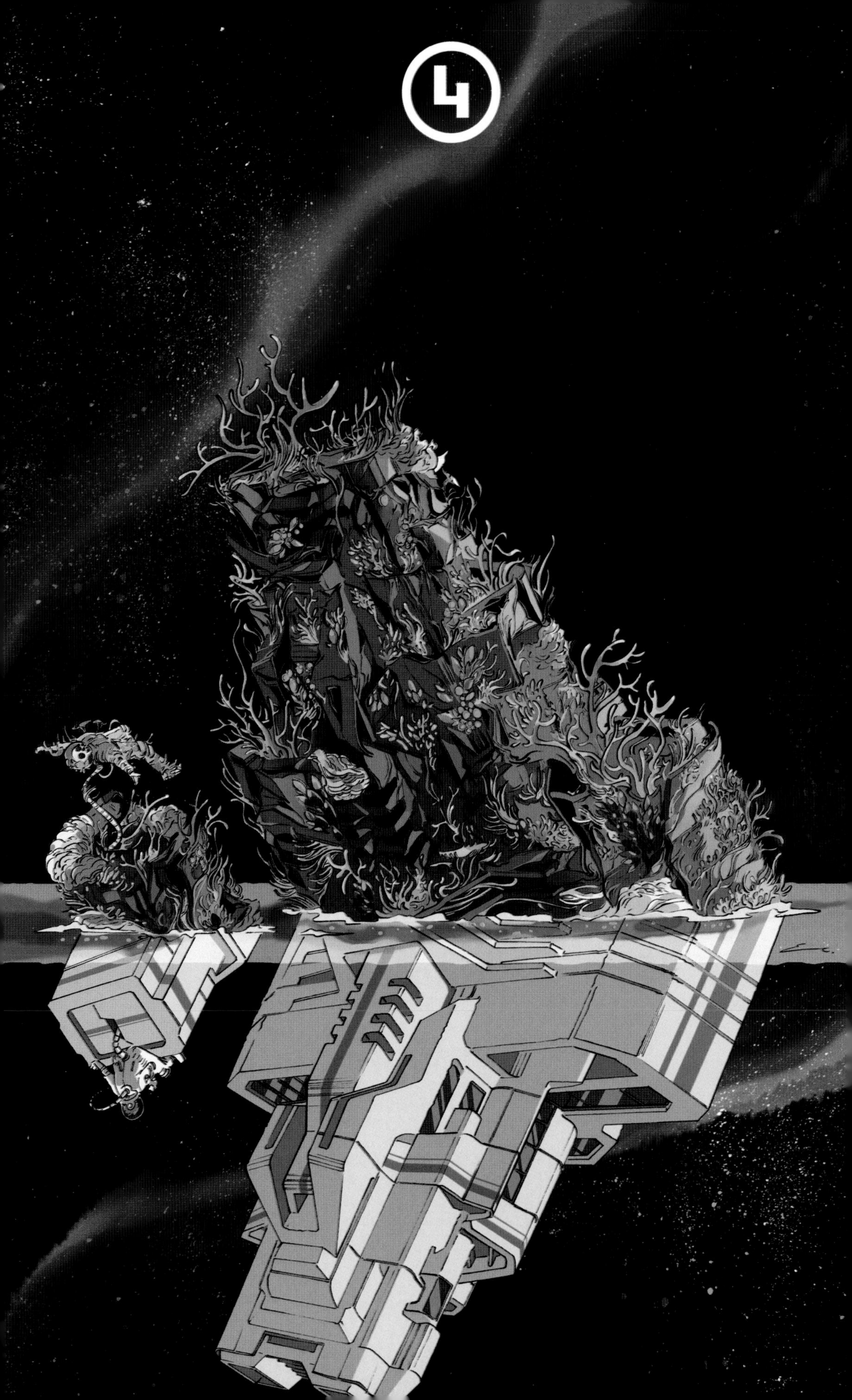
4

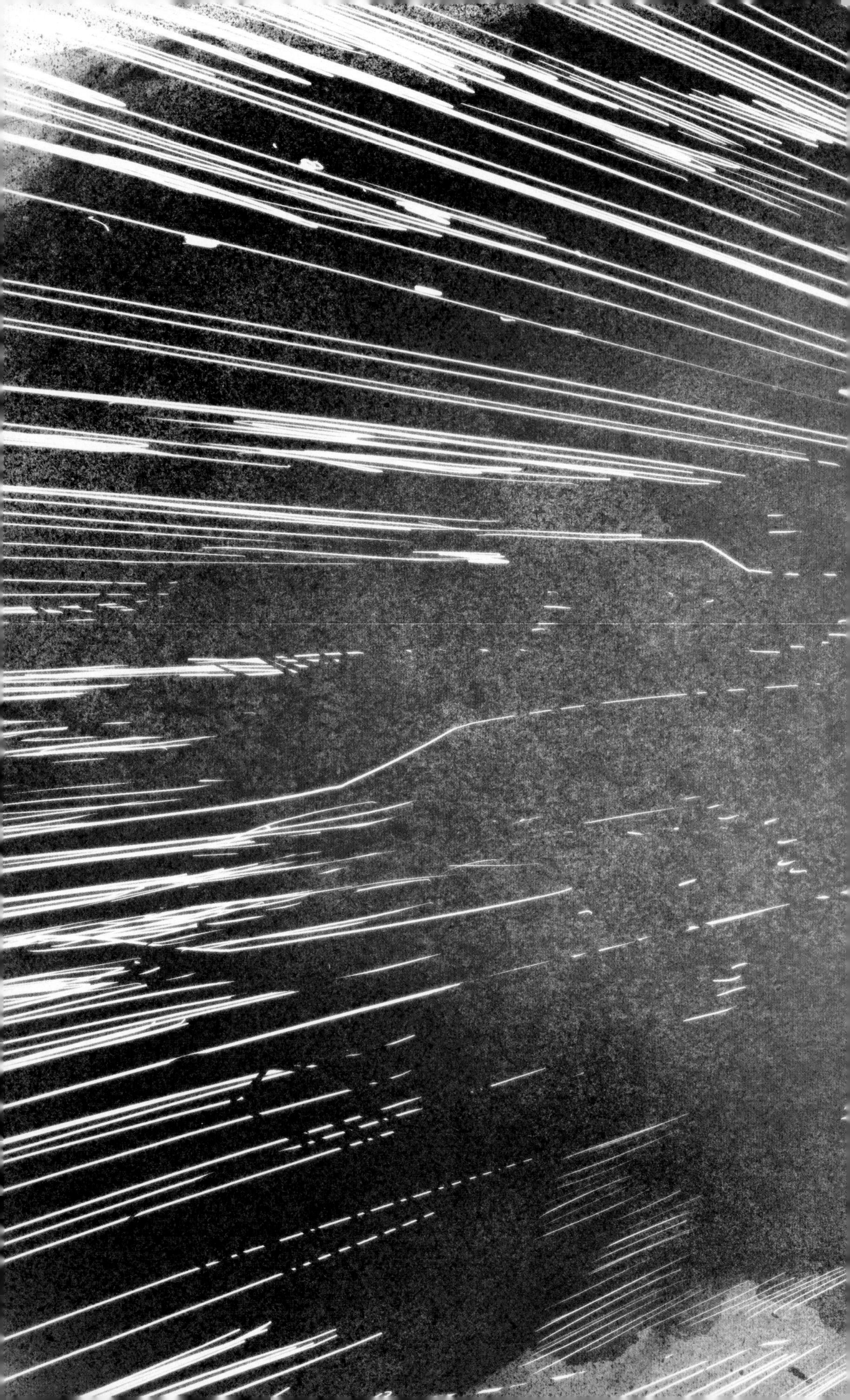

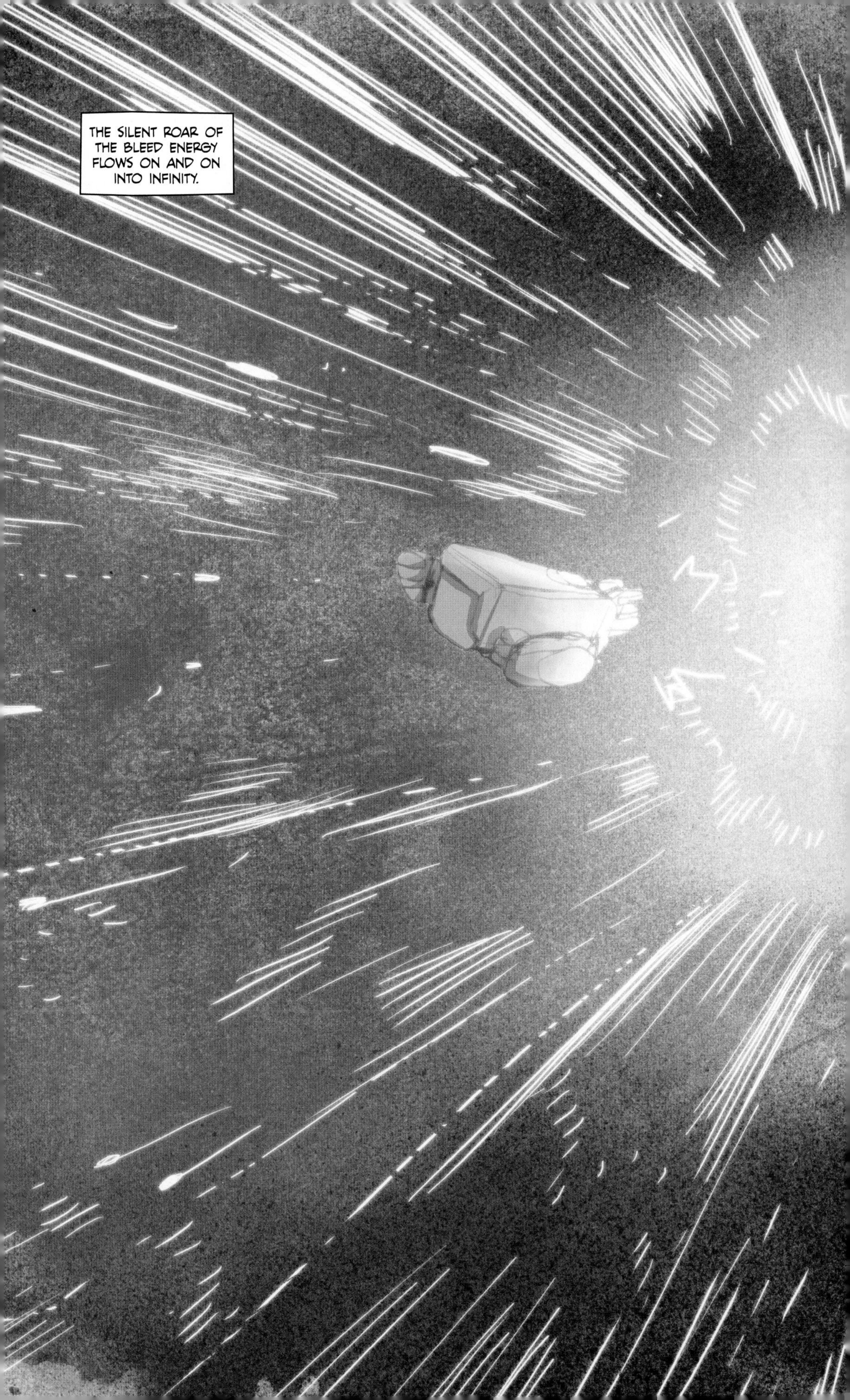
THE SILENT ROAR OF THE BLEED ENERGY FLOWS ON AND ON INTO INFINITY.

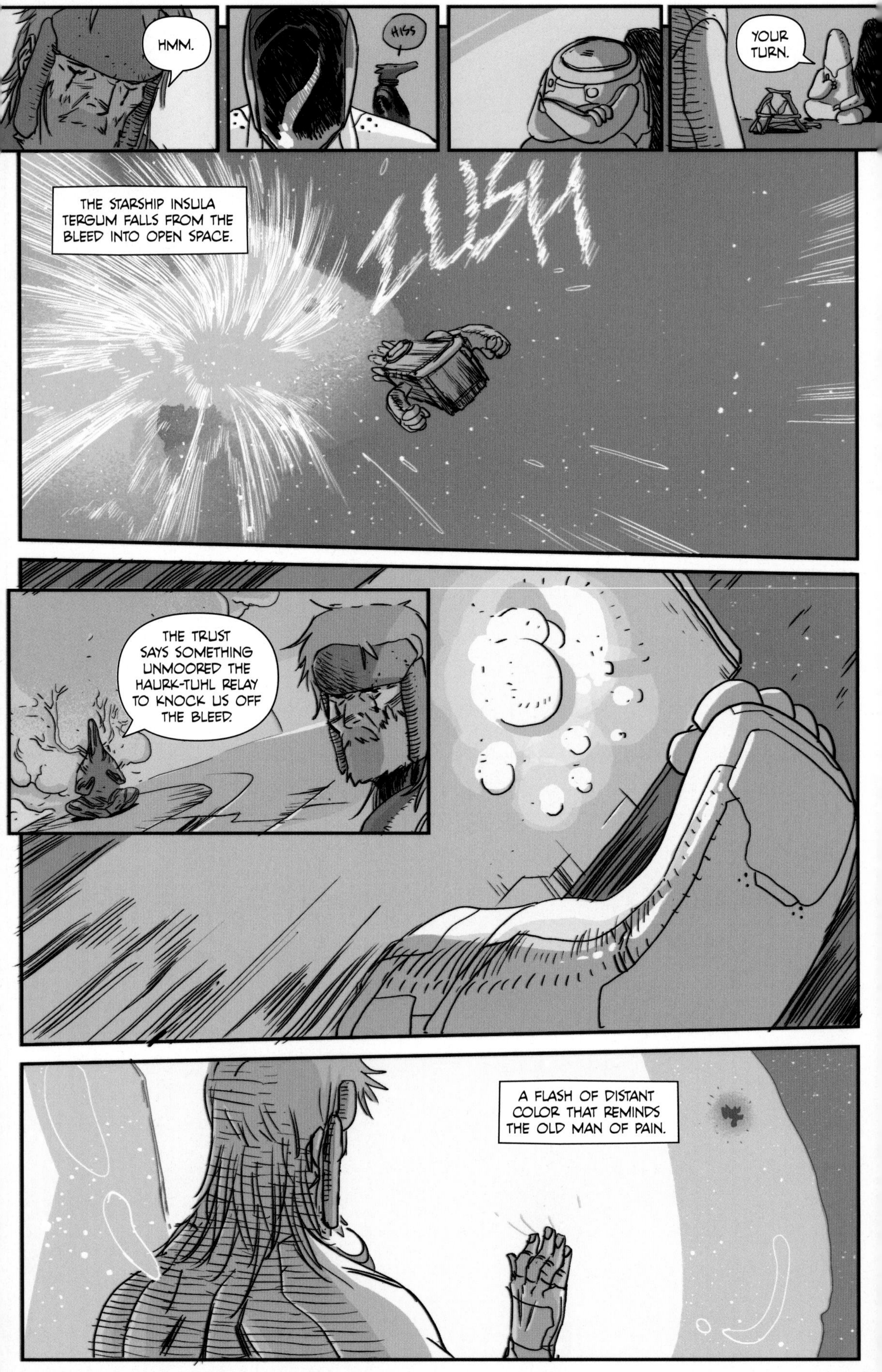
HMM.
HISS
YOUR TURN.
THE STARSHIP INSULA TERGUM FALLS FROM THE BLEED INTO OPEN SPACE.
ZZSH
THE TRUST SAYS SOMETHING UNMOORED THE HAURK-TUHL RELAY TO KNOCK US OFF THE BLEED.
A FLASH OF DISTANT COLOR THAT REMINDS THE OLD MAN OF PAIN.

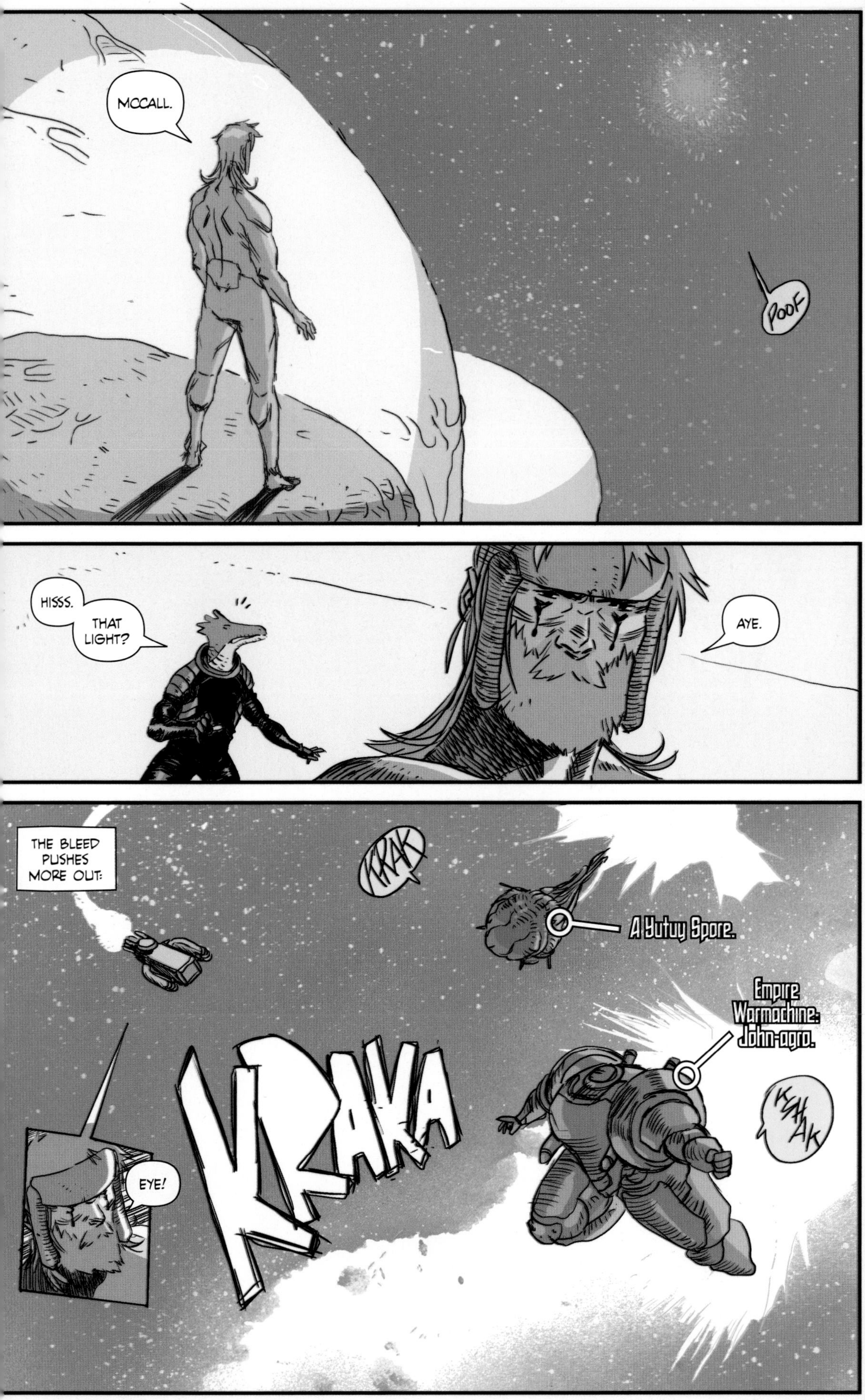
MCCALL.
POOF
HISSS.
THAT LIGHT?
AYE.
THE BLEED PUSHES MORE OUT:
KRAK
A Yutuy Spore.
Empire Warmachine: John-agro.
EYE!
KRAKA
KSHAK

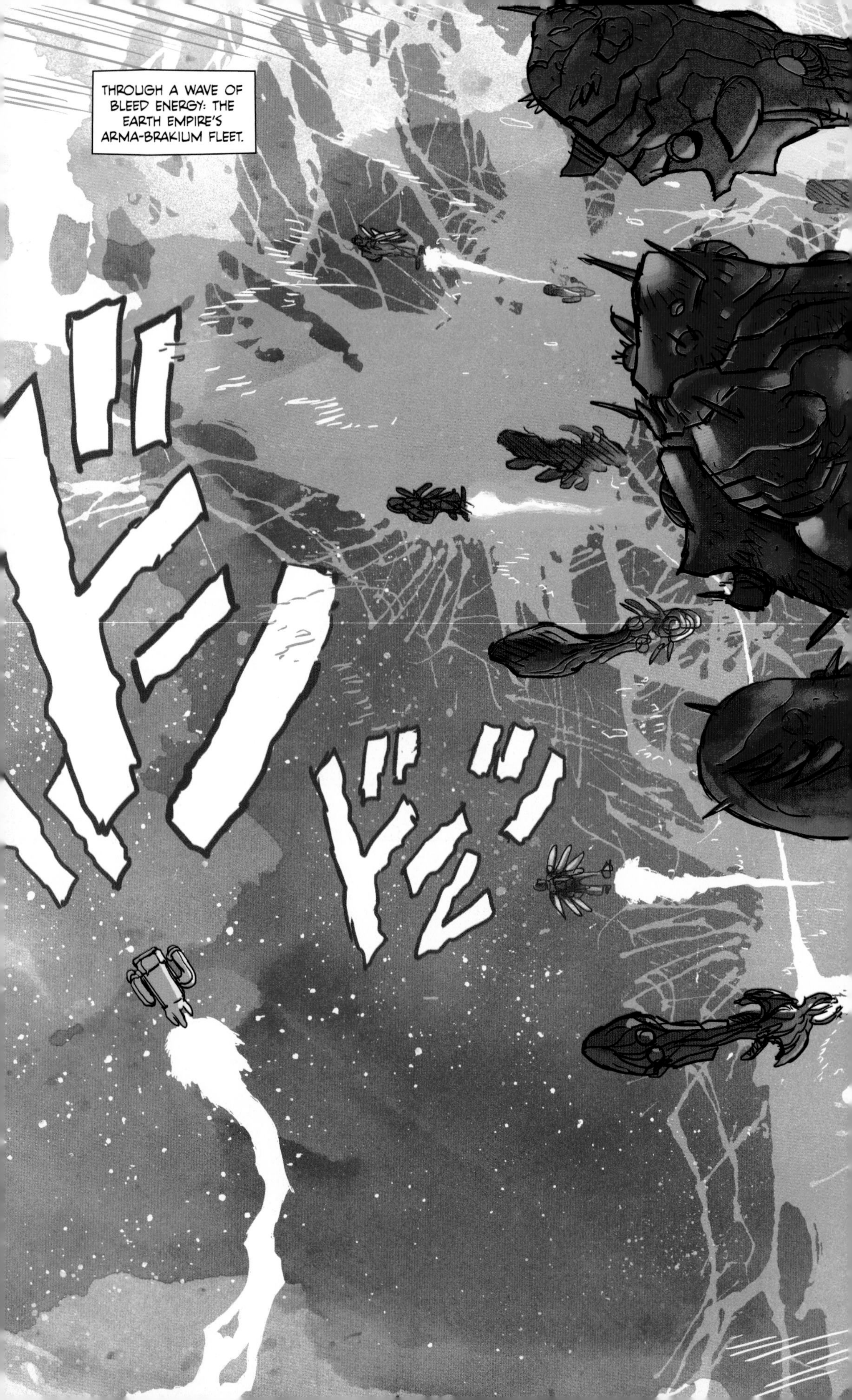
THROUGH A WAVE OF BLEED ENERGY: THE EARTH EMPIRE'S ARMA-BRAKIUM FLEET.

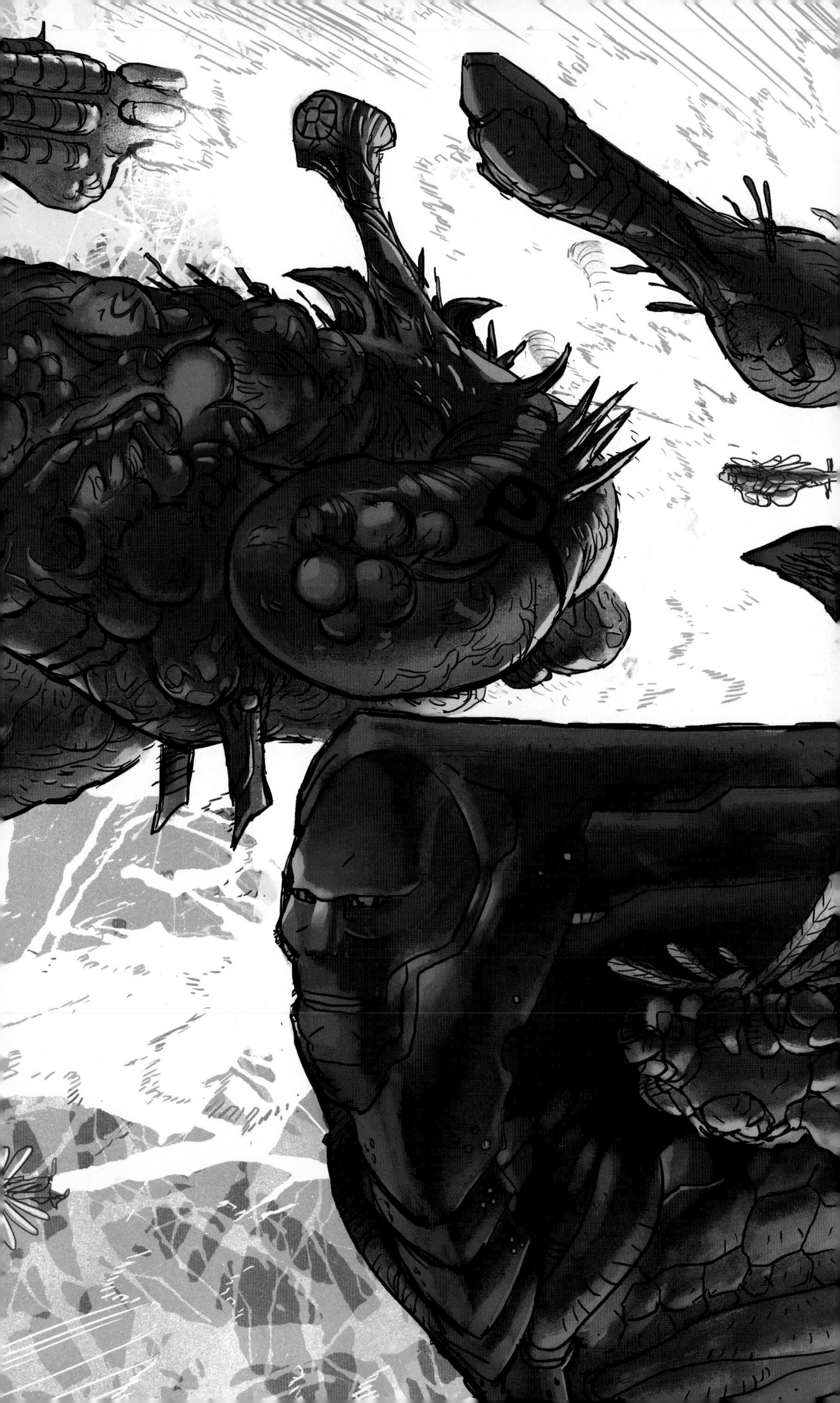

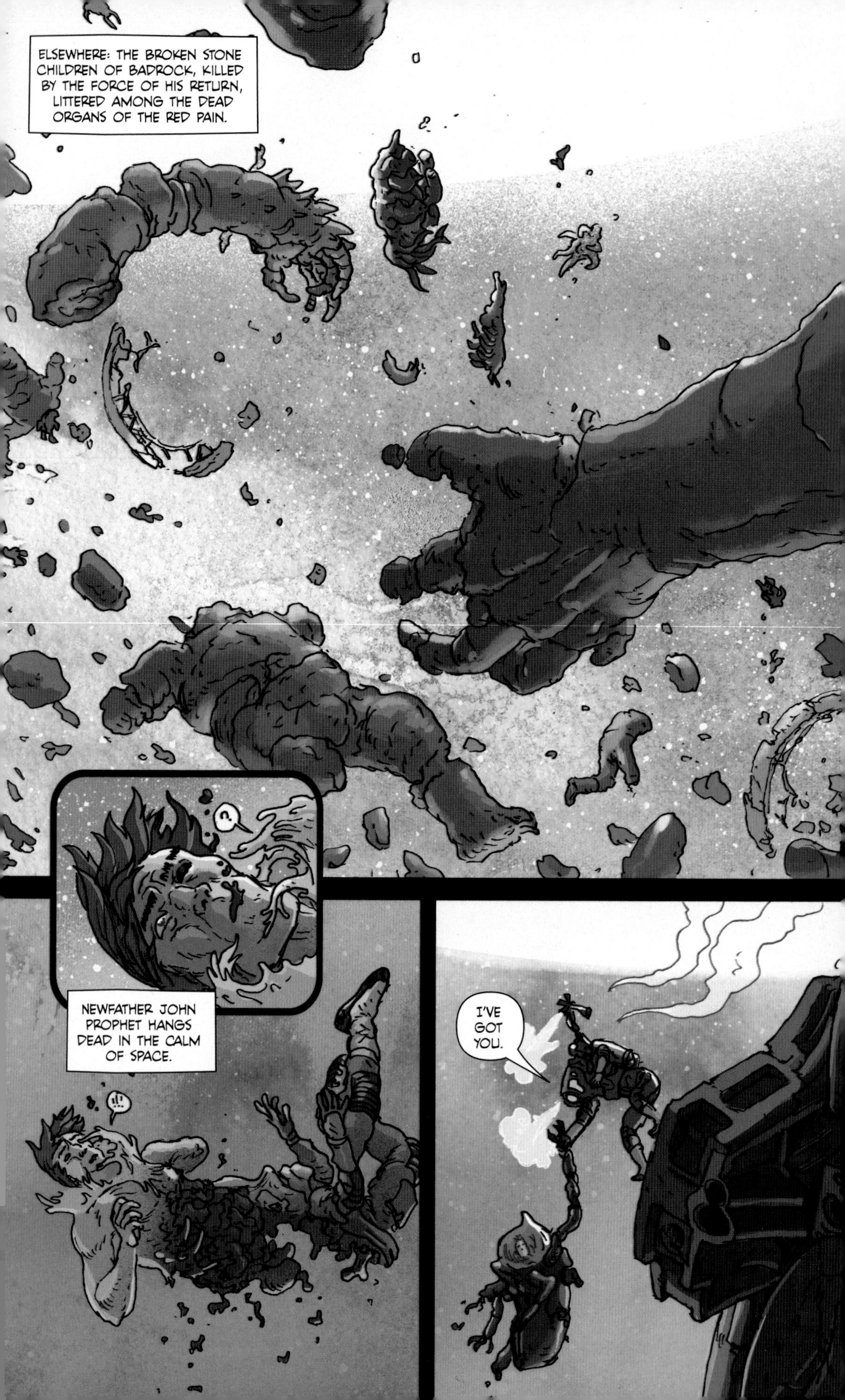
ELSEWHERE: THE BROKEN STONE CHILDREN OF BADROCK, KILLED BY THE FORCE OF HIS RETURN, LITTERED AMONG THE DEAD ORGANS OF THE RED PAIN.
?
NEWFATHER JOHN PROPHET HANGS DEAD IN THE CALM OF SPACE.
!!
I'VE GOT YOU.

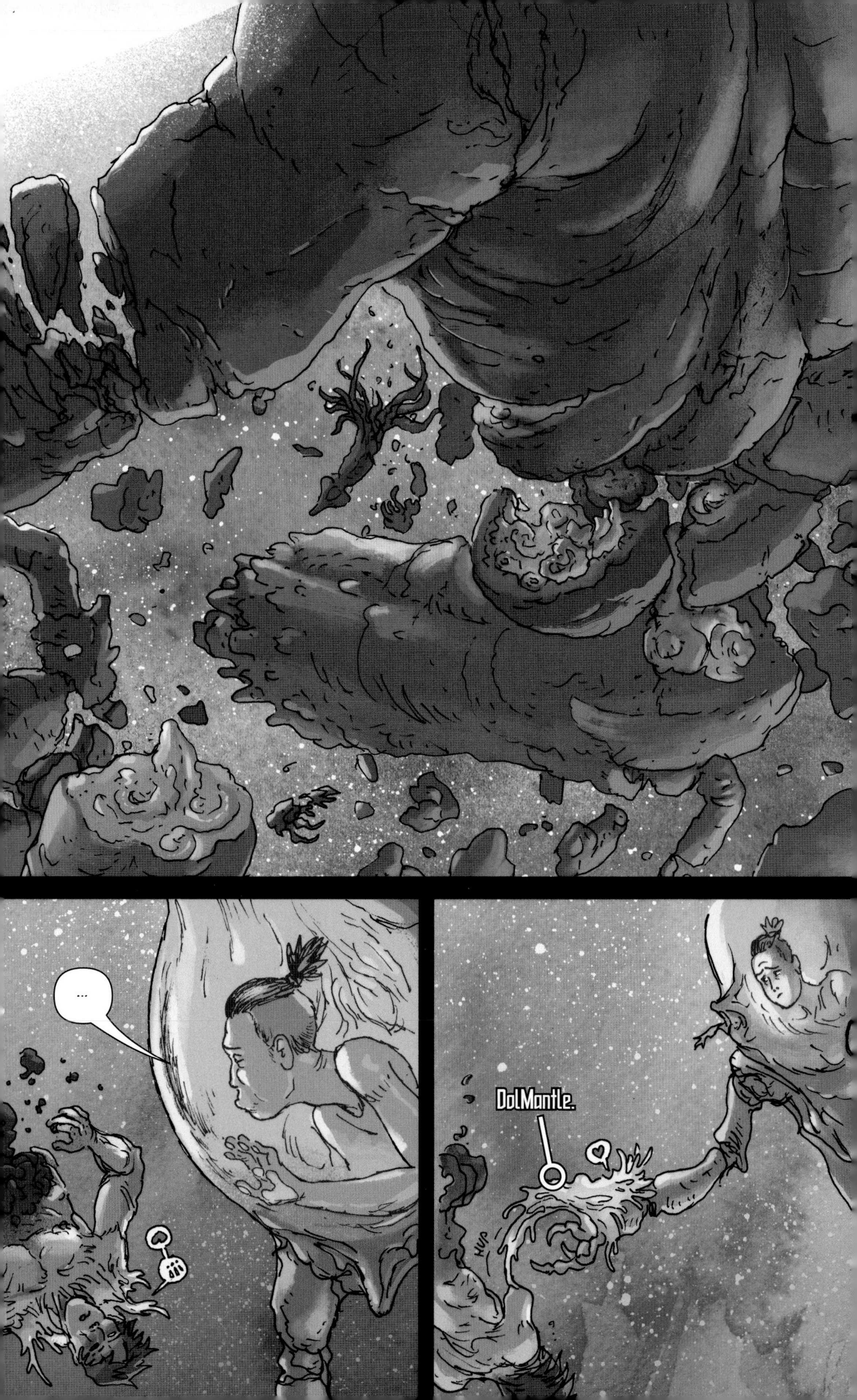
...
DolMantle.
HUP

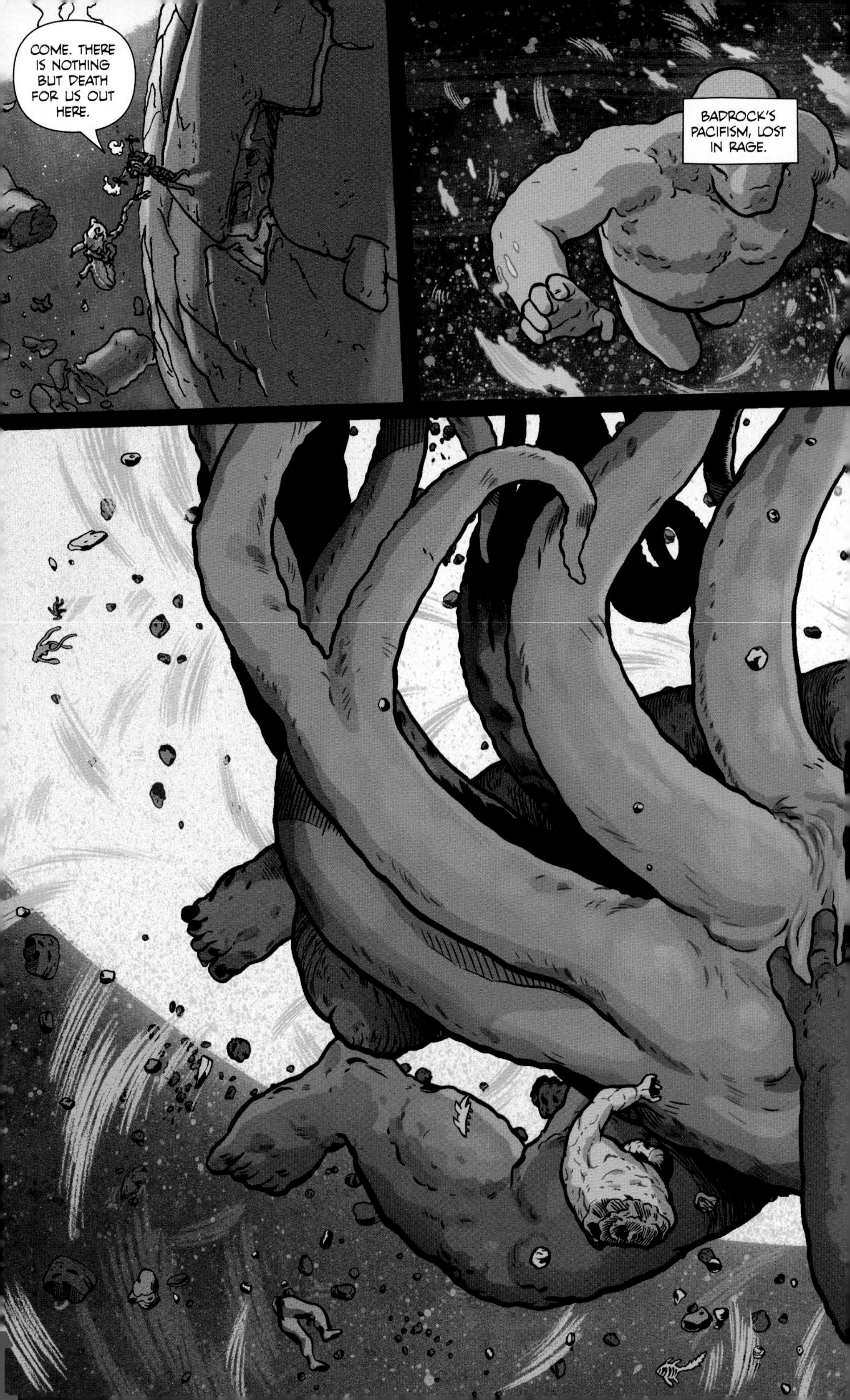
COME. THERE IS NOTHING BUT DEATH FOR US OUT HERE.
BADROCK'S PACIFISM, LOST IN RAGE.

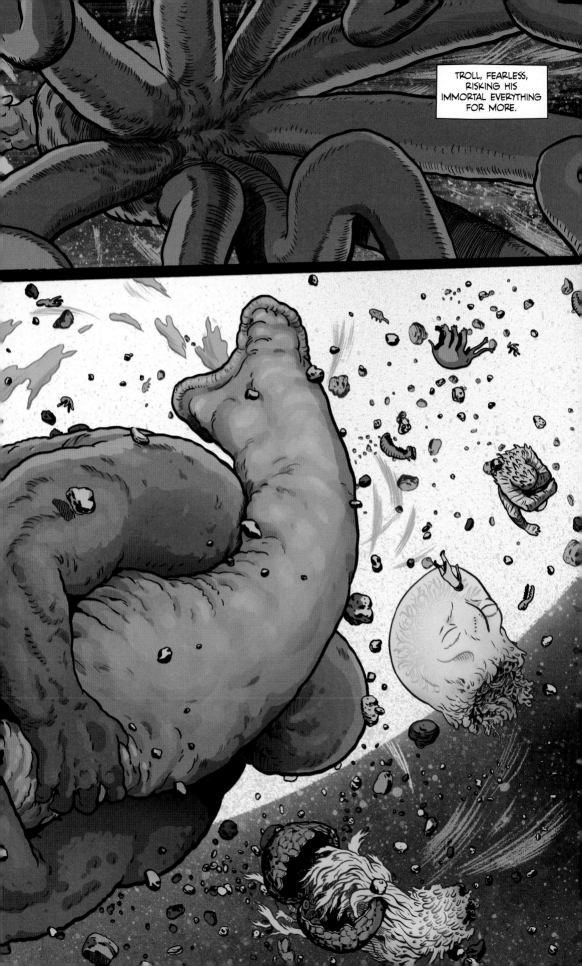

TROLL, FEARLESS,
RISKING HIS
IMMORTAL EVERYTHING
FOR MORE.

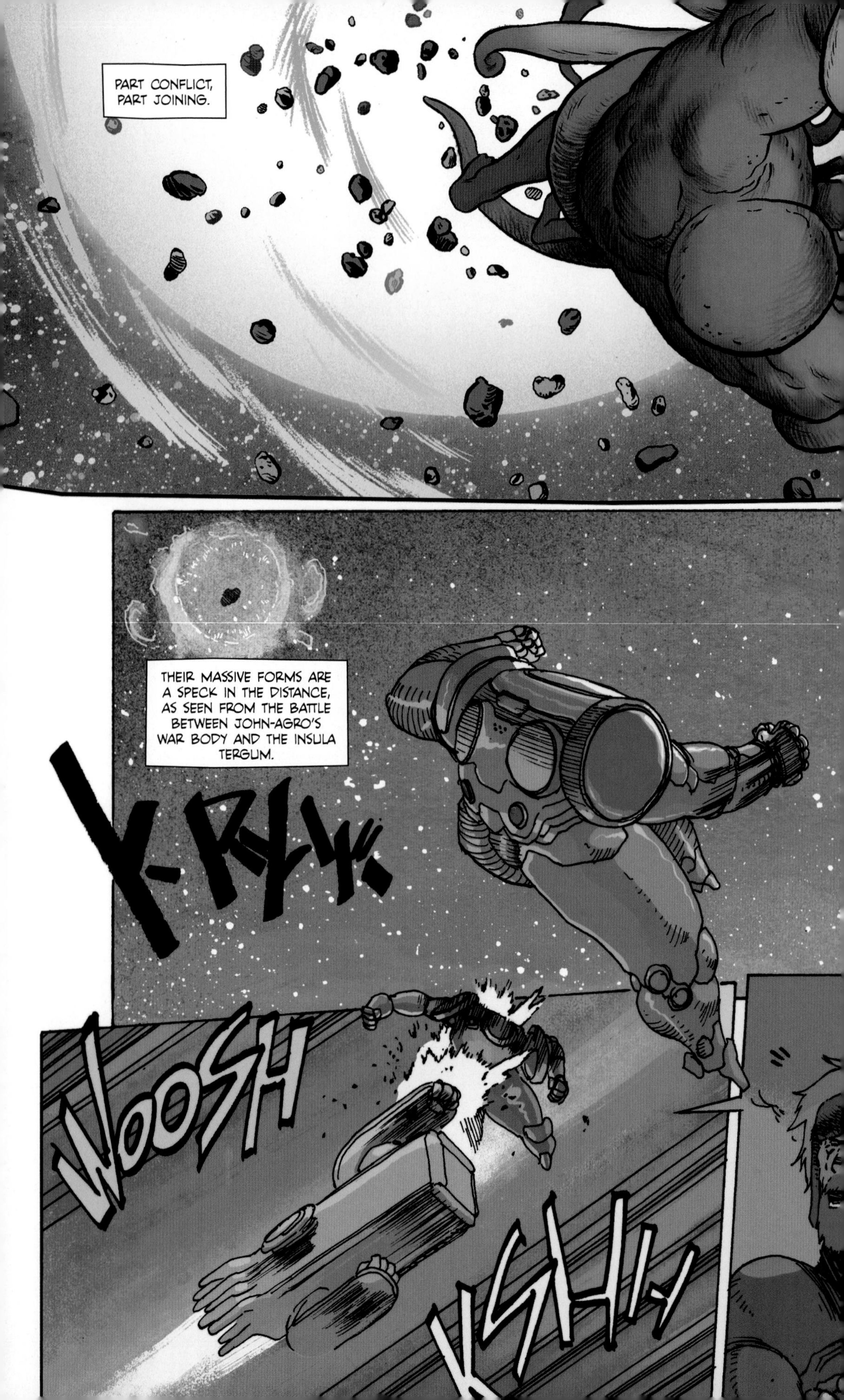
PART CONFLICT,
PART JOINING.
THEIR MASSIVE FORMS ARE A SPECK IN THE DISTANCE, AS SEEN FROM THE BATTLE BETWEEN JOHN-AGRO'S WAR BODY AND THE INSULA TERGUM.
WOOSH

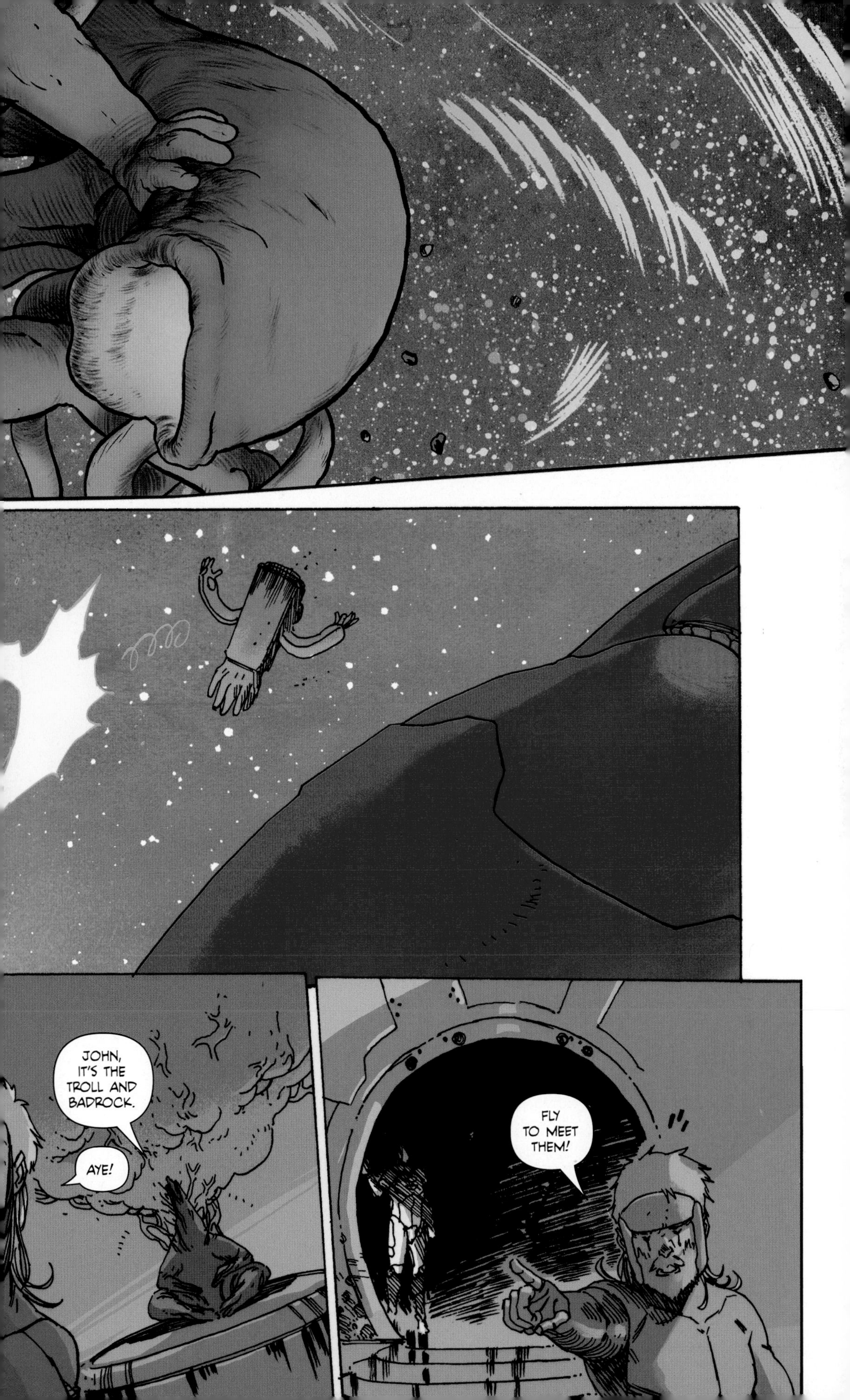
JOHN, IT'S THE TROLL AND BADROCK.
AYE!
FLY TO MEET THEM!

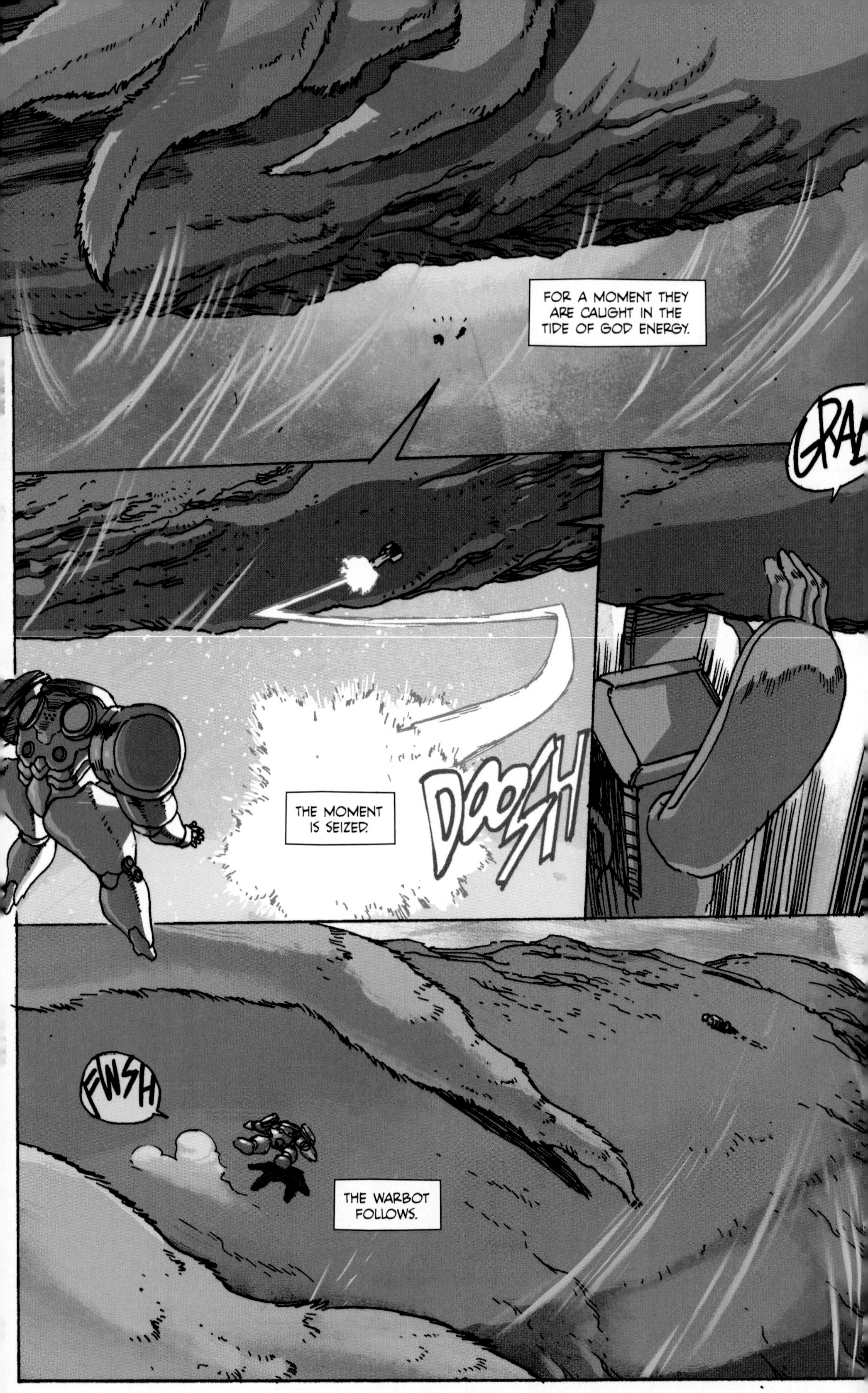
FOR A MOMENT THEY ARE CAUGHT IN THE TIDE OF GOD ENERGY.
GRA
THE MOMENT IS SEIZED.
DOOSH
FWSH
THE WARBOT FOLLOWS.

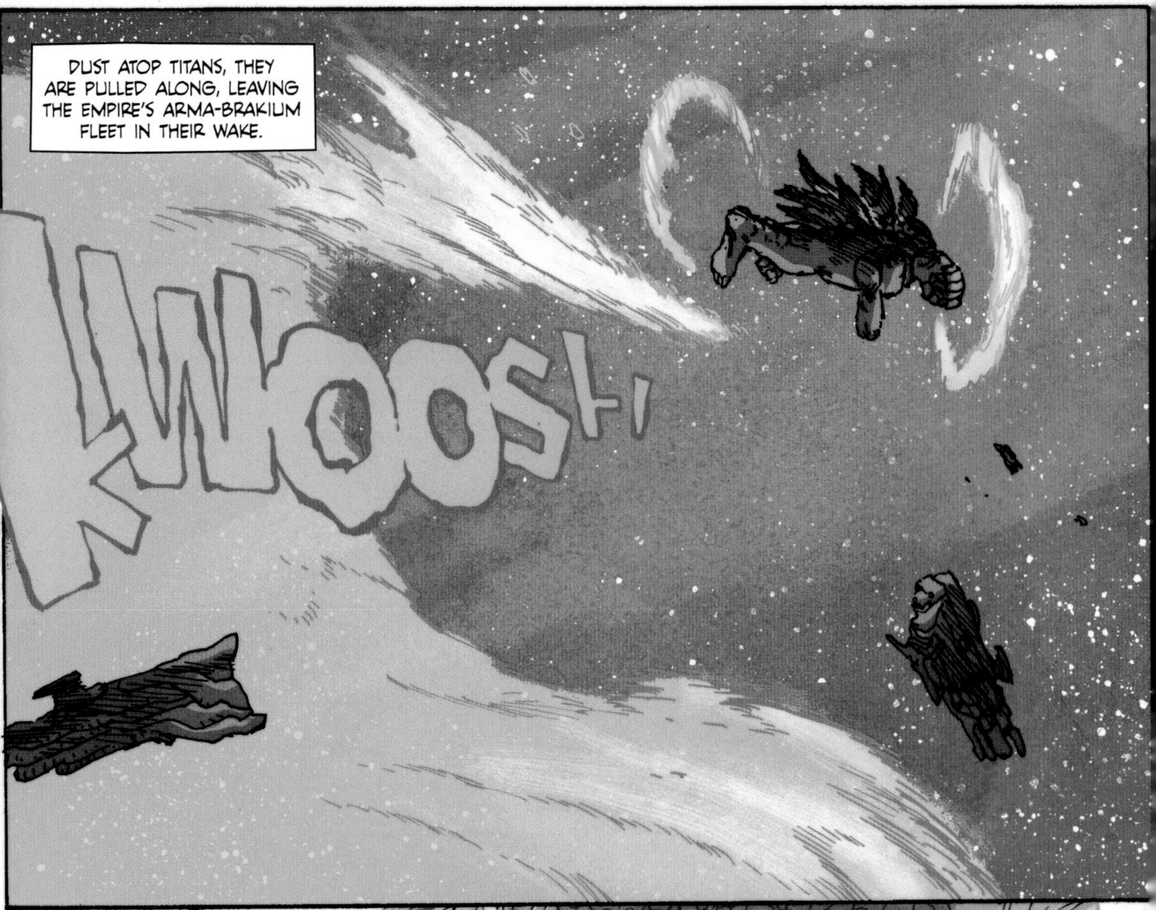
DUST ATOP TITANS, THEY ARE PULLED ALONG, LEAVING THE EMPIRE'S ARMA-BRAKIUM FLEET IN THEIR WAKE.
KWOOSH!

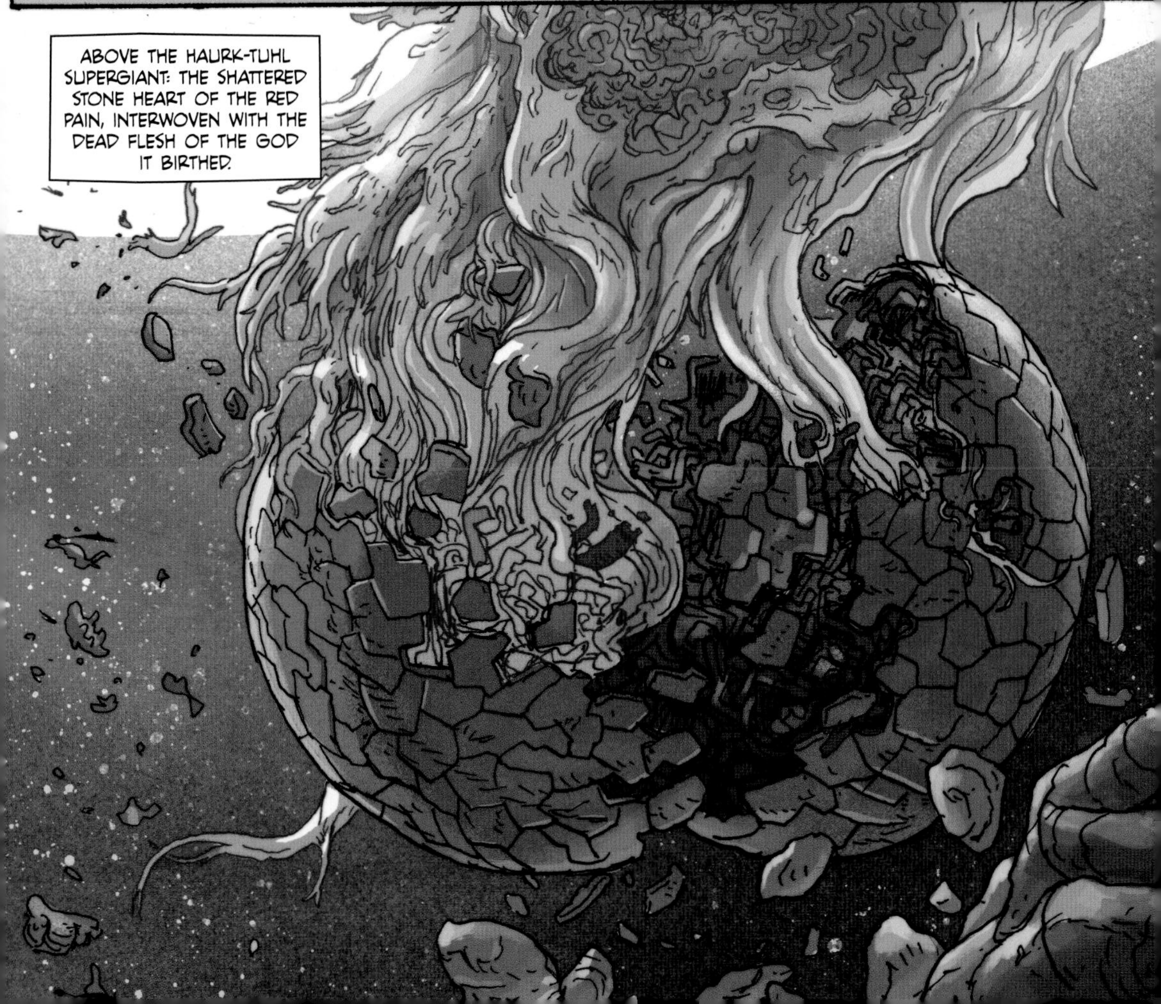
ABOVE THE HAURK-TUHL SUPERGIANT: THE SHATTERED STONE HEART OF THE RED PAIN, INTERWOVEN WITH THE DEAD FLESH OF THE GOD IT BIRTHED.

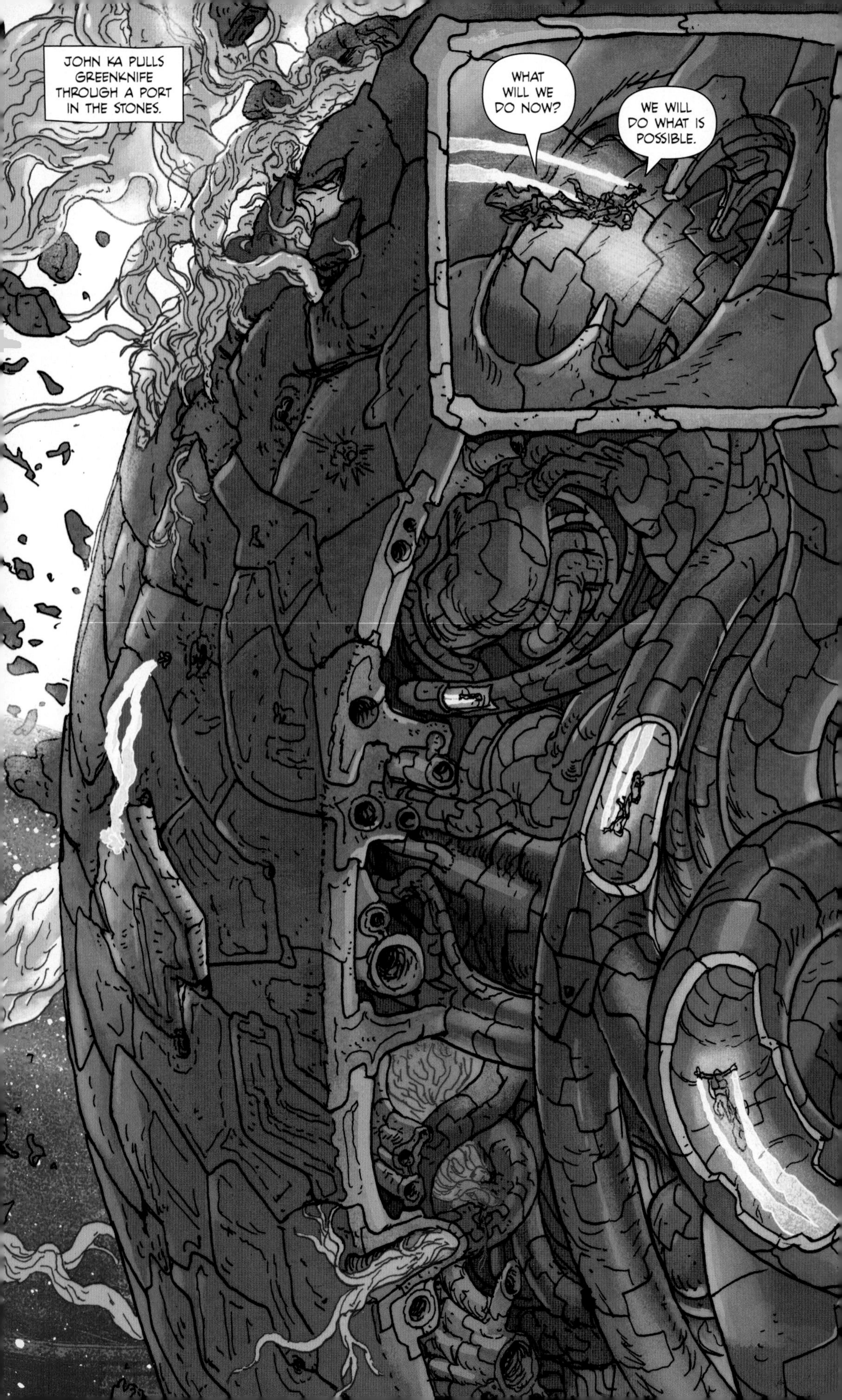
JOHN KA PULLS GREENKNIFE THROUGH A PORT IN THE STONES.
WHAT WILL WE DO NOW?
WE WILL DO WHAT IS POSSIBLE.

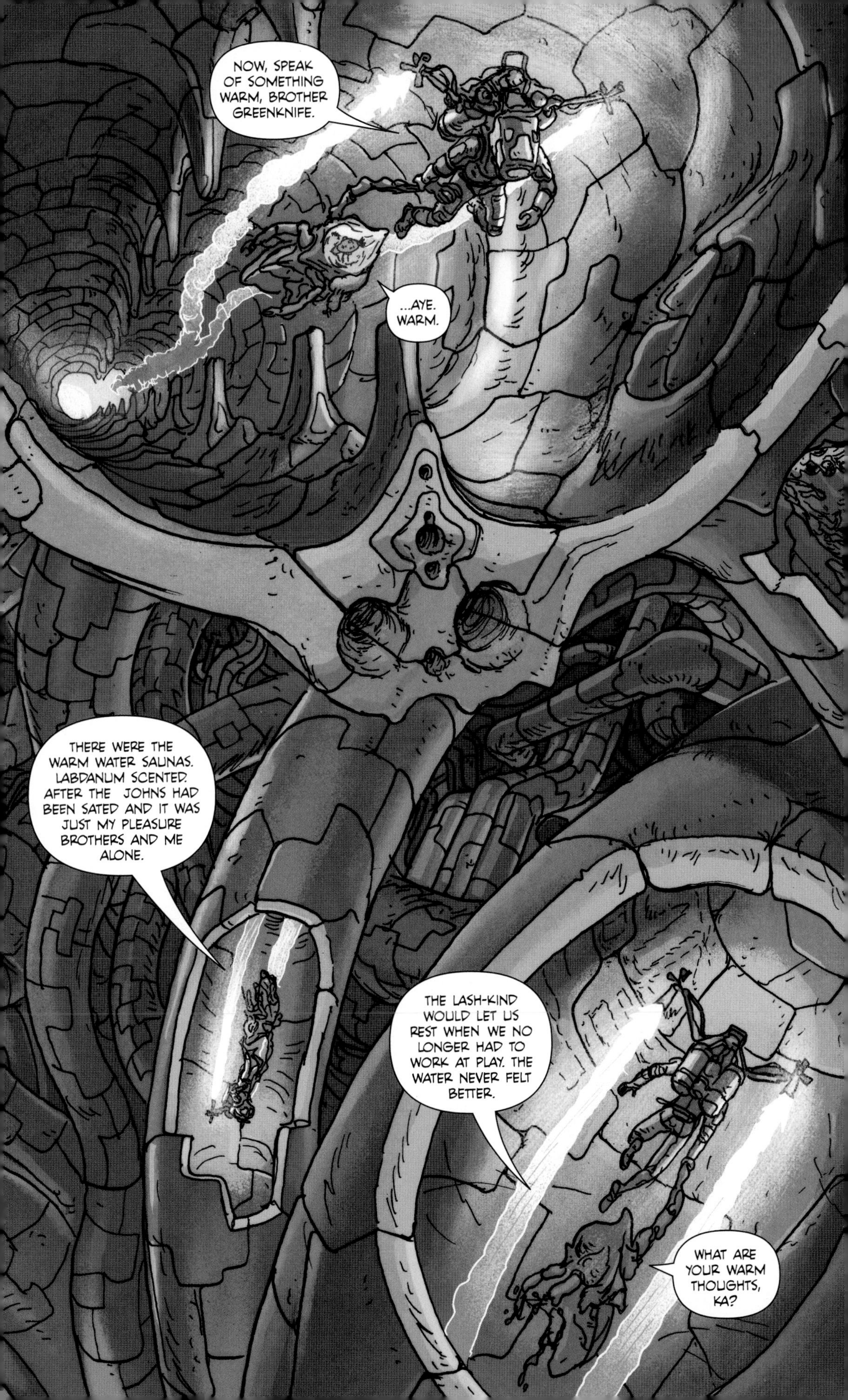
NOW, SPEAK OF SOMETHING WARM, BROTHER GREENKNIFE.
...AYE. WARM.
THERE WERE THE WARM WATER SAUNAS. LABDANUM SCENTED. AFTER THE JOHNS HAD BEEN SATED AND IT WAS JUST MY PLEASURE BROTHERS AND ME ALONE.
THE LASH-KIND WOULD LET US REST WHEN WE NO LONGER HAD TO WORK AT PLAY. THE WATER NEVER FELT BETTER.
WHAT ARE YOUR WARM THOUGHTS, KA?

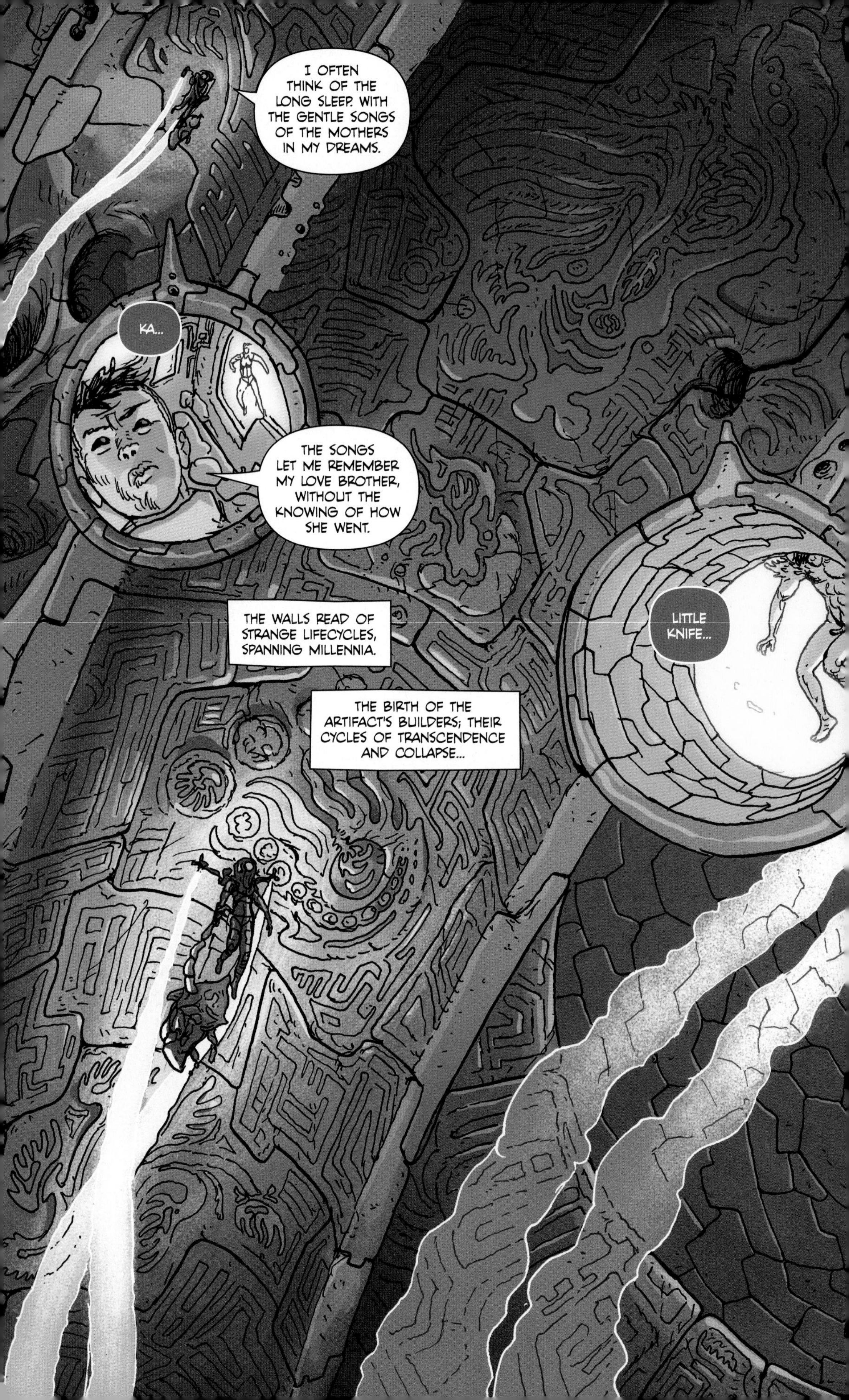
I OFTEN THINK OF THE LONG SLEEP. WITH THE GENTLE SONGS OF THE MOTHERS IN MY DREAMS.
KA...
THE SONGS LET ME REMEMBER MY LOVE BROTHER, WITHOUT THE KNOWING OF HOW SHE WENT.
LITTLE KNIFE...
THE WALLS READ OF STRANGE LIFECYCLES, SPANNING MILLENNIA.
THE BIRTH OF THE ARTIFACT'S BUILDERS; THEIR CYCLES OF TRANSCENDENCE AND COLLAPSE...

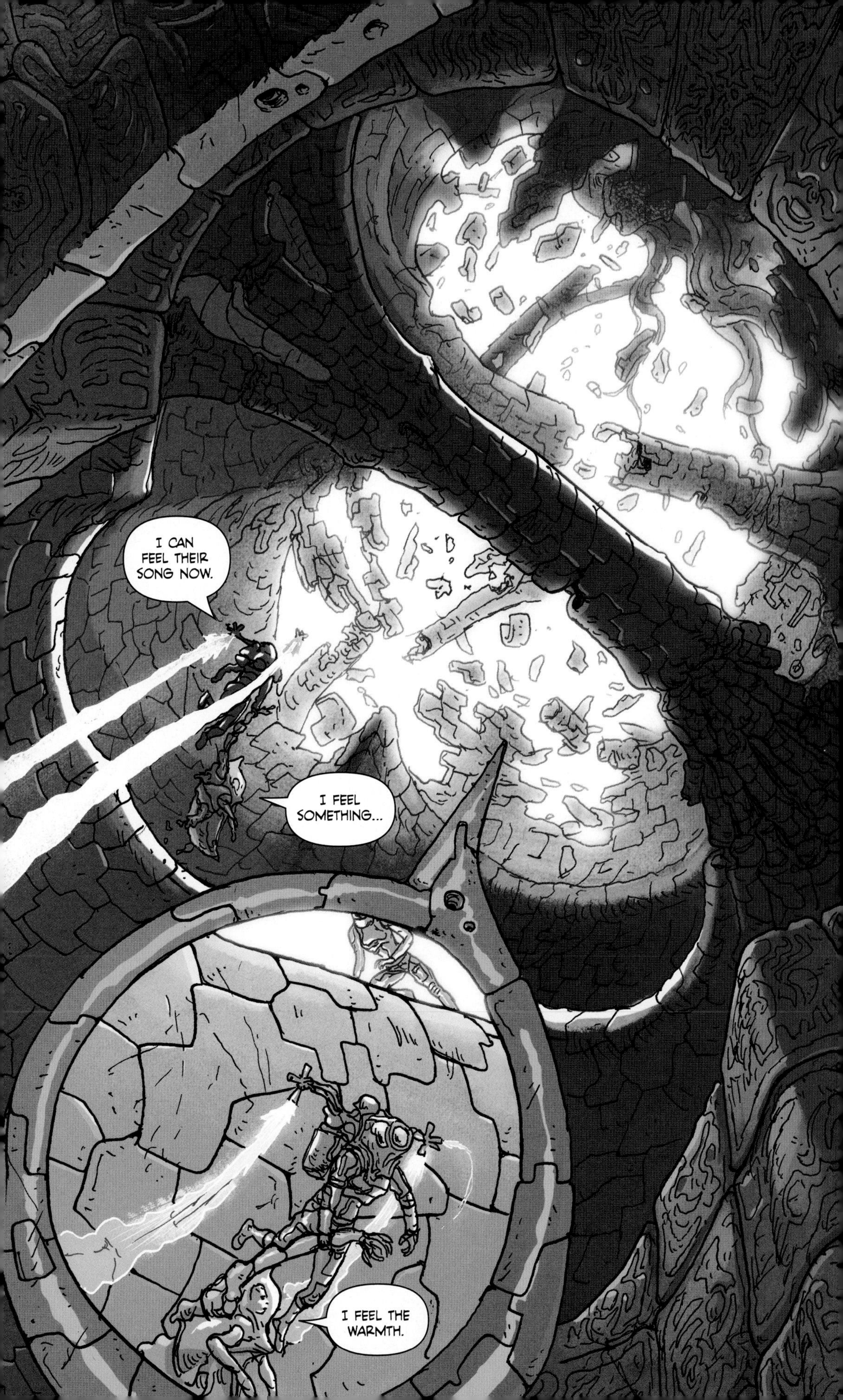

I CAN FEEL THEIR SONG NOW.
I FEEL SOMETHING...
I FEEL THE WARMTH.

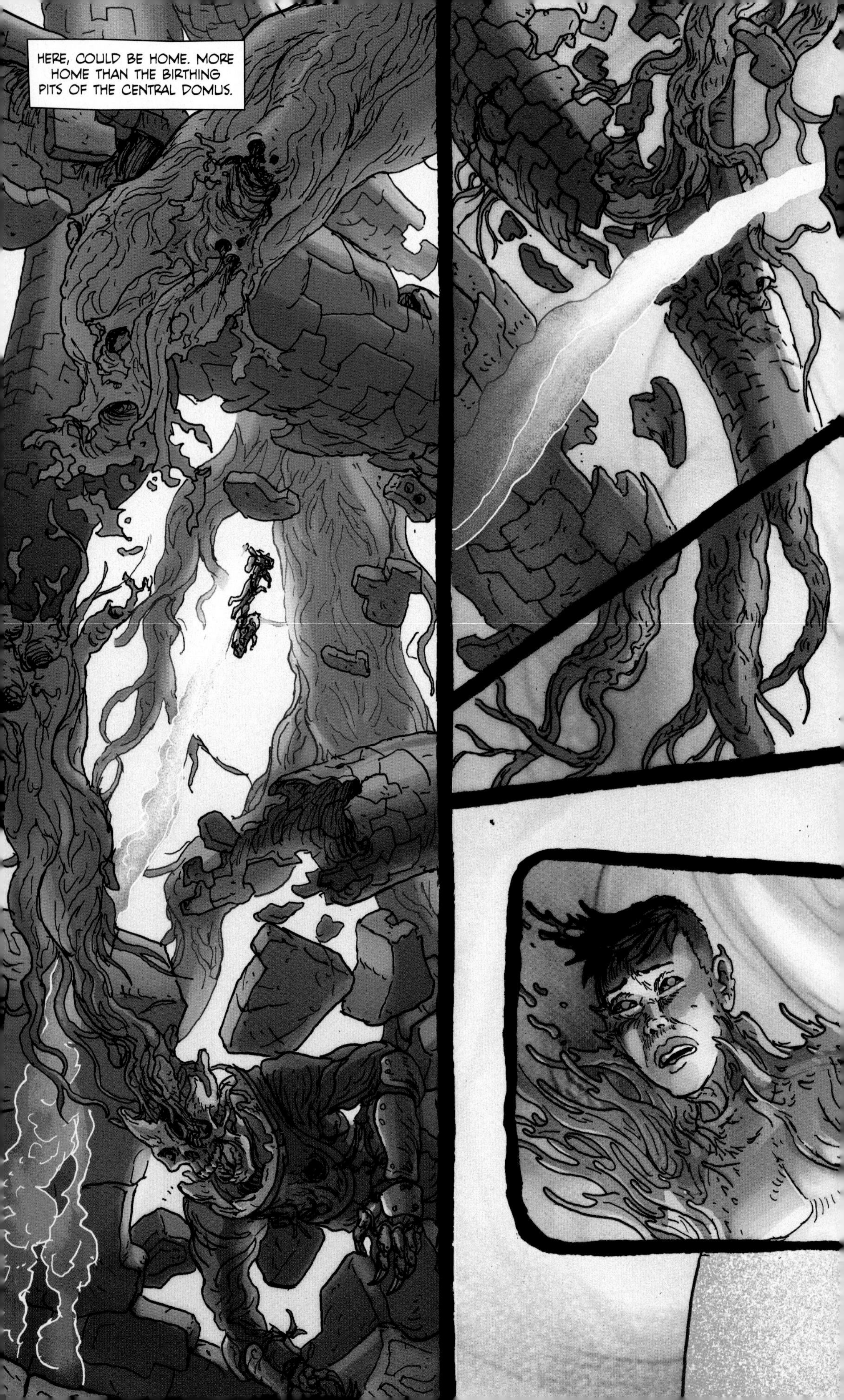
HERE, COULD BE HOME. MORE HOME THAN THE BIRTHING PITS OF THE CENTRAL DOMUS.

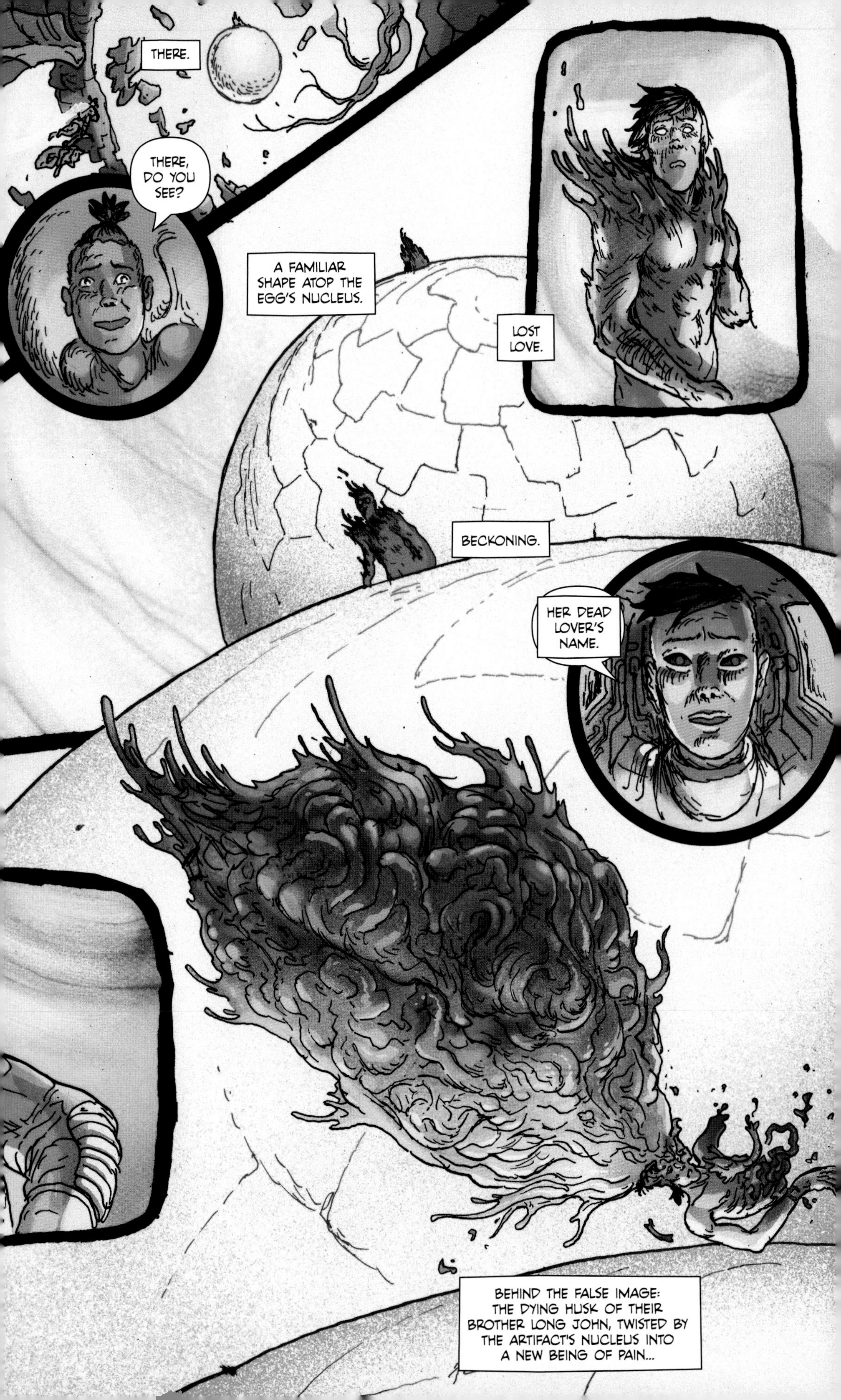
THERE.
THERE, DO YOU SEE?
A FAMILIAR SHAPE ATOP THE EGG'S NUCLEUS.
LOST LOVE.
BECKONING.
HER DEAD LOVER'S NAME.
BEHIND THE FALSE IMAGE: THE DYING HUSK OF THEIR BROTHER LONG JOHN, TWISTED BY THE ARTIFACT'S NUCLEUS INTO A NEW BEING OF PAIN...

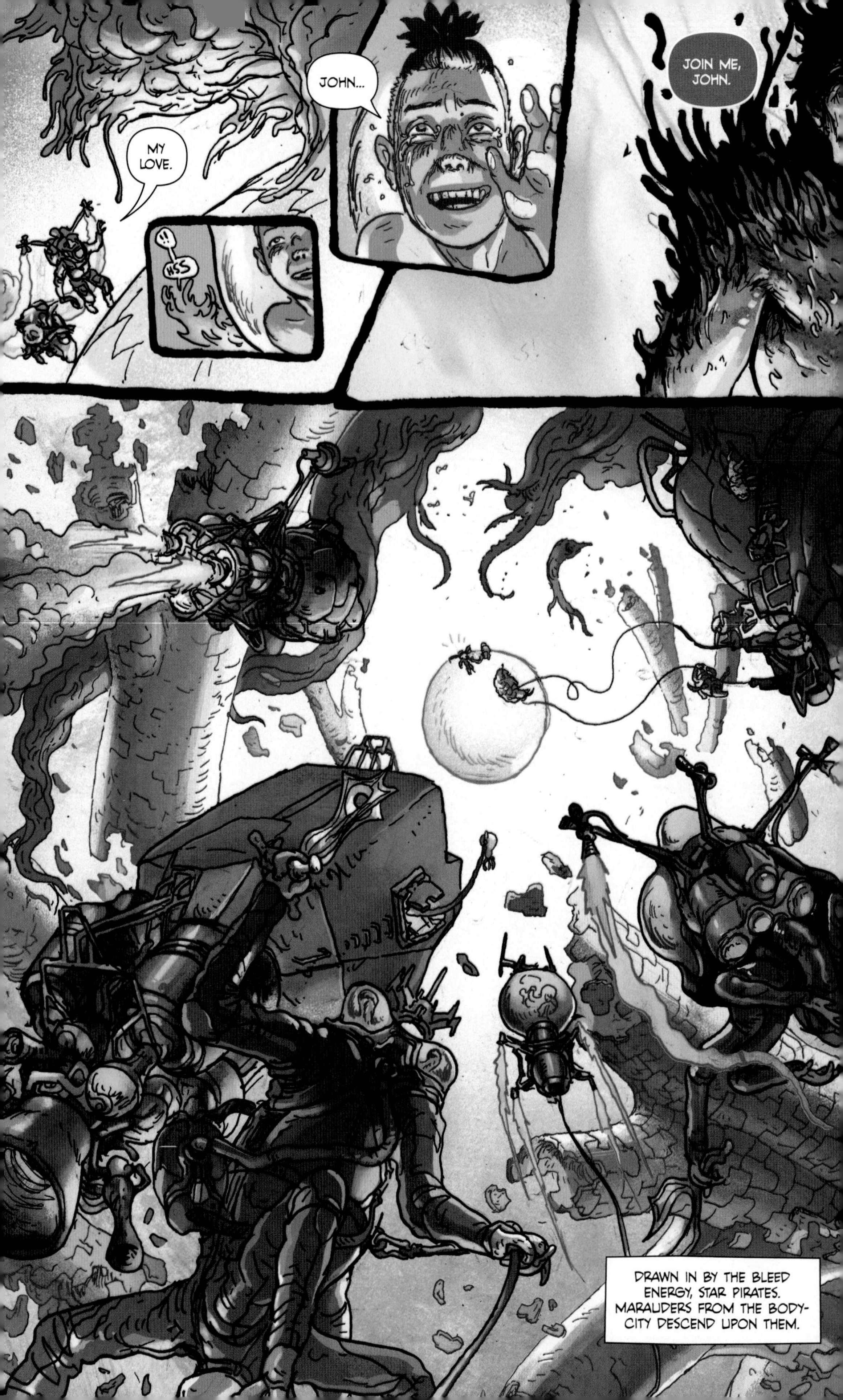
MY LOVE.
JOHN...
!!
HSS
JOIN ME, JOHN.
DRAWN IN BY THE BLEED ENERGY, STAR PIRATES. MARAUDERS FROM THE BODY-CITY DESCEND UPON THEM.

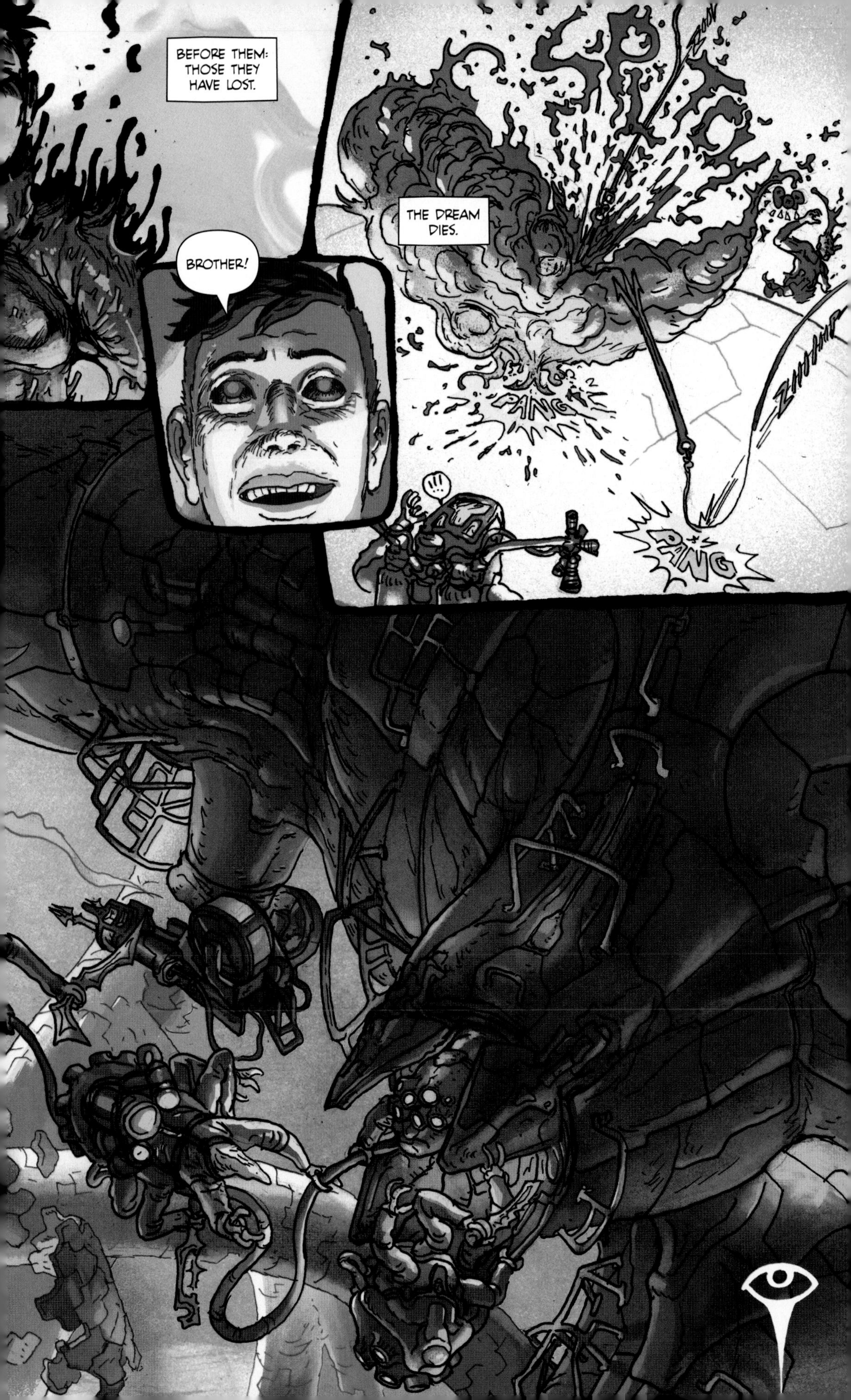
BEFORE THEM: THOSE THEY HAVE LOST.
BROTHER!
THE DREAM DIES.
POP
PANG
!!!
PANG

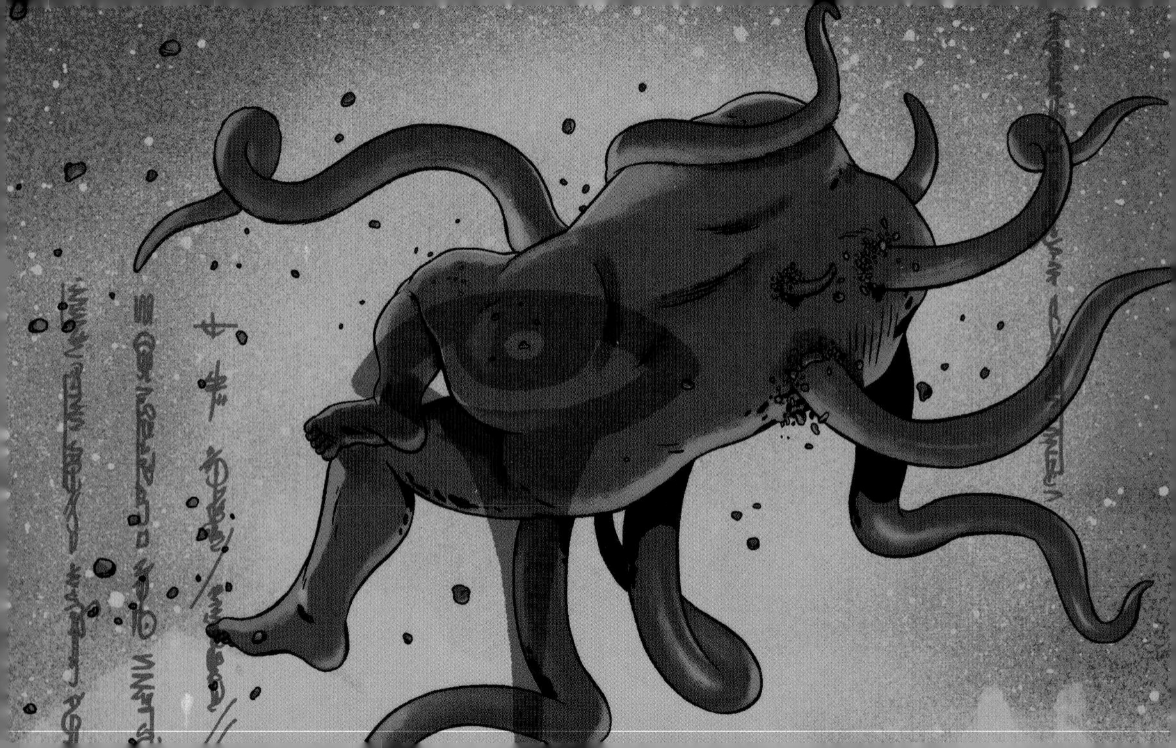

5

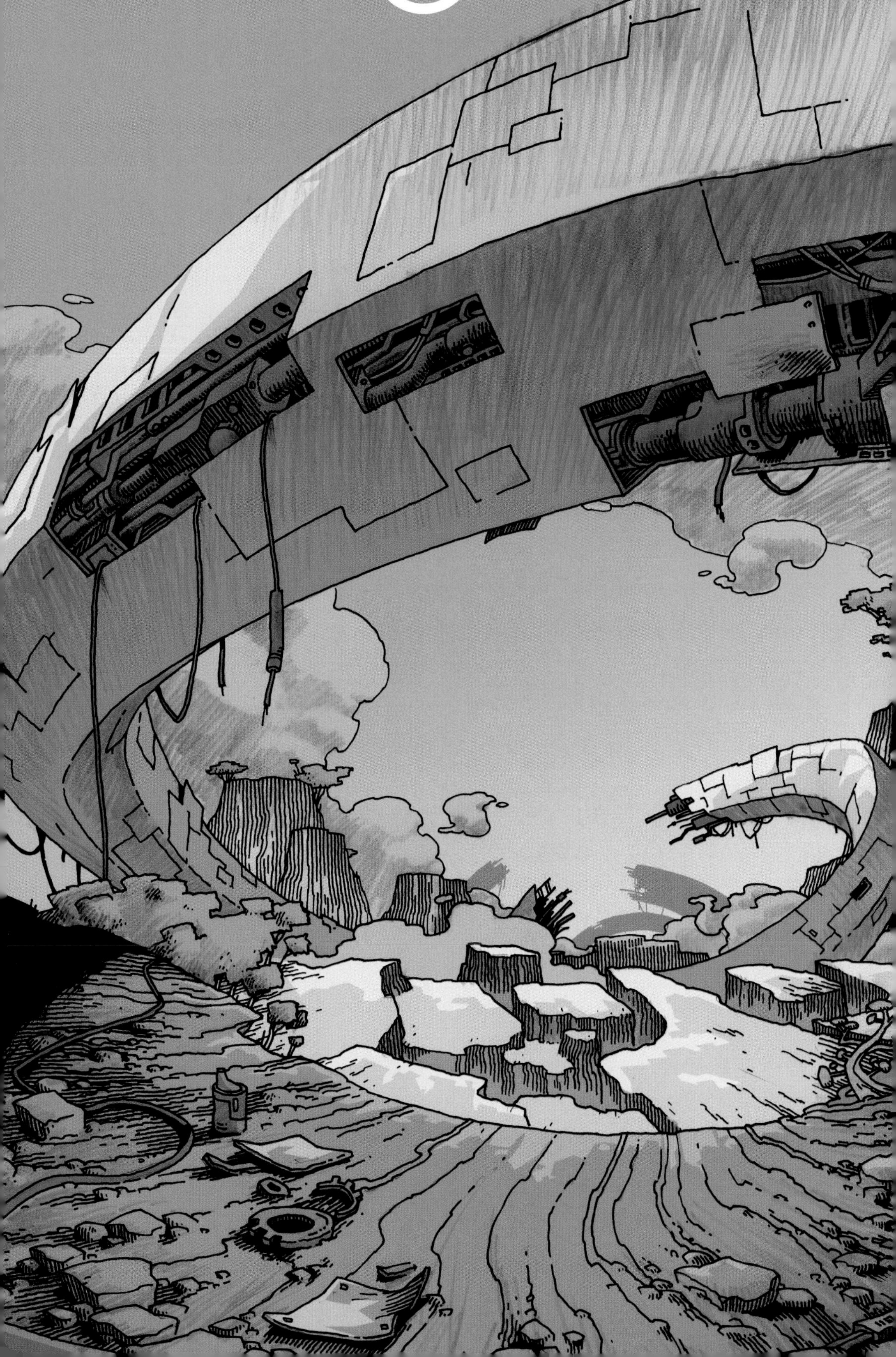

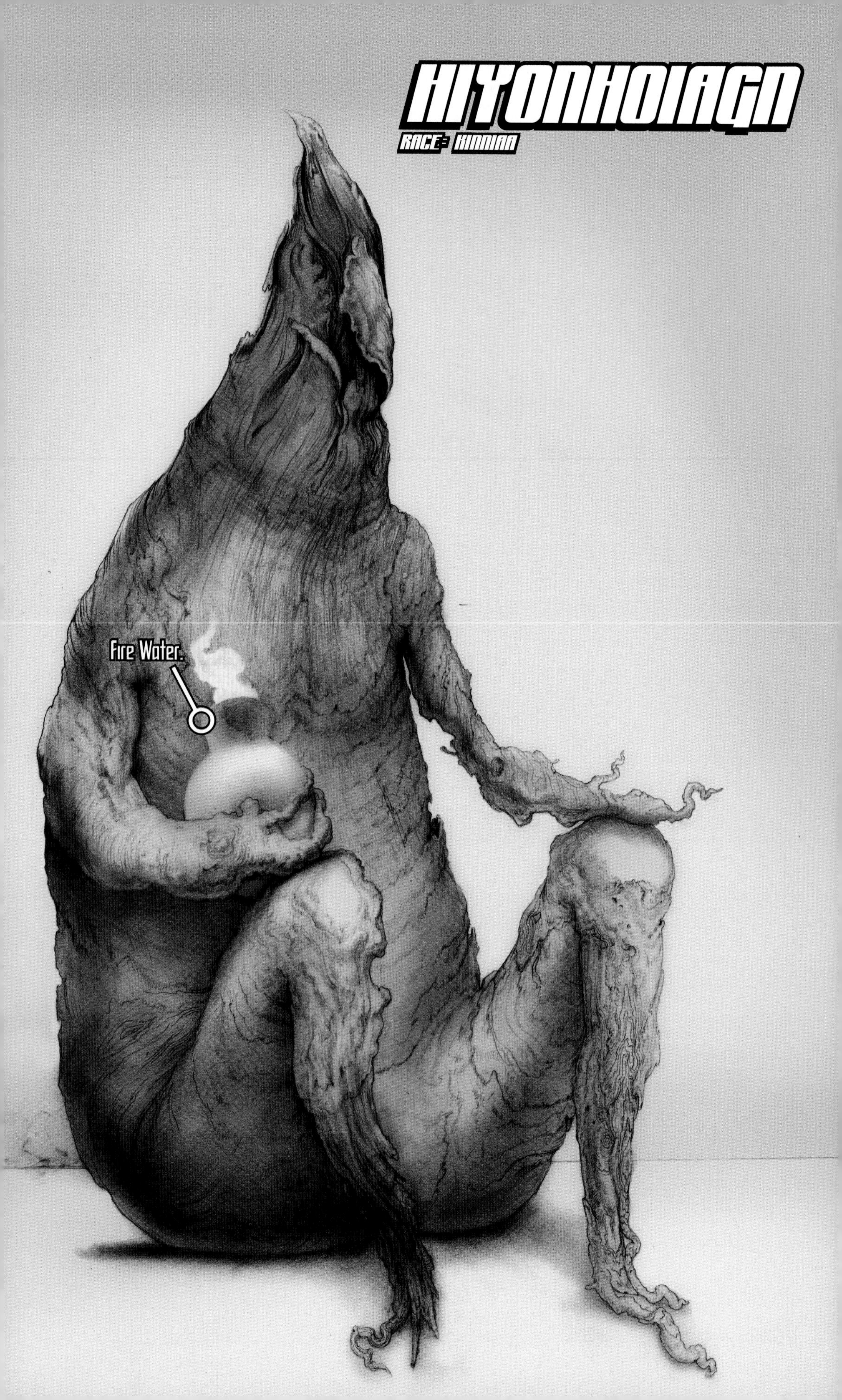
HIYONHOIAGN
RACE: KINNIAA
Fire Water.

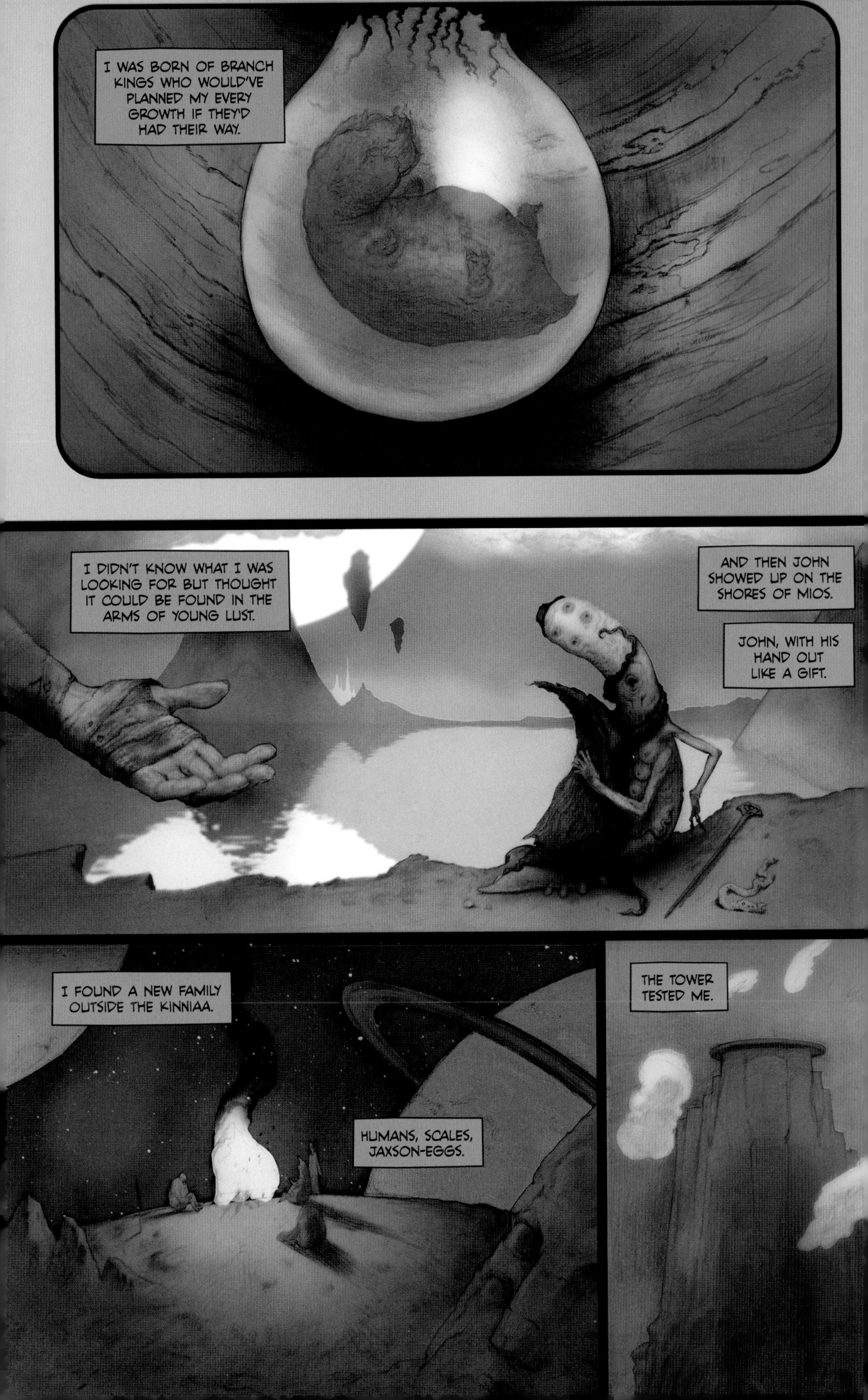
I WAS BORN OF BRANCH KINGS WHO WOULD'VE PLANNED MY EVERY GROWTH IF THEY'D HAD THEIR WAY.
I DIDN'T KNOW WHAT I WAS LOOKING FOR BUT THOUGHT IT COULD BE FOUND IN THE ARMS OF YOUNG LUST.
AND THEN JOHN SHOWED UP ON THE SHORES OF MIOS.
JOHN, WITH HIS HAND OUT LIKE A GIFT.
I FOUND A NEW FAMILY OUTSIDE THE KINNIAA.
HUMANS, SCALES, JAXSON-EGGS.
THE TOWER TESTED ME.

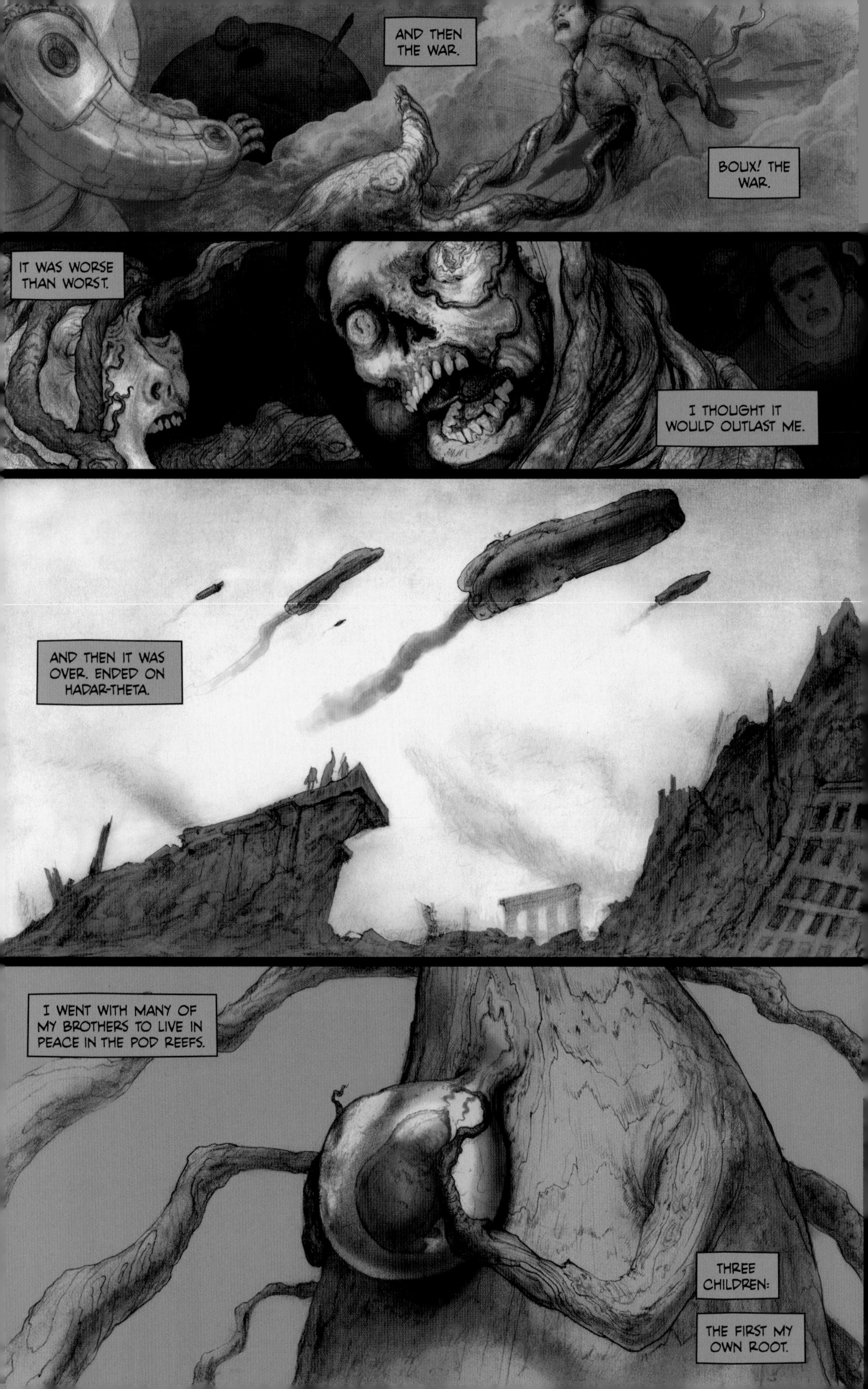
AND THEN THE WAR.
BOUX! THE WAR.
IT WAS WORSE THAN WORST.
I THOUGHT IT WOULD OUTLAST ME.
AND THEN IT WAS OVER. ENDED ON HADAR-THETA.
I WENT WITH MANY OF MY BROTHERS TO LIVE IN PEACE IN THE POD REEFS.
THREE CHILDREN:
THE FIRST MY OWN ROOT.

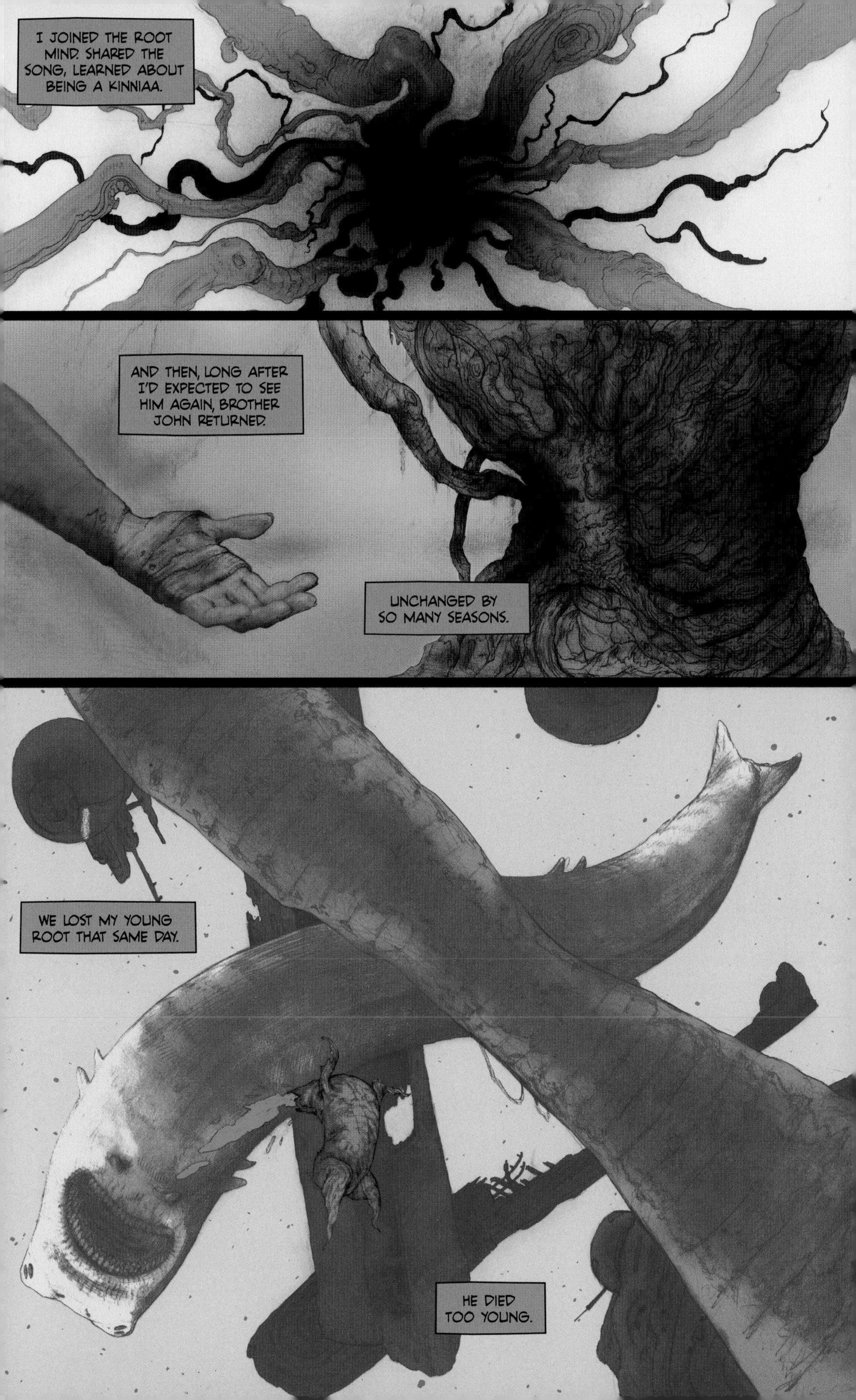
I JOINED THE ROOT MIND. SHARED THE SONG, LEARNED ABOUT BEING A KINNIAA.
AND THEN, LONG AFTER I'D EXPECTED TO SEE HIM AGAIN, BROTHER JOHN RETURNED.
UNCHANGED BY SO MANY SEASONS.
WE LOST MY YOUNG ROOT THAT SAME DAY.
HE DIED TOO YOUNG.

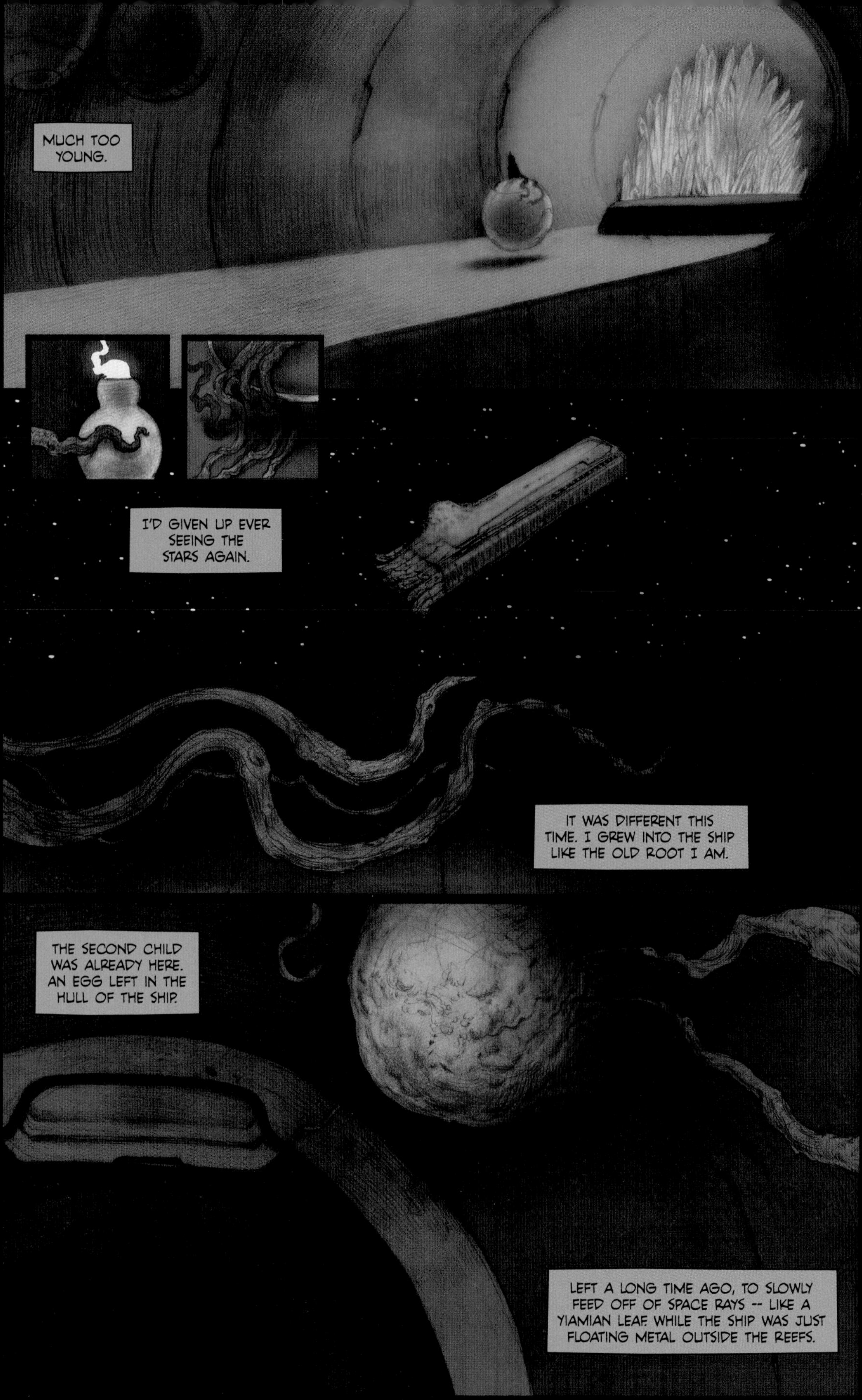
MUCH TOO YOUNG.
I'D GIVEN UP EVER SEEING THE STARS AGAIN.
IT WAS DIFFERENT THIS TIME. I GREW INTO THE SHIP LIKE THE OLD ROOT I AM.
THE SECOND CHILD WAS ALREADY HERE. AN EGG LEFT IN THE HULL OF THE SHIP.
LEFT A LONG TIME AGO, TO SLOWLY FEED OFF OF SPACE RAYS -- LIKE A YIAMIAN LEAF WHILE THE SHIP WAS JUST FLOATING METAL OUTSIDE THE REEFS.

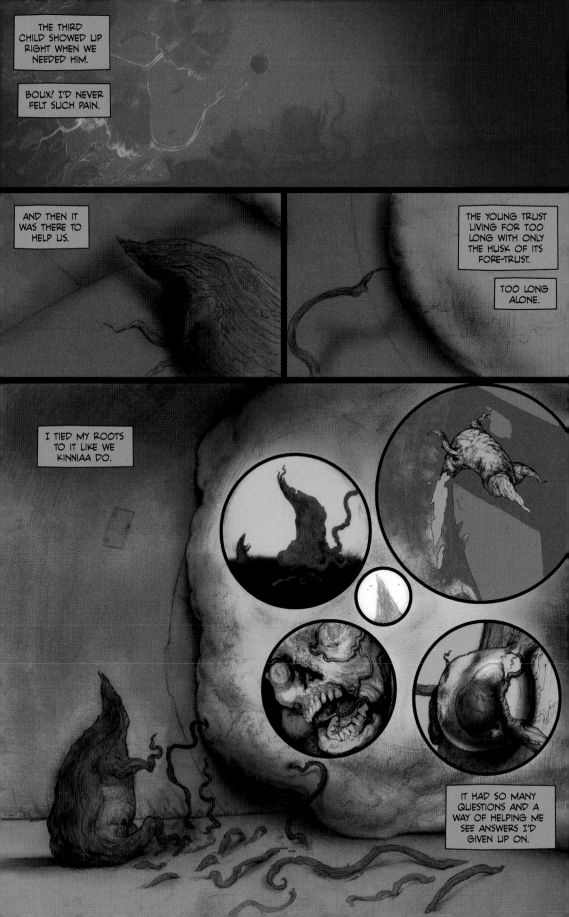

THE THIRD CHILD SHOWED UP RIGHT WHEN WE NEEDED HIM.

BOUX! I'D NEVER FELT SUCH PAIN.

AND THEN IT WAS THERE TO HELP US.

THE YOUNG TRUST LIVING FOR TOO LONG WITH ONLY THE HUSK OF ITS FORE-TRUST.

TOO LONG ALONE.

I TIED MY ROOTS TO IT LIKE WE KINNIAA DO.

IT HAD SO MANY QUESTIONS AND A WAY OF HELPING ME SEE ANSWERS I'D GIVEN UP ON.

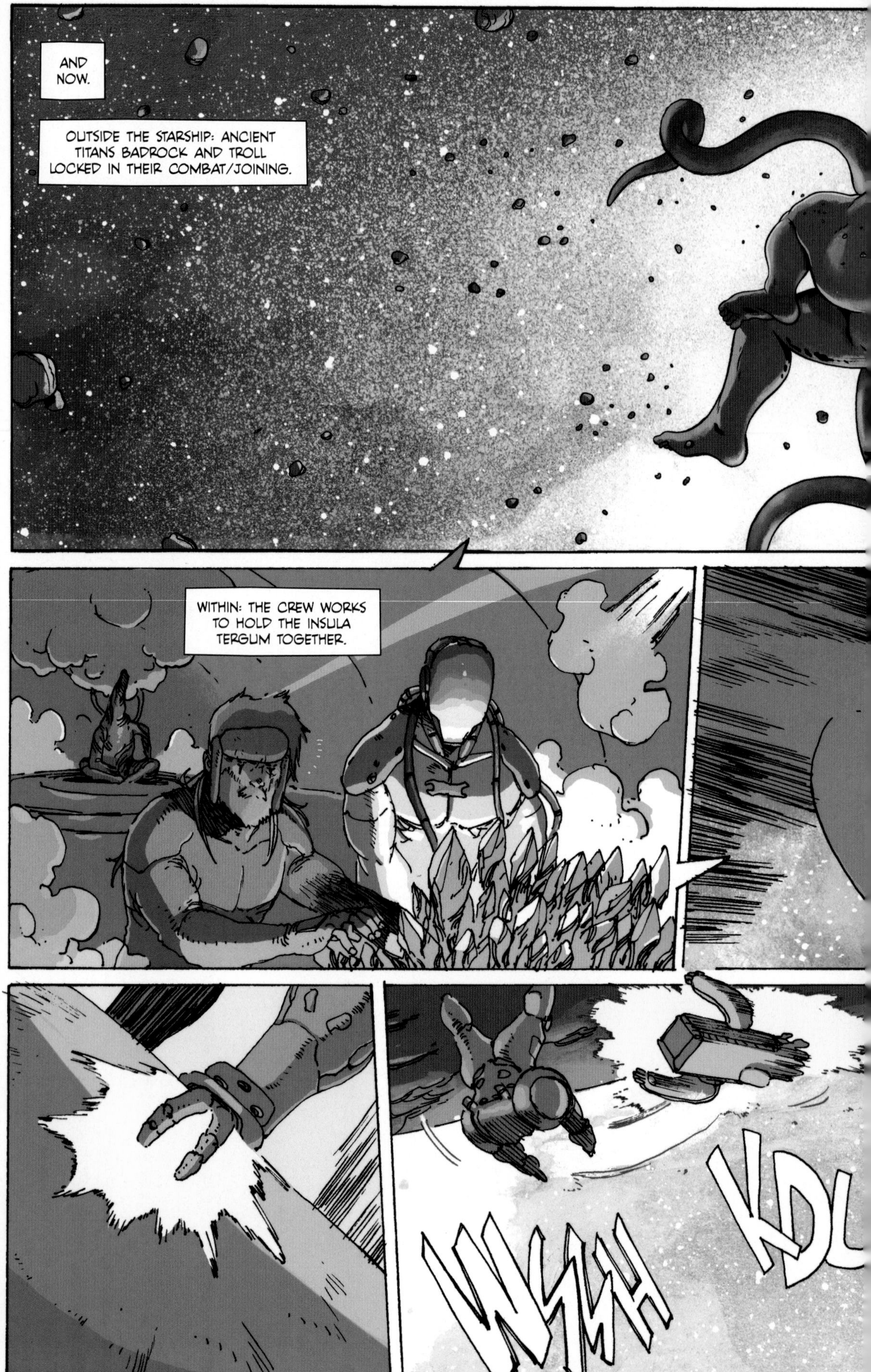
AND NOW.
OUTSIDE THE STARSHIP: ANCIENT TITANS BADROCK AND TROLL LOCKED IN THEIR COMBAT/JOINING.
WITHIN: THE CREW WORKS TO HOLD THE INSULA TERGUM TOGETHER.
WSSH
KDU

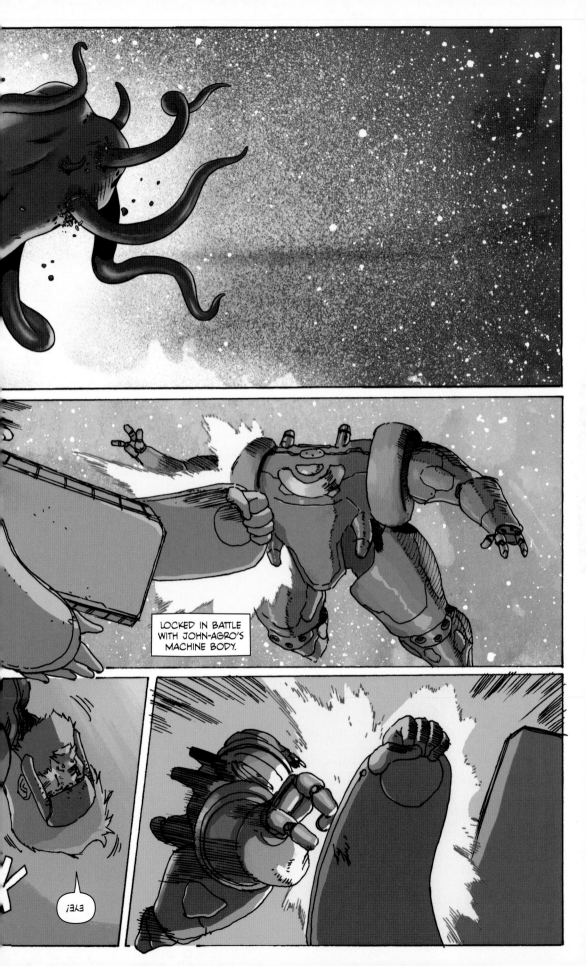

LOCKED IN BATTLE
WITH JOHN-AGRO'S
MACHINE BODY.

EYE!

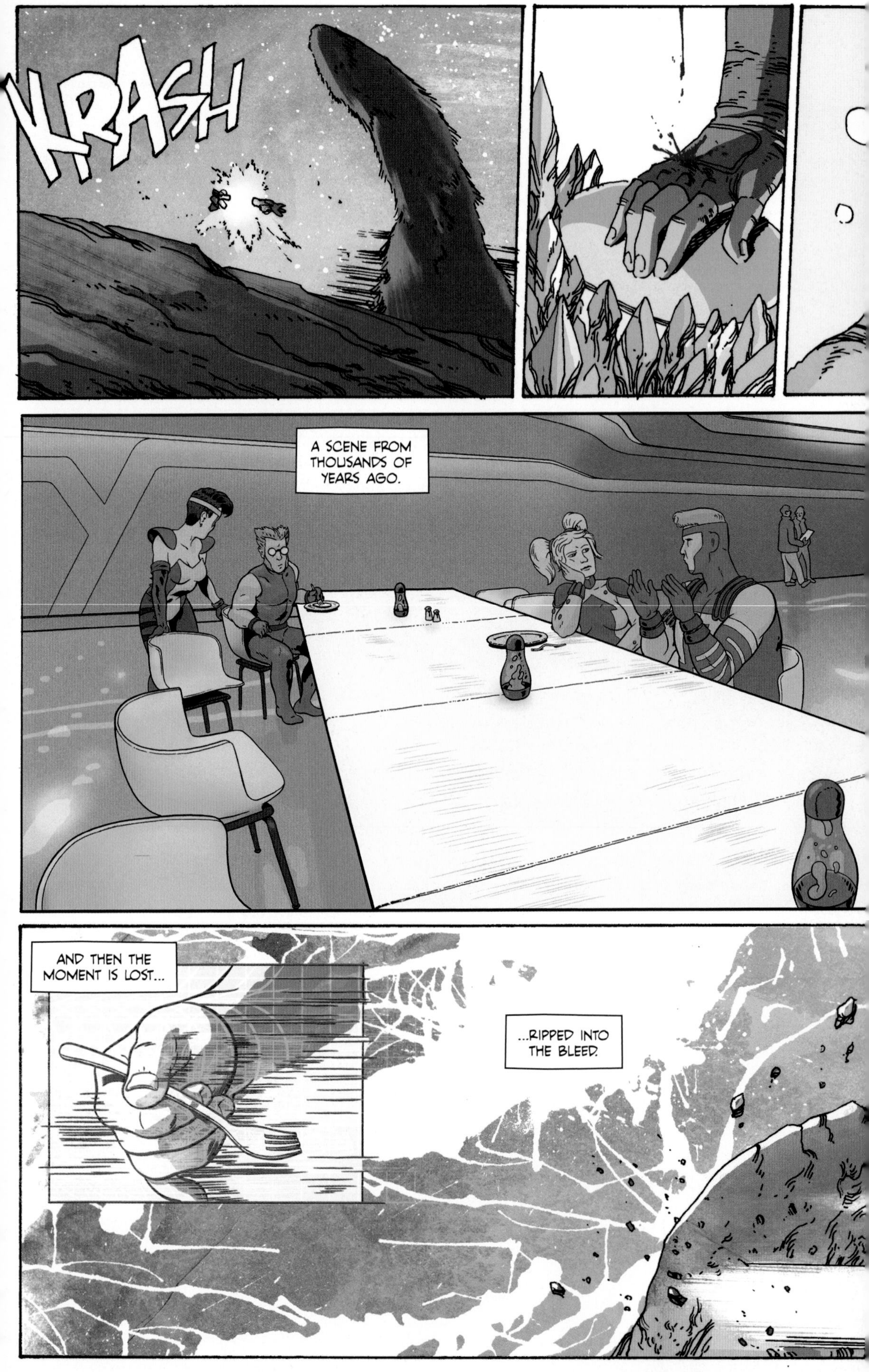
KRASH
A SCENE FROM THOUSANDS OF YEARS AGO.
AND THEN THE MOMENT IS LOST...
...RIPPED INTO THE BLEED.

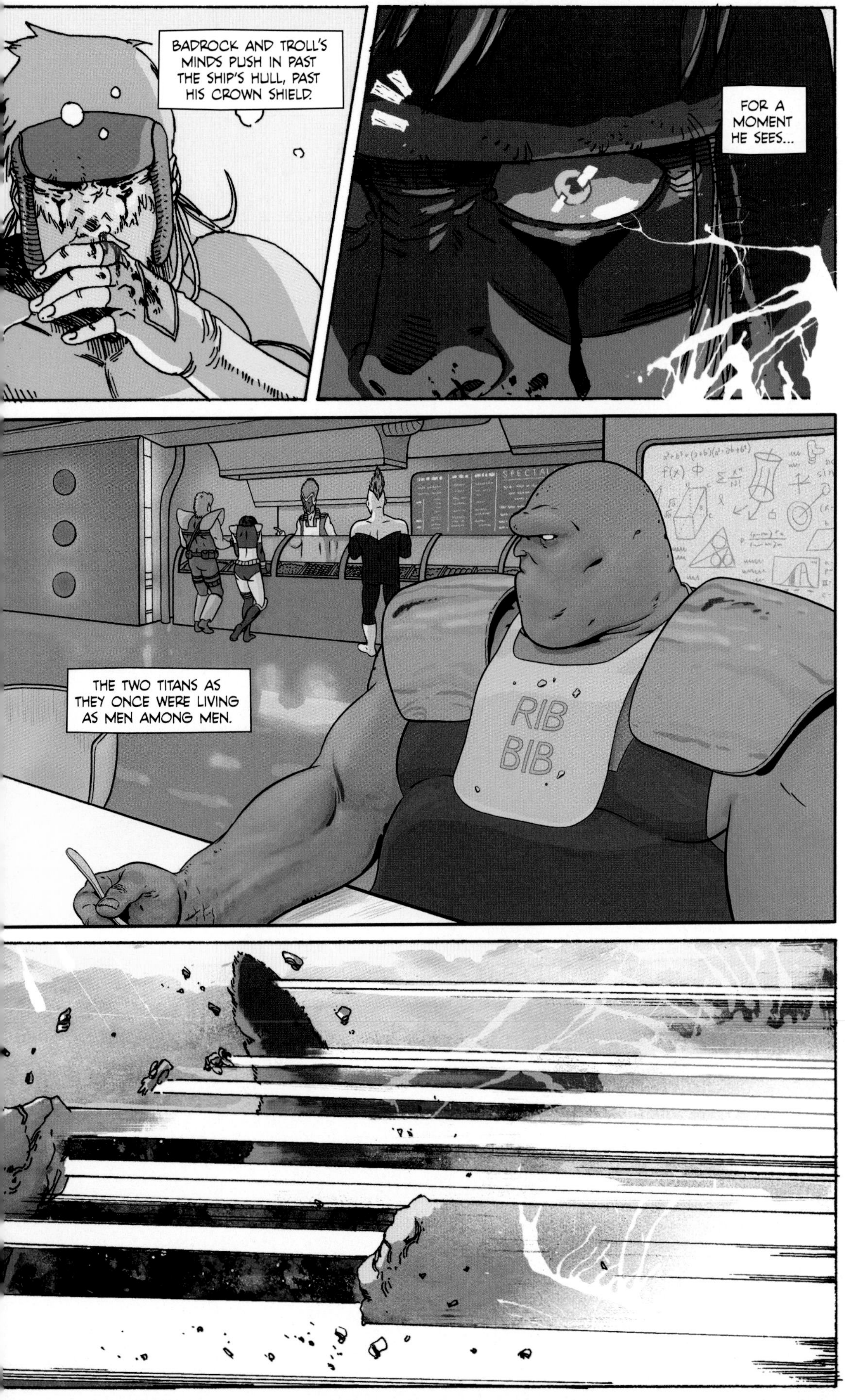
BADROCK AND TROLL'S MINDS PUSH IN PAST THE SHIP'S HULL, PAST HIS CROWN SHIELD.
FOR A MOMENT HE SEES...
SPECIAL
THE TWO TITANS AS THEY ONCE WERE LIVING AS MEN AMONG MEN.
RIB BIB.

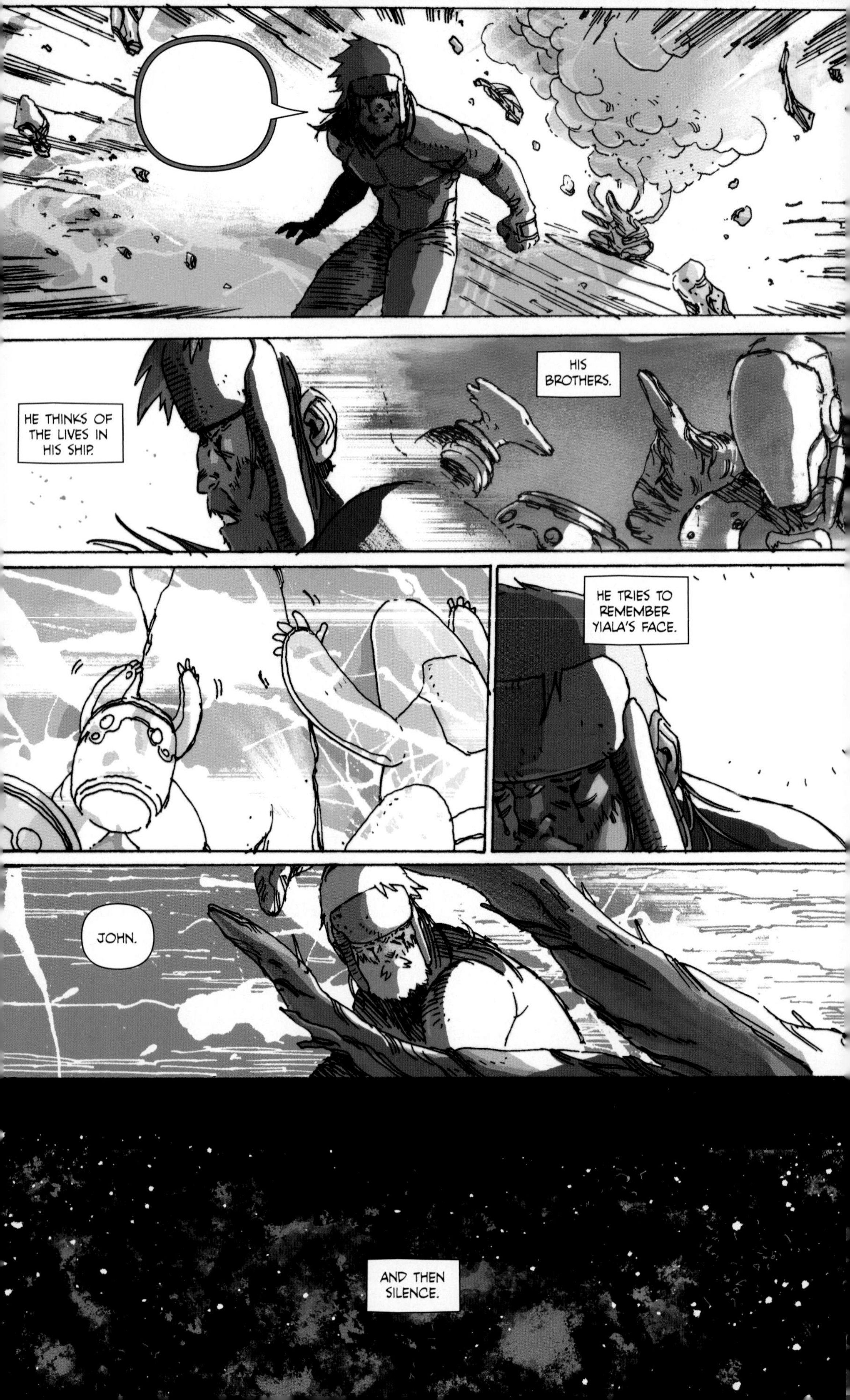
HE THINKS OF THE LIVES IN HIS SHIP.
HIS BROTHERS.
HE TRIES TO REMEMBER YIALA'S FACE.
JOHN.
AND THEN SILENCE.

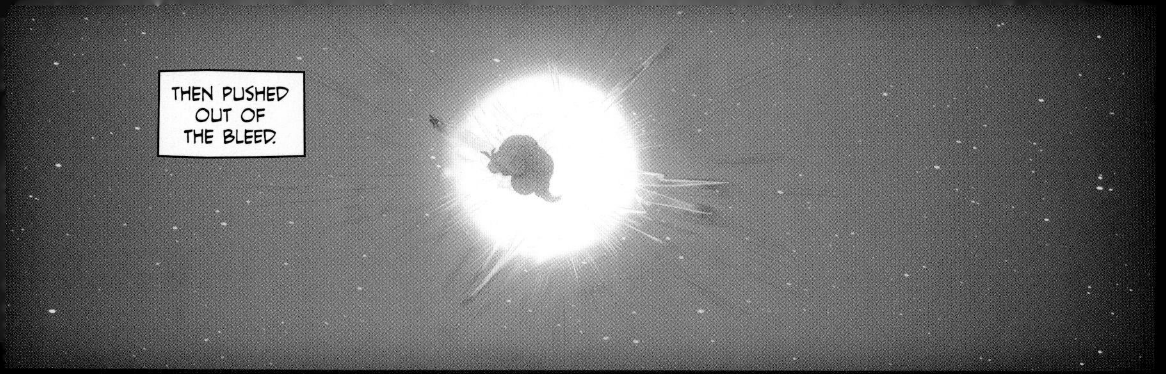
THEN PUSHED OUT OF THE BLEED.

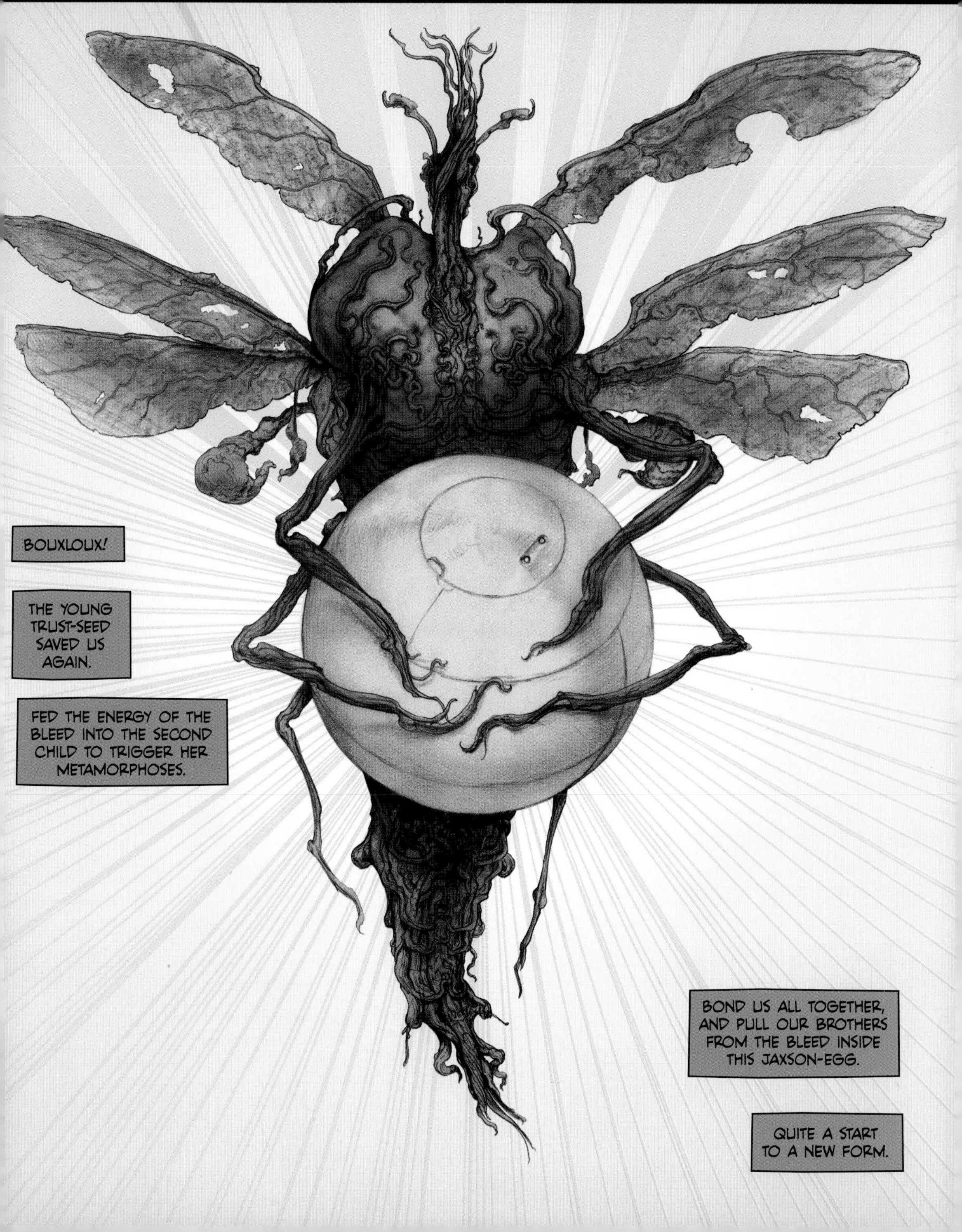
BOUXLOUX!
THE YOUNG TRUST-SEED SAVED US AGAIN.
FED THE ENERGY OF THE BLEED INTO THE SECOND CHILD TO TRIGGER HER METAMORPHOSES.
BOND US ALL TOGETHER, AND PULL OUR BROTHERS FROM THE BLEED INSIDE THIS JAXSON-EGG.
QUITE A START TO A NEW FORM.

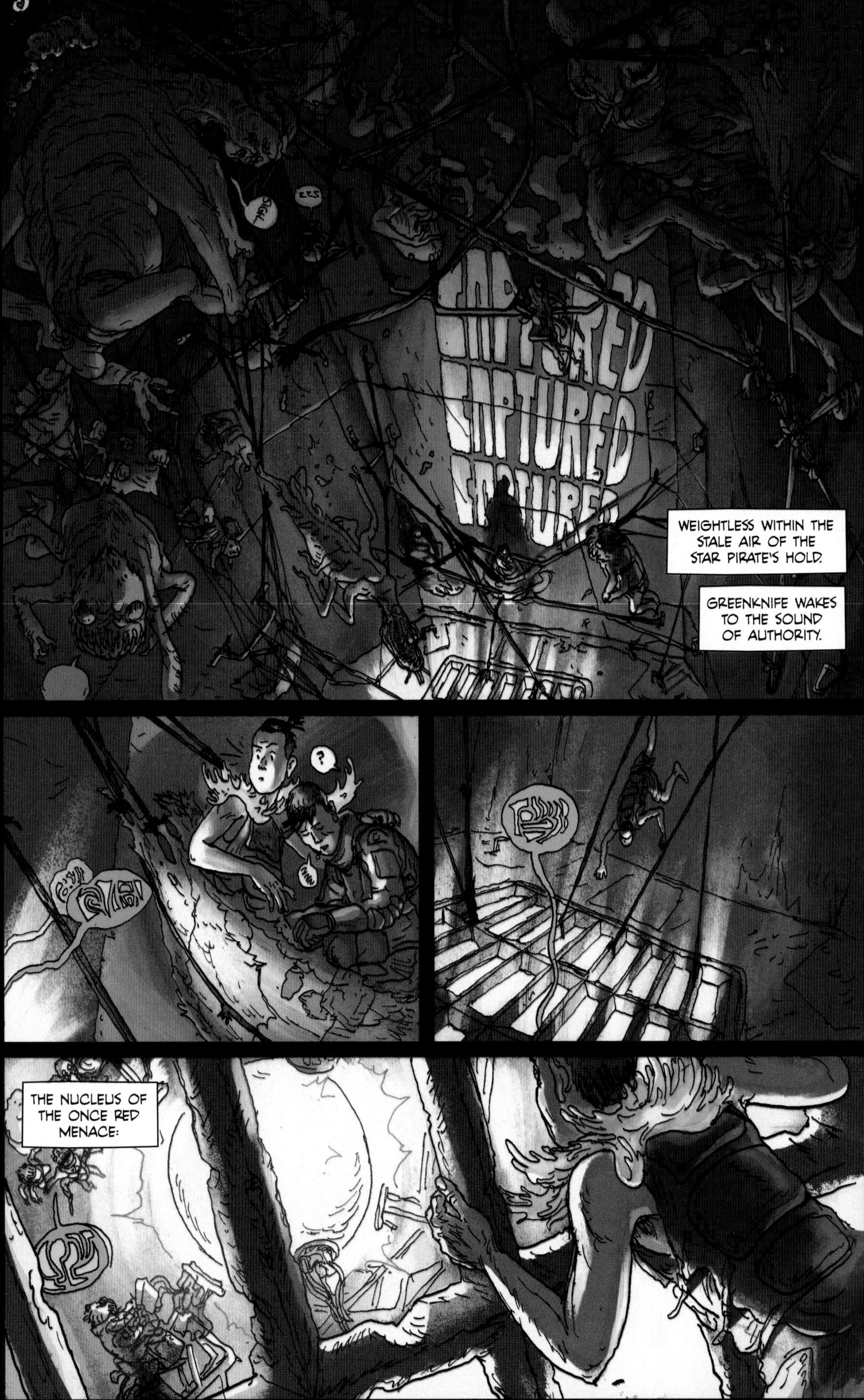
WEIGHTLESS WITHIN THE STALE AIR OF THE STAR PIRATE'S HOLD.
GREENKNIFE WAKES TO THE SOUND OF AUTHORITY.
THE NUCLEUS OF THE ONCE RED MENACE:

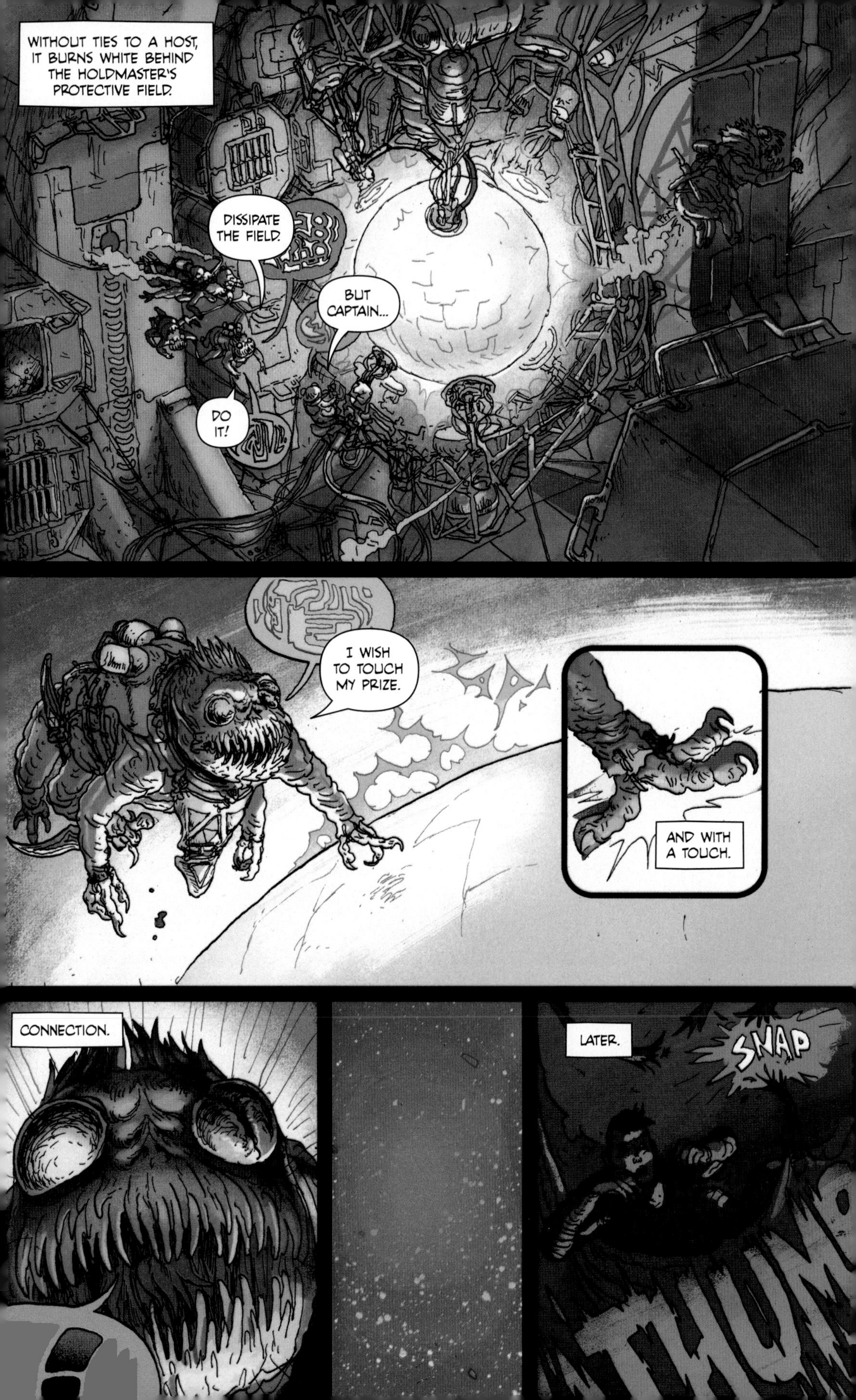

WITHOUT TIES TO A HOST, IT BURNS WHITE BEHIND THE HOLDMASTER'S PROTECTIVE FIELD.
DISSIPATE THE FIELD.
BUT CAPTAIN...
DO IT!
I WISH TO TOUCH MY PRIZE.
AND WITH A TOUCH.
CONNECTION.
LATER.
SNAP
THUM

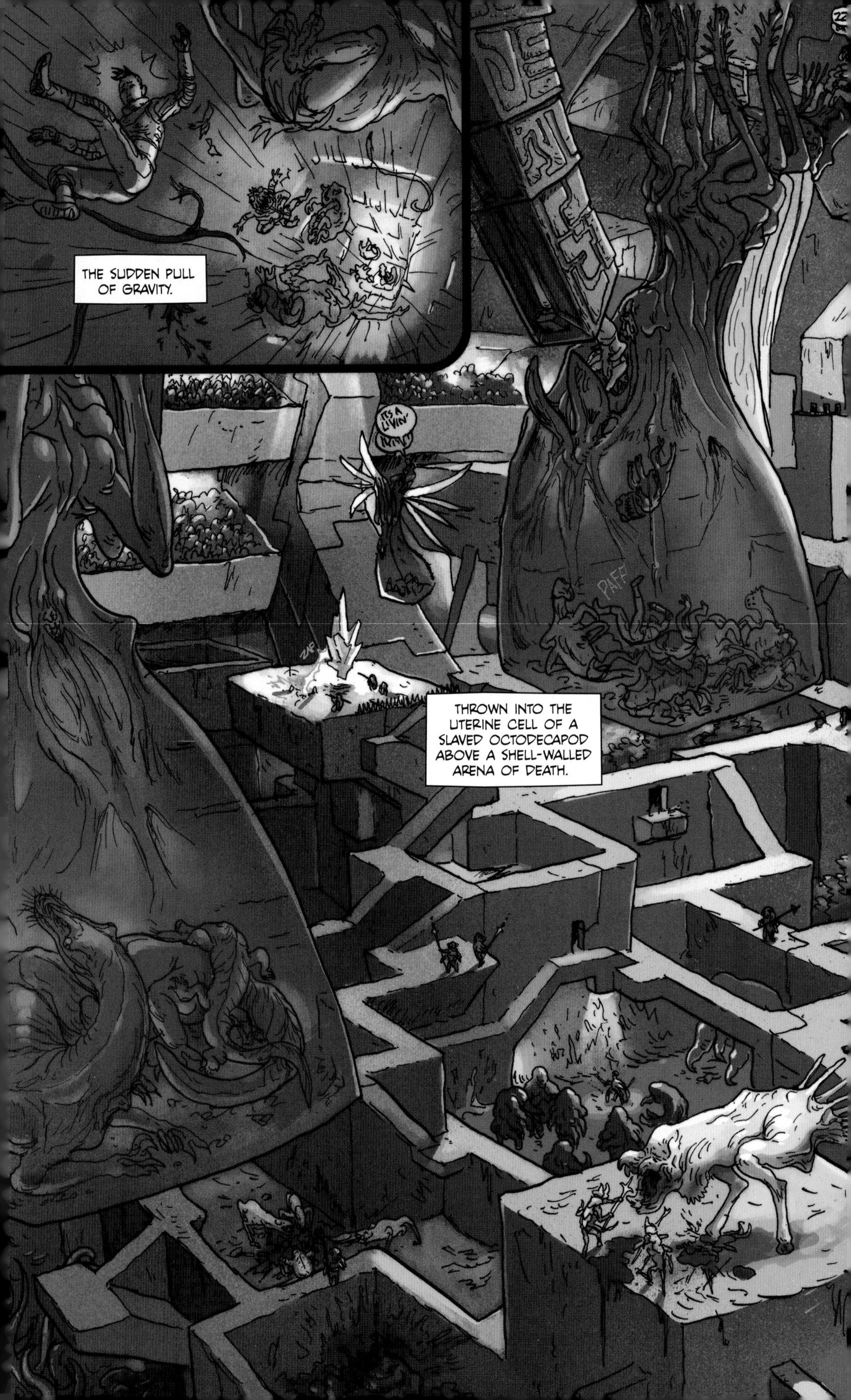
THE SUDDEN PULL OF GRAVITY.
IT'S A LIVIN'
PAFF
THROWN INTO THE UTERINE CELL OF A SLAVED OCTODECAPOD ABOVE A SHELL-WALLED ARENA OF DEATH.